D1313568

A WORLD
OF LOVE

A WORLD OF LOVE

MAGGIE FRANCIS CONROY

Kensington Books
http://www.kensingtonbooks.com

To Casey, Meghan, Nadia, Ana, and Alesia.
And, of course, to Mom.

ACKNOWLEDGMENTS

I can always tell first-time authors by their acknowledgments section. It usually includes every person they have ever known and is longer than some of the chapters. (Perhaps this is in case their first book is their last book.) So, please bear with me while I do the same thing.

Thanks to Elizabeth Cavanaugh for taking a chance with my story and explaining the publishing world to me. Thanks to Tracy Bernstein for explaining the publishing world to me the second and third times, and for walking the tightrope between editing my writing and paralyzing me with fear; I appreciate your patience. Thanks to Jessa Vartanian for prying the manuscript from my arms the first time I asked her to read it, and for all her moral support during the middle stages of "book labor."

Karyn Dorcak, Sharon Wong, Kim Haley, and Tobie Smith have been more than supportive throughout this process—when I couldn't do my "day job" because I was bleary-eyed from a late night of piecing together another chapter. Marnie Morrison deserves my thanks for being a "second mommy."

In addition to this book, our family in its present state would not have been possible without Bee Brown, Marge Hurwitz, Bev Lamphere, Diana Revutsky, and the many other adoption professionals, teachers, doctors, social workers, therapists, and health care professionals who have interacted with our family. These are all people who take to heart the phrase "It takes a village . . ."

This is my opportunity to let my family and friends know—in print—how much I appreciate their love and generosity of spirit. Thank you all.

Our story is by no means meant to be a roadmap of what to expect in a foreign adoption. I'm simply relating our experience from my personal perspective. International adoption regulations, laws, and costs are in constant flux and every adoption agency has its own style and outlook. Therefore, while there are similarities, please remember that every adoption is unique. My profound hope is that this book will help others to consider adoption—whether international or domestic—as a viable option for growing their families and enriching their lives.

INTRODUCTION

February 24, 1995

I was tucking Nadia into bed when she looked at me and said, ``Mom, when I was in Russia I thought about having a mommy sometime. Then they tell me I will have a mom and a dad. But I never thought I would have a whole family! Now I have a mom and dad and sisters and grandpa and grandmas—everybody—forever and ever.'' She looked at me grinning, so happy with herself for winning this prize—an entire family.

Nadia's family—our family—is an ordinary one. My husband, Casey, and I live in a quiet, tree-lined Northern California suburb. We both work outside the home and spend most evenings and weekends attending our kids' school functions and sports activities. Our lives aren't that different from millions of other over-thirty-and-fast-approaching-forty couples. What I've learned, though, during an amazing three-year period in our lives, is that ordinary people can accomplish extraordinary things when they give in to chance and change, and take on unexpected opportunities.

Our jump into "extraordinary" began with a simple wish to expand our family—to have a sibling for our daughter, Meghan, who was six at the time. Now we have four beautiful daughters—born on four different continents—and a wealth of anecdotes ready to tell around future dinner tables to embarrass and delight them. Here is our family story.

Chapter 1

THE DECISION

*Six-year-old Meghan often wished
for a sister.*

August 20, 1991

Casey and I made a huge decision today, one that will change our lives.

Although we agree on the origins of other major turning points in our marriage, it depends on who you ask, Casey or me, as to who first mentioned the possibility of adopting a child. We agree that the subject came up during the day of our eighth wedding anniversary. Casey planned a quiet celebratory lunch, which greatly impressed me, the usual instigator of such events. He chose a cozy Italian restaurant. Although situated on a busy downtown San Jose street, the pathway leading to the front door was surrounded by flowering vines and lush, green plants which muffled the city noise. We sat at a table tucked away on the side of the room where we could easily talk about our dreams for the future. Casey claims credit for broaching the subject, but as the scribe of our story, I have priority memory rights. The miracle was that we—for the first and possibly the last time in our marriage—had the same desire at the same time with the same intensity.

We wore our new and lofty idea like a warm quilt, snuggling safe and warm with fantasies of another child, already potty trained, playing happily with Meghan. We laughed together about whether we would adopt a boy or a girl and how old the child would be. We both felt strongly that this newest family member would be found outside the United States. We played with scenarios of a child from Asia—a girl, we decided, about four years old. She was lovely and bright. As the saying goes, ignorance was bliss.

Knowing what I know now, I feel lucky to have been able to dream like this with Casey. Many people view adoption as a last resort after a painful history of infertility. We had the luxury of making the decision solely on the basis of wanting to give a home to a child who already existed. Having had the opportunity to experience our daughter's birth, we could idealize what was involved in taking on a life whose origins were more unknown. Adoption was a theory, an idea, a great solution for having two children closer in age after waiting five years to enlarge our family. It was easy to be optimistic because we had no idea about what adopting a child from another country involved.

It wasn't until weeks later that our warm quilt of unrealistic expectations was shredded and we were forced to face the realities of international adoption. I don't think we really believed it would be as easy as our fantasy suggested. We knew that giving birth the old-fashioned way involved at least nine months of physical and emotional upheaval—and several more months of hormonal imbalance for me—but adoption was its own mysterious process. Although I sometimes felt that an alien being had invaded my body during pregnancy, I loved feeling Meghan twist and punch around inside me. I felt that I was an essential part of her birth. I ate healthy foods (usually), monitored my weight (sadly), and could call my doctor with questions and concerns. I dreamt of litters of puppies arriving on my due date, or of a monster-child born already able to walk, complaining about my parenting skills. But so did all the other mothers I talked with. I had plenty of role models and all the free advice I could handle. My unmistakably pregnant body was an invitation for other women to tell me their birth stories (mostly of three-day labors and C-sections). No matter how daunting the stories or my backaches, I knew I was normal and on the right track.

Adoption was a different story from the beginning. As we were soon to find out, once established in our own adoption process, the only true control we had over our situation was the choice of one unknown over another. Our friends and family couldn't provide the same reassurance and advice for something that was as much a mystery to them as it was to us. Although always supported by loved ones, we were on our own as far as figuring out what to do next.

Now I can recite hundreds of adoption support organizations throughout the country, but when we started our search, we had no idea where to go for information. As is our way of facing new challenges, Casey began thinking about the implications of adding another child to the family, and I got busy figuring out how to make it happen as soon as possible. I found the yellow pages and looked under "A" for adoption.

The first agency sent us a brochure with beautiful children and families smiling from the pages. In reading their materials, I discovered that it had been started by adoptive parents and that their programs focused mainly on children from South American countries. Their next informational meeting was scheduled for October. October! We couldn't possibly wait four weeks to begin. (Remember, this was in the initial this-shouldn't-be-too-hard-let's-get-moving stage.) I called to reserve a spot in the meeting anyway, but in the meantime I contacted a second agency.

Bee Brown of ACCEPT, a nonprofit adoption and counseling organization, agreed to meet with us as soon as it was convenient. "How about tomorrow?" I asked. I imagined that we would walk into the agency's office and be given photo albums of waiting children. I even entertained the possibility that one child's photograph would leap out at us as *the* child that we were destined to adopt. It would simply be a matter of finalizing the paperwork and meeting the child at the airport. If we got started right away, I figured we could have a child by New Year's Day.

As Casey and I walked into Bee's office, we were both optimistic about what was in store for us. I was on pins and needles, anticipating the possibility of seeing my future child that morning. Casey was much calmer—more curious than nervous. Bee is a charming woman with a refined and assertive British manner. She shook our hands firmly and gave us a warm greeting. We introduced ourselves and told her glowingly about Meghan as we sat in two comfortable chairs in front of her large desk. The walls and shelves of her office were filled with colorful embroidered artwork, an assortment of dolls and figurines, and other intricate crafts representing ethnic cultures from around the world. It took me a few minutes of staring at everything before I could concentrate on what Bee was telling us. The excitement I felt, the contents of the room, and Bee's strong presence gave me the sense of beginning a great adventure.

Bee explained that their program helped people through the adoption process by doing a home study (a social worker's report regarding whether or not a family will be able to care for and support a child), helping with the immigration paperwork, and then in finding and coordinating efforts with an appropriate adoption liaison for the chosen country.

Then it was reality time. "Before we go any further," she said in her crisp BBC accent, "I'd like to ask why you have chosen to adopt a child."

This was a logical question. What was the real reason we wanted to adopt a child over having one biologically? There wasn't just one answer. I didn't know what Casey might be thinking, but I was wondering how in the world to explain briefly something that I didn't really understand myself. What if I didn't come up with an answer that was acceptable? Could we be turned down for not having a good enough reason? *Why did I want to adopt?*

Myriad thoughts ran through my head. I wanted to adopt because giving a home to a child who might not otherwise have one made me feel needed; because I wanted Meghan to have a sibling close in age; because I didn't care about "doing diapers" again; because I had experienced a wonderful pregnancy already but wasn't enamored with labor; because I knew there were already enough children in the world that needed homes; because the "idea" of adoption seemed right.

"I want to adopt because I know I can love another child," I finally said quietly, hoping she would accept my true, but simplistic, answer.

Bee looked over at Casey.

"I want Meghan's sibling to be closer in age and I don't care about doing the baby thing again," he said.

Bee nodded and smiled.

"Whew," I thought, relieved. "It wasn't a trick question." I started to feel more confident.

"Where are you in the adoption process?" Bee asked.

"We're just beginning," I told her. "You're the first person, other than my mom, we've discussed this with."

Between smiles directed at each other, we told her of our newly formulated adoption scenario. We explained that we were interested in adopting a child of around four or five years of age and that we were hoping for a program that wouldn't have a long wait since we already had a child and were anxious to enlarge our family. Being the professional that she is, Bee immediately sensed that we knew nothing about what we were in store for. Our education began.

"This will be extremely difficult," she told us. "It can take months just to find a child, and then you must be prepared to travel to the country at a moment's notice. You may have to stay in the country for as long as the paperwork takes, possibly leaving the child and returning when the courts are ready to finalize the adoption."

Our smiles dimmed a bit, but we felt we could handle this.

"These children have a right to retain knowledge of the culture they were born into," Bee went on. "If you adopt an older child, there may be emotional problems to deal with. The child could be from an orphanage or from the streets. Either way, they have been given up and will have had a difficult beginning. Many of these children are malnourished. Some may have developmental delays or physical limitations."

We were starting to understand the complexity of international adoption.

Bee continued, "Would you be willing to accept a child with special needs?"

"What kind of special needs?" we asked.

"Well, special physical needs can run the gamut from a cleft palate to blindness to missing limbs," she answered. "There are also children with severe emotional needs from various forms of abuse or abandonment. You must think about what kind of child you are willing to accept because the agencies who place these children need to know. The good news is that children over three years of age are harder to place in the adoption world, so your waiting time may be less."

Finally, some good news. But why are older children harder to place? What were we capable of dealing with as far as raising a child with special needs? My head was humming with unanswered questions. My fantasies were starting to dissolve.

Bee leaned closer as she began to discuss finances. "Have you considered how much an adoption will cost?" she asked gently.

"Oh, don't worry," I answered brightly, glad that at least *this* wasn't going to be a stumbling block. "Casey's company has an adoption program that will reimburse us for up to three thousand dollars of adoption expenses."

Bee looked concerned. "Well, our fees will run about twenty-five hundred for the home study and paperwork. The agency or lawyer facilitating the adoption in the foreign country will have expenses. Travel to the country can be at least another three thousand and most countries have bureaucratic charges as well. The least expensive international adoptions run around ten thousand dollars—they usually cost considerably more."

I felt a lump forming in my throat. Three thousand dollars had seemed like a huge amount of money to us. Finally, I said, "Well, we'll just have to work things out financially as we go." (I had absolutely no idea how we could possibly raise that kind of money.)

"Have you considered a county domestic adoption?" Bee asked. "The expenses are considerably less."

We explained our fears of bonding with a child that might be taken from us if the biological parents changed their minds. We told her of friends who had lost an eight-year-old boy after he had lived with them as their son for over a year. His biological mother, who had not wanted custody of him during his first seven years of life, would not sign the final relinquishment papers. Our friends and their adopted son were devastated. Watching the suffering of this sensitive child—who thought he had finally landed in a stable home only to discover that he would be uprooted once again—was an experience I will never forget. To his adoptive parents, his removal from their home was unbearable. They moved away from the area shortly after, unable to stay in a place that represented such grief.

"Even though I know this doesn't happen often, we aren't willing to take the chance that it could happen to our family," I said.

I was now vacillating between a feeling of we-can-do-it to complete despair over the impossibility of it all.

Bee began to tell us about the different countries with adoption programs. "We've both envisioned adopting an Asian girl," Casey told Bee. There was no specific reason for this choice. Maybe it was because Casey has always been interested in Asian culture. And our religious beliefs are ecumenical and have always had a strong Asian influence from Buddhism and Hinduism.

Bee looked at a list of programs available in Asia. Vietnam was closed and very difficult to work with even when open. China required a $5,000 "gift" to the government—in cash—right up front, which made it a very expensive program.

"In many Asian countries the people can't understand why a

couple would want to adopt a girl," Bee explained, "especially if they already have a girl and don't have a boy. It makes them suspicious. There have been rumors that people are adopting girls from Asia as servants. Girls over three available for adoption are hard to find because many are sold for prostitution."

I wanted to cry. I knew there were millions of children in the world who needed homes. Why was the adoption process so difficult? No wonder more people didn't adopt. How could governments use their children as a means of raising money from foreigners? The problem wasn't a lack of children needing homes, it was the bureaucracy.

"How do you feel about adopting a black child?" Bee asked.

"Fine. We would love to adopt a black child."

Then we learned of the problems of white families adopting black children. There are organizations that do not want black children being raised by white parents. "Are you willing to send the child to a black church? Are there other black families living in your neighborhood? These are all things to consider."

India was a possibility, but it had a two- to three-year waiting list for children adopted into non-Indian homes. "Too long," I said. "We cannot possibly wait two years to add to our family. It wouldn't be fair to Meghan to have the process drag out so long." (It was easy to use Meghan as an excuse; the truth was that I didn't want to wait that long.)

"How about Russia?" we asked. We both have a great interest in Russian history from our college days and friends had gotten us involved in a Russian sister city program.

"Russia is closed to adoptions. How about South America?"

We hadn't considered South America. We didn't know much about the continent's history or have any connections with the culture. But we were open to any country.

Bee discussed several South American options. Colombia piqued our interest because adoptions are handled through a Social Services program instead of through lawyers. (Both Casey and I had an ingrained "collective unconscious" distrust of lawyers and weren't enthused about dealing with one from another country.) It was one of the less expensive programs and the waiting time was supposedly shorter than other South American countries.

Bee showed us photos of children who had been placed through her agency, giving us a sense that if other parents could manage an international adoption, then so could we. But the parents in the photos looked older and wealthier than Casey and me. They looked sure of themselves. Secure. Surely they had been better informed when they'd started. What had they expected? What led them to choose adoption? Were they as confused at their first meeting as we felt? They all certainly looked happy now.

Finally, Bee ended our meeting by telling us we didn't have to decide on the country right away. If we were interested in pursuing an international adoption, we could call and set up an appointment with Marge Hurwitz, the social worker.

We were two very different-looking people when we left that office. I felt like a zombie—shocked and confused. Casey was overwhelmed. Bee had painted the grim reality, and although we felt as if our ideals had been shattered, we were still determined to continue and adopt a child—weren't we?

We walked down the block to find a place to eat. We were both very quiet for a while. Then my floodgates opened. "Why did she have to be so negative?" I cried. "I should have known things wouldn't be quite as easy as I imagined but this isn't what I expected at all. Why does it have to be so hard? How can we possibly raise ten thousand dollars?"

As we walked, we shared our fears and frustrations with the interview. But as we talked, we also began to see the positive things that Bee had mentioned. They had been hard to see during the conversation amid all the shocking truths, but they were there. Bee hadn't been negative so much as she had been "straightforward." Wouldn't we rather know what we were up against from the start so we can be more prepared and make a wise decision? The children we saw in the pictures were wonderful—and wasn't that the point of all this, a child to join our family? What important life change is easy?

We went back and forth feeling confident and dismal toward our prospects, but the bottom line emerged: We both wanted this adoption to happen. We were in it together. Somehow—together—we would make it work.

Later that day, we signed an agreement with ACCEPT, wrote out a check for $500, and made our first appointment with Marge. We had begun.

Chapter 2

HOME STUDY

*December 11, 1984, the day after
Meghan was born.*

November 14, 1991

Marge is coming to the house today to complete our home study. I'm a wreck.

Nobody with closets as messy as mine wants her home studied. And it wasn't just our home that was going to be scrutinized but the stability of our marriage, our parenting skills, and (gulp) our finances. Why hadn't anyone cared about these details when I gave birth to Meghan? (Well, aside from my mom.) No one showed up at our front door to make sure I knew what I was doing and whether or not I had a good home waiting for my expected baby. As long as we paid the doctor's bill, we were okay. But now we had to be financially sound and fiscally responsible. We were given a binder full of forms to fill out, to prove our fitness as parents.

As much as I understand the importance of making sure children are placed in good homes, it is still a bit degrading to feel as though your future as a parent is in the hands of a social worker you have never met before.

In our case, the social worker, Marge, made us feel good about our decision to adopt from the start. She interviewed Casey and me together—and then separately—about our reasons for wanting to adopt a child, to make sure we both wanted the same thing. Marge made it clear to us that her foremost goal was to place as many children as possible. Her job wasn't to decide whether or not we deserved a child but to educate us and make sure a child would be safe in our family. Our financial status was taken into account primarily to prove that we could take care of another child's basic needs without government assistance. She helped us focus clearly on the real reasons we wanted to adopt a child, and I knew after the first visit that she would help us achieve our dream.

I cleaned for a week before Marge's visit to our house. Even though I trusted her, my grandmother's voice echoed in my head. "Remember, Margaret, you are judged by the order of your household. Cleanliness is next to Godliness." I worried about rumors I'd heard about social workers sometimes looking through garbage containers to check for liquor bottles or smutty magazines. I thought Marge might be required by some law to check every aspect of our home for suitability. I was almost disappointed when she glanced through the house, commented on how nice Meghan's room was, and began to write up her report over tea. "Don't you want to see under the beds?" I wanted to ask. "I could move the stove out for you to see where I swept for the first time in my life—you wouldn't believe what I found back there!"

But by that time Marge seemed comfortable that we weren't hiding any secrets. In fact, she knew we weren't because during our meetings in her office we confessed every transgression we had ever committed. Casey stole a guitar from a kid when he was in high school. I was taking Prozac to keep a chemical imbalance in check. We had thousands of dollars' worth of student loans we were paying off. We let family skeletons out of the closet—how Casey's father is a recovering alcoholic, the depression that runs in my family. Things never discussed during polite conversations in the Midwest were brought up during our meetings with Marge. But apparently it was nothing compared to what she had heard before. "Every family has their history," she assured us. After confessing to stressful times in our marriage, Marge said she would be more concerned if we *didn't* have some imperfections. "It's the couples that come in and insist that they've never had a disagreement that I worry about."

Marge wrote out her reports by hand in front of us as we answered her questions. She did this, she explained, so that we could not only know right away what was being written about us, but also so that we could correct any misunderstandings. The easy questions were first; name, date of birth, occupation, annual income, height, weight, color of eyes, and so on until enough basic information was on paper that any Internal Nationalization Services (INS) staff person could picture our faces and lives vividly in his mind.

We told Marge about our childhoods.

Mr. Conroy was born January 26, 1959 in Oregon, the second of six children. . . . Mr. Conroy feels his childhood years were secure and happy. Mrs. Conroy was born November 12, 1956 in Iowa, the middle of three children. . . . Both parents have always been loving and supporting.

When we met individually, Marge asked me what had brought me to this point in my life. I stopped and reflected. The main reason I moved to California at age twenty-five was because of a single line in a college brochure stating that all students in the graduate psychology program at the College of Notre Dame in Belmont, California, must experience personal therapy firsthand. When I was young, I received the clear message that only people who needed to be locked up in an attic go in for therapy or, God forbid, see a psychiatrist. Major problems were not discussed. Our unspoken, but fully understood, family rule was that if you never mentioned something, it didn't exist.

"Well," I thought after finishing the brochure, "it isn't that I'm confused and emotionally lost. I'm just curious about family dynamics." In my doing-things-the-hard-way pattern, I moved 2,000 miles away (not knowing a single soul in California), took out several student loans, and began a career in mental health just to understand my own. My family wasn't any more dysfunctional than any other family with more than one member in it; I just couldn't find a direction for my life. I was living on my own, working as a legal secretary—a job I was fortunate to get with my newly acquired degree in fine arts—and madly in love with a young man who was nowhere near ready to commit to a permanent relationship. Things were not turning out as I had planned, which hurt, even though I had never had a real plan in the first place.

I had called the college and asked the student who answered whether I could enroll midyear. As fate would have it, she mistakenly assured me that entering the program early would not be a problem and sent me all the application forms. Luckily for me, when I arrived in February 1981, the office of admissions made an exception and allowed me to begin classes a semester early and stay in a college apartment with two other students.

Meanwhile, Casey was trying to finish a double degree in history and English. He had been at the college since graduating from high school and now lived on campus as a resident assistant. Because of a scheduling mix-up, he was going to have to spend an extra semester taking one final course before he could graduate. So, I arrived early, Casey stayed late, and we met soon after at the student mailboxes—me frantically hoping to find a letter from home, and Casey with a gorgeous brunette named Lisa by his side. Although it would make this story more interesting, I'm sad to report that it wasn't love at first sight.

Neither one of us was thinking much about a new relationship. I was still infatuated with my Iowa boyfriend and knew I would only be able to get over him by being as far away as I could get without crossing an ocean. Casey had recently broken off a relationship himself and liked his freedom. But since Notre Dame was a small campus and Casey was the only other person living there who was close to my age, we found ourselves meeting more and more and becoming good friends. There's nothing quite like a relaxed college atmosphere filled with long esoteric discussions, late nights working on term papers, and the feeling that you're learning how to save the world, to help people grow closer. Since our only responsibilities consisted of getting to class on time and to the dining hall before it closed, we had the luxury of getting to know each other through hours and hours of intense and heartfelt conversations. In a way it was the therapy I had come to experience. I shared parts of my life with Casey that I had never been able to share with anyone. I gradually came to realize that I wanted, and needed, a steady and committed relationship and that such a thing was possible. The first time Casey told me he loved me I didn't know what to say. Having someone love me felt exciting and frightening at the same time, but I grew to like it and to return his faith in love. Two years later we were married in a lovely outdoor wedding ceremony with a potluck reception. ("If that's what they do out there in California, I guess it's okay," my mother had sighed.)

The first year of our marriage, I began an internship at a local hospital. I was assigned to a therapy group working with children who were having "adjustment problems" and who had been identified as being "emotionally disturbed." I had absolutely no idea what this meant (I still don't) but was eager to give these kids lots of love and attention. "If they know someone cares, I'm sure they will respond," I reasoned. Besides, I was almost finished with my course work so I was sure I could handle whatever emotional problems these unfortunate children might have. I went into the situation thinking that no child could possibly have more life experience than I did. I was wrong. The group consisted of "latency-age children," so-called because the developmental stage roughly between the years six and eleven is a period of time when sexuality is deeply buried. (Casey and I soon referred to them as the not-so-very-latent kids.) The first day my intern instructor introduced me to a boy who looked about nine years old. "Johnny," he said, "this is Maggie, and she is going to join our group today."

"Hi, Johnny," I said with a smile, bending down to eye level with him, as instructed in class. "How are you doin' today?"

"Fuck you, bitch," he hissed. Turning away, he stomped off and flung himself into a chair.

"Oh, dear," I said, looking at my instructor, not quite able to stand up right away.

"Welcome to group," he said, extending his hand.

My real education with children began at this point. My experience until then had been, I realized, only play. Now I had to get to know kids that no one else wanted to know, and to find out how to reach them through barriers of hurt and anger. I learned that my sometimes-silent family was paradise compared to what many children live with at home. My confused feelings about the world paled in comparison with the trials these youngsters faced on a day-to-day basis. I learned to value the love I had been given throughout my childhood, and began to understand the immense responsibility involved in raising a healthy child. I soon learned that I wasn't going to cure these children of their personal demons, but that I might give them a small inkling of the truth: they were good and worthwhile people.

I learned that it takes a whole family structure to nurture and love a child. No matter how hard we tried, we were with these children a limited amount of time. These kids were identified as *the problem* but often they were the healthiest member of an out-of-control family. Parents or guardians often wanted us to *fix* their kids so they wouldn't cause more trouble, but were unwilling to be a part of the solution. My real training in mental health had begun, and with experience, I learned to reach out to these kids and see them as individuals and not as "good kids" or "bad kids." After my internship ended, I was hired as a mental health worker to continue with the group and I took part-time work in a pre-school to fill out my days.

As much as I learned, and as highly as I valued my work, when I was about to give birth sixteen months later, I decided that the atmosphere at the hospital was too stressful for a new mother. Since most of the kids were moving on to an older group, I moved out of the mental health profession and found a full-time position with a preschool that would allow Meghan to attend with me when she was old enough.

I have always been able to work wonders with other people's kids and had plenty of advice for the parents of "my children." I felt sure that having my own was going to be a cinch. I was used to being able to coax any child out of a tantrum while his parents stood by helplessly. As a teacher, I knew exactly what to do in every situation and was eager to share my expertise. Then I became Meghan's mother and, with her help, became much humbler and more empathetic. God had smiled and given me the one child who seemed to puzzle me at every turn. It was especially degrading when she was older and behaved much better for her new preschool teachers than she ever would for me. I felt I should call up every parent I had ever dealt with and give them a formal apology.

Meghan spoke her first words at six months and began testing any rule we came up with as soon as she was able to understand that rules existed. She was an amazing baby and, as a toddler, was a force to be reckoned with in our newly established family. I now understand that Meghan was our training ground for future parenting challenges—an advanced course in patience. At the time, though, I couldn't understand how our combined genetic makeup had created the one child that I couldn't keep up with. It helped me to assume that her strong personality was Casey's fault, but my mother dashed that concept with a confession. "I'm sorry, Margaret," she said during a weekly phone conversation. "When you were a little girl, I survived by hoping you would someday know what I was going through. It sounds like my wish was granted." Casey's mother later revealed wishes along the same lines for him. A double whammy!

The idea of a second child rarely came up. For the first five years of Meghan's life we were convinced that one child was more than we could handle properly. But now Meghan was getting older and we were much more experienced parents. When she started school full-time, I took a job as art director for the Children's Discovery Museum in San Jose. Although I produced artwork for children's programs, I wasn't working with children all day. I felt I had the energy I needed for another child of my own. "We're both ready and feel like we can handle anything," I said.

"Thank you," said Marge, and began writing.

> *Ms. Conroy was awarded her B.A. degree in 1980. . . . She met Casey while earning her M.A. degree at College of Notre Dame in California. She has worked in the fields of education and psychology. . . .*

Our home study would have been bound in volumes if Marge had written everything we told her. But she was a pro at cutting to the chase. Later, she told us that it was our ability to be open and flexible that convinced her that we would be able to successfully adopt. Knowing that someone was reviewing my life, I tended to blow small things—like every decision I had ever made—out of proportion, and with every word out of my mouth I wondered, will this be the thing that gets us rejected? The only thing worse would have been my paranoia had I not been forthright and honest during these initial meetings.

In his meeting, Casey told Marge of his interesting career path. Casey had begun his search armed with a degree in history, high hopes, and lots of experience waiting tables, and ended when he accepted the first job he was able to find—a copier salesman. (Casey once told me of a professor who commented that a liberal arts education provides you with the ability to appreciate the finer things in life and a value system such that you will never be able to afford them.) He hated working in sales. His manager tried to convince him that the "hard sell" was the only way to get by in a competitive market. Casey wasn't exactly a "hard sell" kind of guy. Needless to say, he didn't last long in his new profession.

His next foray into the working world was as an energy conservationist. He was to inspect residential conservation construction work such as weather stripping, insulation, and installation of new appliances. If the work was done properly, the homeowners would qualify for energy conservation loans and rebates. He enjoyed this job because he was able to educate himself and others in a field that was of interest to him. After three years, though, he felt as if he had learned all he could and longed to be able to work in the corporate world.

Casey began calling anyone he knew who worked in the corporate world—which in the San Francisco Bay Area generally meant high-tech firms—and asking about their company and their work. He was a good listener and discovered what they liked and disliked about their jobs. He always ended the conversation asking for names of anyone else he could talk with. After about twenty-five of these informational interviews over the next six months he got a referral for some freelance writing work at Apple Computer. For a year, he worked on projects for Apple, learning and then honing his technical writing skills. He worked hard and got a full-time position as a writer in one of Apple's training organizations. By the time of his home study interview with Marge, he was an instructional designer and project manager working on interactive training for the Macintosh computer.

> *Mr. Conroy was employed in several jobs before accepting a position with Apple Computer, Inc. where he has worked for five years doing technical writing and developing computer training.*

Both Casey and I talked about our child-rearing methods— time-outs instead of spanking, positive instead of negative reinforcement, consistency, consistency, consistency—and again about the challenges of raising Meghan. "One minute she's the sweetest child on earth, and the next, she's the most stubborn creature I've ever encountered," said Casey.

"If one of us says, 'no,' she will wait and ask the other. We have to constantly be on guard and work together for fear she'll outsmart us," I added.

"How wonderful to have such an independent and intelligent child," Marge said with a knowing smile. "She sounds like a very normal six-year-old."

> *The Conroys' biological child, Meghan . . . is witty, very bright, and verbal. They both enjoy raising their daughter and both contribute to all facets of her life. They both believe consistency, compassion, and good listening skills are important for being good parents.*

I couldn't believe what a great couple we made on paper.

. . . She is a lovely, sensitive, and intelligent person.
. . . He is warm, bright, and articulate.
. . . They provide an emotionally safe and stable home environment
and many enriching activities.
. . . Both are physically fit and very active. . . .
. . . I highly recommend the placement of a little girl with this lovely
and mature couple.

"Wow, we really sound like good people," I beamed at Casey. "Now *I* want to be adopted by us!"

After our glowing report, we were ready to let Meghan in on our plans. I knew she had always wanted a sister or brother—I didn't know how she would react to the real thing. Especially an older child who would be big enough to get into all her important *stuff*.

Everyday family talk normally happened at the kitchen table, on the way out the door, or in Meghan's room before bedtime. So, when we sat Meghan down in the living room, she knew right away that something was up.

We presented the news in the best possible light. We had broached the topic before in a theoretical way, so we reminded her of the bunk beds we had talked of buying. She would be gaining a sister, a playmate, a confidant. We emphasized what a great "big sister" Meghan would be—wasn't that exciting?

Meghan looked at us as if assessing this new information, then said, "Okay, cool."

"Do you have any questions?" I asked, prepared to answer any objections or concerns.

"Yeah, I have one."

Casey and I leaned forward.

"Do I get the top bunk?"

We breathed a sigh of relief. But where was that six-year-old curiosity we were so familiar with—the Meghan who wanted to be consulted regarding everything from meal menus to sock selections? Evidently, the idea itself—in the absence of an actual child—didn't offer much excitement or threat. After a short pause, she asked another question.

"Can I go outside and play now?"

With Meghan in on our news, we thought everything about our adoption plan was in place, ready to go, under control. Little did we know that our "major decisions" had just begun.

Chapter 3

WAITING

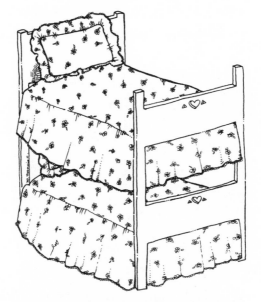

*The bunk beds and our family were
ready for a new family member.*

February 8, 1993

Today we went to the Colombian consulate in San Francisco to have our papers authenticated. ``Authenticated'' means having a Colombian official stamp each page for $15.00 per stamp. When we got home there was another form waiting for us from Colombia— three pages, double sided, and all in Spanish. It will never end. I'm beginning to wonder if I'm destined to fill out adoption forms for the rest of my life.

An eighteen-month, all-expense-paid sabbatical in Hawaii would fly by. The eighteen months before I turned thirty went by at warp speed even with me dragging my heels all the way. But eighteen months seems like forever when you are trying to adopt a child. It's enough time for two nine-month pregnancies, back to back, but with no assurance of results. Don't get me wrong; it wasn't as if we were lounging around doing nothing. These were eighteen months of paperwork, fingerprints, paperwork, interviews, paperwork, consulate seals, paperwork, physical exams, paperwork, reference letters, and of course, paperwork. And not just paperwork in English but paperwork in Spanish, too. Every time we thought we were beginning to understand the process of adoption in Colombia, we would learn something new.

We finished our home study work with Marge in late November. We were still gathering up the other INS information we needed to submit, going to the court house for our marriage certificate, writing to our home states for birth certificates, and gathering reference letters from friends. After our home study was sent off to the INS, we were referred to an Oregon organization called PLAN that would facilitate our work with the Colombian Social Services. After we signed a contract and filled out more forms, we were directed to a Colombian woman named Mercedes, who would be our liaison. In June 1992 we visited Mercedes at PLAN while on a visit to Casey's folks in Portland. I was hoping that she might give us an idea of who our child might be. "Maybe," I thought, "they have already identified someone for us."

We felt as if we had been extremely busy and had accomplished great feats of bureaucratic magic. She let us know right away that we had only scratched the surface. Part of the problem was our misunderstanding of the "adoption clock." When we were told a time frame—six months to process a child for adoption, for example—we assumed that it meant from the time we *requested a child*. What it really meant, we were to find out, was six months from the time every iota of paperwork was finalized, authorized, notarized, and any other "proceduralized" thing that could be done to a legal document. *That's* when the clock starts ticking. We knew we wouldn't change our minds and decide not to adopt, but some people do, and so we learned that our case wouldn't even be considered until everything was turned in. We were taking our time at first, thinking that since they had to prepare the child, we would be ready about the same time our little girl would be. We figured that if the Colombian government wanted something sooner or had a child available for us, they would let us know. We were wrong, and after our discussion with Mercedes, we realized that we had to be much more aggressive in getting our paperwork finished.

When we returned to our car, I began to cry. "I feel so stupid," I moaned. "Why does it have to be so complicated? I just want another child. What are we doing wrong? No wonder more people don't adopt—why should they go through this hassle? I'm trying to do something I don't understand until I've done it wrong. Why didn't Mercedes explain it would be this hard? Why can't she make it easier?"

Casey held me in the car until I ran out of complaints and tears. "We'll do it," he assured me. "Nobody can make this easy. We just have to take things one step at a time. Mercedes can only do so much; she can't change the system for us."

"Well, at least she's seen us in person—we're not just a file anymore," I said, feeling spent. "I hope she liked us."

When we returned from our meeting with Mercedes, we were sure of one thing. It was up to us to get our act together and finish up our end of the process before the squeaky wheels of adoption would begin to turn. I called ACCEPT and asked to talk to Bev, the woman who handles the paperwork. "I know you've explained this stuff a hundred times to me over the phone, but I'm coming in and I'm bringing my binder of forms. Please, I beg you, let me stay in the office until every one of these is filled out."

"I thought you'd never ask," she said drolly, glad for a possible reprieve from my daily calls.

To complicate matters further, we were given the opportunity to buy our first house. My mother offered to help out with part of the down payment while housing prices and interest rates were low. Fate, testing our limits for change, had created another huge learning curve for us: escrow, homeowners insurance, property taxes and all the other minutiae of buying a house. The house we found was a Spanish-style, stucco home located in a good neighborhood but on a busy street (the reason we could afford it). It was small—two bedrooms, one bath—but we figured that the chance to own our own home outweighed the disadvantage of our two girls having to share a bedroom. Besides, it had beautiful hardwood floors, charming hand molding throughout, and a newly designed kitchen. We didn't need a huge house, we reasoned. If we only knew.

Another road block for us was that Colombians had a different sense of time and bureaucracy than Casey and I. If the Colombian Social Services office ran out of money for postage, they simply wouldn't mail anything until their next postage allocation. At first, I took it all in stride. But as the months rolled by with endless snafus and hang-ups, I became more and more frustrated. Meanwhile, Mercedes moved to the East Coast. We received all our information and instructions from her by telephone and her accent was so thick that I was lucky if I understood half of what she said.

"I warned you it wouldn't be easy," Bee reminded us.

"You'll get through it, you always do," comforted my mother.

"I know it's hard to wait," said Marge.

"Will it really ever happen?" asked Meghan.

"Are you still trying to adopt?" asked neighbors.

Eventually, friends didn't ask questions anymore. They knew I would tell them if I had any news and they didn't want to upset me. Actually, I missed talking about it. Like I said, when I was pregnant, my baby was a constant source of discussion. But you can only discuss your latest police clearance for so long. Most people don't want to hear about the ins and outs of the Colombian foster care system—and who can blame them? You can't give a baby shower for an anonymous mystery child who may arrive a year from now. The first Thanksgiving after we had decided to adopt, I made the announcement to friends and family that next year at this time we would have another child. The next Thanksgiving, I wasn't making any predictions and was feeling very sorry for myself. But at least by then we had finished the last form. All that was left to do was wait, which turned out to be much harder by far than completing any of the paperwork.

My career was in flux along with everything else. I decided to leave my job at the children's museum to pursue the goal of being self-employed. I figured that I could make more money if I worked as a designer and art director on an independent contractor basis. I'd have flexible hours when we traveled to Colombia—if that day ever arrived—and could spend more time with Meghan and her new sister. More time, more money, better working conditions ... Anyone reading this who is self-employed is laughing his head off right about now. But I thrived on the challenge. The effort to find a steady flow of corporate clients and to learn the fine art of running a business helped keep me occupied in a positive way while we waited for a referral. Later, Casey left Apple and we joined forces to create Conroy & Conroy, a communication and design firm. Casey created the "words" and I created the "pictures." We had to do without the company adoption bonus we'd been planning on, as well as all the wonderful benefits that Apple had provided (finding our own health insurance was painful), but working for ourselves was satisfying and our company grew. Now, if only our family could.

Finally, in March 1993—eighteen eternal months from the time we began the adoption process—we got the call we had been waiting for. Except that it wasn't quite what we had expected.

Chapter 4

MARIA

*Our initial photo of Maria resembled
me when I was a toddler.*

Letter from Mercedes, March 1993

Dear Casey and Maggie:

I am sending to you the information and a color copy photograph of the child I told you about over the phone and I think for her age is the most appropriate for you to consider.

I want you to take your time reading the information and let me know.

We had a referral—a child available for us to adopt—at last. It was for a three-year-old girl named Maria. But there was a catch. Maria was undersized and had rickets and various other health problems. She had been born the ninth child of a poor farm woman who refused to acknowledge her birth. The mother claimed that she had never been pregnant and had no idea where Maria might have come from. She refused to care for her new baby and her husband spent his days in the fields trying to earn a living and grow enough food for his family. Therefore, Maria's sisters tried as best they could to care for her. But Maria failed to thrive and became malnourished. Eventually, Social Services came and took her into foster care. It was unknown what effect the lack of nourishment would have on her long-term growth and development but she seemed to be happy. Would we like to see her picture?

"Can you send it FedEx?" I cried.

"Slow down, Maggie," cautioned Casey.

When the package containing Maria's picture arrived, I tore it open immediately and gasped. This was our child. She was beautiful. Her eyes—dark brown eyes—looked just like mine when I was her age. We couldn't tell exactly how little she was, but the man's leg that was next to her in the picture looked enormous.

We scheduled a meeting with our pediatrician right away to ask about the effects of malnutrition—not something we had ever had to think about before. After reviewing Maria's sketchy medical history, she was cautious.

"I can't tell you how much the lack of food and her failure to thrive has affected her brain," Dr. Morgan told us. "Maria could have learning difficulties, but that doesn't mean she can't lead a productive and happy life."

"What about her size?" Casey asked.

"She might always be small for her age, but barring other unknown conditions, with a proper diet and medical attention she should be relatively healthy."

I sat wondering what "relatively" meant. Casey asked a stream of medical questions.

"Here's the bottom line," she finally told us. "Maria is a high-risk proposition. I can't tell you what might lie ahead concerning this child's health. You have to decide if the high probability of medical and learning problems are acceptable for your family."

We thanked Dr. Morgan and drove home without saying much. I stared at Maria's photo, clasped tightly in my hand. I didn't want to lose this child.

We'd known that most children who were in the care of Social Services would have some kind of health problems, we just hadn't anticipated facing what we then considered a high level of risk. I felt depressed that, after all this time, we were having to make a decision that felt uncomfortable. How could we accept a child joyfully into our family with so little information?

When we were filling out our paperwork for Colombia, we had to answer a questionnaire about what special needs we would be willing to accept in a child. I can't describe how hard it was to answer those questions. Would we be willing to raise a child with one arm? A blind child? How about a child who had been sexually or emotionally abused? What about multiple handicaps? What was our family threshold for dealing with special needs?

How were we supposed to know? When Meghan was born, I hoped for the best, but knew I would have to find a way to cope with whatever challenges she might have. Even a baby who is born perfect may develop serious medical problems in the future. I certainly wasn't asked to make a decision to have a child by taking into account every genetic glitch that might possibly occur. But now we were being asked to knowingly choose the degree of imperfection we could tolerate. Now we had to decide whether to accept Maria, a child of flesh and blood, who would arrive with a multitude of health problems. She was much more than a line item on a form.

I had already made up my mind. It was made up the second I saw Maria's picture. Casey wasn't as sure.

"Her health problems just mean she needs us," I said.

"Oh Maggie, try to be rational about this child," Casey said.

"She's already had one mother turn her away."

"I'd like to wait for a referral that isn't so risky."

"But we've worked so hard and waited so long for *this* referral."

"If Maria has serious health problems, will we have the money we'll need for all her medical bills?"

"We'll find the money somehow."

"What if we spend so much time with Maria that Meghan feels pushed aside because she's healthy?"

"Turning her down could be turning down something fated to be."

"It could be fate that we've been given the opportunity to think about this rationally."

"Does our child have to be perfect for us to love her? She probably won't be a brain surgeon. Is that important?"

"No, but we've got to consider what adopting this child will mean to our family."

"How will we *ever* know for sure if a child is right for us based on a one-page Social Services report? We don't know what the future holds."

"I'm concerned. I want to be careful."

"I love this child."

"I can't fall in love with a picture. I need to know more."

"I can't wait for another referral. What if we get put on the bottom of the list?"

"Then we wait. I'd rather wait and be sure I'm making the right choice."

"I love this child," I said.

"I know," Casey sighed, taking me into his arms.

"I love this child."

"I know."

Sometime late that night, a decision was made. My conviction was very strong and Casey knew from experience what a powerful force that could be. The adoption process had worn us both down and we wanted to get on with our lives, even if that meant accepting something we weren't completely prepared for. Casey wanted to be practical, but confessed to me that his heart was telling him that we wouldn't have discovered Maria if we couldn't handle what she would bring to our family. We both felt sure that no matter what the outcome, we would learn a great deal from her. So, a marathon twenty-four hours after we had received the picture and information on Maria, we called the Colombian adoption agency and accepted the referral. Neither one of us had slept.

I spent the next days on a "baby high." We showed Maria's picture to Meghan. I shopped for clothing to take to Colombia. We began making travel plans. I found a photograph of myself when I was three years old and sent it along with Maria's to family members and close friends. The photos were practically identical.

Finally, after all this time, people had something to get excited about. We had a real child to celebrate and to prepare for. But fate is a funny thing. Two weeks later we got another call from the agency. Because of her special needs, the Colombian Social Service workers had given Maria's information packet out to several agencies—all at the same time. So, many other families had been considering Maria at the same time we were. "How sad for those other families," I thought.

How sad for us, it turned out. At that very moment, another couple, already in Colombia, was finalizing Maria's adoption. She would be their child, not ours.

The news felt like a physical blow. I wanted our agency to correct this horrible mistake. I wanted them to convince this other family—whom I pictured as unscrupulous baby-snatchers—that a terrible mistake had been made, that we were already this girl's parents. I was stunned that a child could be promised to more than one family. I was angered at the callousness of Colombian Social Services, whose attitude, in my mind, was "better luck next child." What kind of sadistic behavior was this? I was furious with the agency worker bearing the news. "How could this happen?" I cried into the phone, long-distance, to someone I'd never met before. *"How could you let this happen?!* Has this ever happened before? Aren't there laws to protect people from this sort of thing!"

"We had no idea," the agency worker answered calmly. "We feel awful about this, but you have to realize that Maria has been placed with loving parents. She will have an excellent home."

My mind wasn't ready to acknowledge this reality. *We* were to be her loving parents! I wanted to know more—maybe I could figure out a solution; visitation, open adoption, I was grasping at straws. "What country do they come from?" I asked. "What are their names? Can we write to them to see how Maria is?"

Of course we couldn't have any of this information, and later it seemed ridiculous—even to me—to have asked. But at the time it was very important for me to know. I wasn't ready to give up the idea of Maria.

I cried. I couldn't quit crying. I was crying for Maria, for the months of paperwork and waiting, for the anxiety, and for the hope we had put into this process to find her. It wasn't supposed to happen this way. I began to blame Casey and myself. If we had said yes the moment we were told about Maria and had taken the first plane to Colombia, would we be the family finalizing an adoption? I knew my feelings weren't justified. I knew I was being petty and selfish. I should be thanking God that Maria had a home at last and didn't have to wait one more day for loving parents. I should have thanked God that I had Meghan and Casey to love. I should have been able to see the whole picture, but I couldn't. I was infuriated at the Colombian Social Services people for allowing another family to take our child. I was angry at Mercedes for not being more informed when she gave out a referral. I was mad at ACCEPT for not protecting us. I was upset at family and friends for not knowing exactly how I felt, and at the world for expecting me to continue my daily routine. And I was especially incensed with myself for having thought I could control a situation that was completely out of my control. I was swallowed up by my own feelings of failure, grief, and ineffectiveness.

Casey's disappointment and grief were quite different from mine, and at the time I saw that as a betrayal. While he was trying to be strong for Meghan and me, I wanted him to be as upset and as hurt as I was. It was easier for him to accept that Maria wouldn't be our child. He had never bonded with Maria's photograph the way I had. He had chosen to wait until it was certain before committing his heart. I envied and hated his ability to do this. Instead of comforting me, his strength angered me!

I think the power of my emotions surprised Casey. He actually felt a bit relieved that the universe had taken this unknown special needs child out of our lives and into the home of another family who might have even better resources to help her grow to her potential. He was accepting this as the latest turn in our path. Why wasn't I? Because I had to grieve first. In my mind I had lost a child, a child that had attached herself to my body as if she had always been there. No one could understand why I felt so passionate about a child I had never held in my arms or even seen in person. A social worker later told me she thought it was ridiculous how people let themselves bond with a mere photograph of a child. I didn't even answer her, knowing that she would never be able to understand that, sensing the presence of a child's soul, and therefore bonding with that child, can happen at any time; and for some people it can happen after seeing a "mere photograph." It had happened to me with Maria.

Eventually, I was able to take a certain joy in Maria's good fortune, even though I still wanted physical proof that she was happy and thriving in her new home—proof I can never hope to receive. My selfishness began to transform into an even stronger resolve to give a home to another child. I began to see Casey's way of handling our loss as different and not as bad or wrong.

Looking back now, I think losing Maria was, in a way, like a miscarriage. I've heard all the advice and well-meaning comments people make in that situation: "Miscarriage is nature's way of preventing a deformed baby from being born." "You can always try again for another child." "Better to happen early in the pregnancy than later." "At least it wasn't a *real* child yet." Now I know these comments don't help a grieving mother. I just say, "I'm sorry for your loss." The gift I received from Maria was empathy and understanding. I will always love her.

Chapter 5

DIANA

Our first glimpse of Nadia.

From a list of adoption agency requirements, 1993

H. **Police clearance.** *You can obtain an NCIC search at the State Police which details your police record, or lack thereof. This will involve them taking your fingerprints on their forms and running a check. (This is not to be confused with the fingerprints for INS and their check. These are two separate processes.) Make some phone calls first so they know what you need, and you know when you can get it. Since it must be notarized, this clearance might only be available during certain hours in some counties. If possible, couples should get one clearance for both parties; if not possible, individual clearances for each are fine (just more expensive to authenticate).*

Marge gave me a stack of adoption magazines filled with adoptive parents' stories. "Read these," she told me. "It will help you put things in perspective. In all the years I've worked in the adoption field, I've never had a persistent family fail to adopt a child. I've never had a family wait longer than two years. Don't give up."

The stories gave me hope. I was amazed to see what people had gone through to give a child a home. Some adoptions appeared easy—beginning to end, just a few months of paperwork. "So it really can happen that way," I marveled. Other stories were ridiculously complex: months, sometimes years, of waiting in a foreign country for a newly adopted infant to be released into the United States or programs closing just days before a child was to be allowed to leave the country. These stories were a testament to an amazing force that drives a person through the most traumatic of circumstances to find a child to nurture. The brave families I read about had such a strong desire to have a child that they poured all their financial and emotional resources into a quest for parenthood. If they could do it, often under much more daunting circumstances than ours, then so could we.

My newfound insights sound very noble. The truth was, I still called Bee at least once a week and whined about how hard it was to wait. I felt a bit guilty if I let a day go by without at least making *some* effort to bring my child home. It was as if I could feel that she was somewhere waiting for me to find her.

Casey took the constant delays in stride. He was a much better example of our religious beliefs in trusting "a perfect time for everything." I, on the other hand, was a fallen practitioner and saw Casey's ability to go on with life as usual as a huge character flaw. I wanted him up when I was up, and down when I was down. We were doing a familiar marital dance and kept stepping on the other's toes. I was impatient and in constant motion; Casey was laid back and going with the flow. I've found that even when two people love each other, they aren't always on the same path at the same time. In the end, things usually balance out, but the interim can be hell.

The news from Mercedes was discouraging. There was great upheaval in the Colombian Social Services administration. People she had known and worked with for years were leaving, being replaced by people who had no idea who she was. It was taking her days just to get through to the new replacements. "They have moved their offices," we were told one day. "Nothing will happen until they get settled."

Then she told us all our paperwork had been misplaced. There was nothing we could do but ask pathetic questions such as, "Well, do they know where they saw the files last?"

Bee understood I needed to stay in motion. She did her best to come up with ideas for groups to contact for support and would call Colombia herself to get more information whenever she could. While I was telling her the sad tale of the lost file, I heard a rustling of papers followed by a long pause, then, "Well, Maggie, I don't know if I should even tell you about this . . ." Another pause. "I just got a letter from a woman named Diana Revutsky. Russia has reopened to foreign adoption and she's starting a new program there. The good news is, she's located in the Bay Area. The bad news is, she doesn't have a track record. Maybe you should call her and see about her program."

I was thrilled. I could do something. I had a task. I called Diana right away.

I was amazed from the start by Diana's energy for her work. Her apparent urgency not to waste a moment was the complete opposite of our experience so far with Colombia, and I loved it! She explained that she was born in the country of Georgia. While helping a friend interpret the complex maze of Russian adoption laws, she had been struck by the desperate need for someone who was familiar with both countries to act as a liaison between the two widely different governments and cultures. Since finding this new passion, Diana had spent the last year developing relationships with Russian orphanages and officials—putting in place a network to help Americans adopt Russian children. The name of her agency was The Russian Liaison, and she was now ready to accept clients. I told her we were hoping to adopt a girl between the ages of three and five, and—to my shock and surprise—she told me she had two girls in that age group she wanted to find homes for. I was stunned. "What are their names?" I asked, trying to sound like a calm, cool, collected woman, deserving of a child. I gripped the phone tighter because my hands were shaking.

"Nadia and Ruta," she answered. Diana began describing each girl, their birth dates, where their orphanages were located, but I can't remember a word she said other than "Ruta" and "Nadia."

I'd like to relate what that first hint of our future child felt like—but the feelings are gone. Only a sense of overwhelming emotion remains. I wanted to ask Diana if I could come over to her office right away but Casey was out of town on business. Instead, we made a date to meet the day Casey returned, and then we said our goodbyes. The phone was barely in its cradle when I screamed with joy and danced around the room. "Oh yes, oh yes," I yelled to the ceiling and walls of the room. "I've got to get hold of Casey!"

Casey was in Arizona delivering a training course to a group of corporate executives. I had to call several numbers before I found someone who could track him down and put him on the phone. "What's wrong?" he asked breathlessly, imagining a major crisis.

"We may have a child!" I told him. "From Russia!"

I can't imagine how this must have felt to Casey. Pulled out of an important training session by his almost-incoherent wife, to hear about not one child, but two children; not from Colombia, but from Russia; and not through Mercedes, but a woman he'd never heard of before named Diana. "Oh, and by the way, honey, we're meeting with Diana on the way home from the airport to see the girls' pictures and read over a possible contract." Kind of makes a guy scared to leave home . . . or maybe just scared to return.

I tried to control my excitement when Meghan got home from school that day. After all, she had heard all about Maria and then that had fallen through. I wanted this to be something we were more sure of before I spoke to her of the possibilities. She was just thrilled to see her mother in such a great mood. We even went out for ice cream—before dinner! Meghan knew enough not to ask questions. She just said, "Chocolate chip, please."

Casey and I could only grin when we first met Diana. (These grins were becoming our default setting.) On our emotional adoption bungie jump, we were definitely on the up-swing, but we both knew that it was a long way down from the platform. Casey was immediately enthralled with Diana's Russian accent and wanted to know how to say hello in Russian. "*Zdrazvooityil*," she answered, and Casey mimicked it back perfectly. I knew then that Russian was going to be a lost language on me. Even hello seemed out of my diction range. "Hi," I said.

Diana was gracious and charming, insisting on getting us cool drinks before we talked. I just wanted to see the pictures. Casey wanted to ask endless questions about her work in Russia. She showed us pictures of children that she was currently placing with other families. They all looked beautiful. "I'd adopt any one of them," I thought to myself. "How wonderful and healthy they look." Finally, she showed us the pictures of Ruta and Nadia. How could we possibly choose? They were both cute, but what did cute mean, and did cute have anything to do with it?

I began thinking up reasons to choose one child over the other:

- My mother's name is Ruth; Ruta sounds a lot like Ruth.
- I had a cat in college named Nadia.
- Ruta is wearing glasses, so she must need us more than Nadia, who appears to see fine without glasses.
- I was a gymnast when I was younger; I was captivated by Nadia Comaneci.

- Ruta's hair is darker than Nadia's. Maybe she will look more like us.
- Nadia looks like she needs a family to comfort her.
- Ruta looks like she needs a family to help her smile.

These profound impressions weren't the best basis for a sound decision. Casey looked as if he was weighing his own impressions with no more luck than I was having. We looked at Diana. "How can we choose?"

Thankfully Diana helped. "Nadia is a year older than Ruta. Soon she will have to go on to an orphanage for older children. Of course it is strictly your choice, but Nadia will have little or no chance to be adopted from the next orphanage." She went on to explain that in the Russian orphanage system there are fewer caregivers as the children get older, and a greater mix of ages. Life can be very hard for the newest children; they are often treated cruelly by older children, who find them easy targets to vent their frustrations.

"I will find a home for both of these girls, but I must act quickly with Nadia."

I looked at Nadia's picture again. I had accepted Maria so quickly. Why wasn't I feeling that same tug with Nadia? She seemed like a sweet child although her hair looked as if it had been cut in a dark closet, with blunt scissors, by a hairdresser who was having a bad day. Diana explained that all the children were given frequent haircuts to keep them from getting lice. Nadia held a doll tightly in her arms as if protecting it from the stranger who snapped the photograph. Her eyes were small and a bit puffy, as if she hadn't gotten enough sleep the night before. Her smile looked fake, tentative, a smile in place by request rather than from happiness. She did look healthy and well cared for, though. What was wrong with me? Where was that tug on my heartstrings?

Although some parents travel around the world to bring home a child they have never seen, most receive a single photograph. That photo of Nadia became our only connection with her. We stared at it often, trying to decipher Nadia's personality from that split second the camera shutter opened into her world. I am thankful that I have never had to be chosen for anything based on a family snapshot or, heaven forbid, my driver's license photo. Imagine a whole life hinging on a good hair day. I tell people now that in a foreign adoption the final decision can be based only on the desire to have a child. Anything else is not reliable information, and that's just the way it is.

I knew that we would have adopted either child. So why were we hesitating? All I can answer is that we were protecting ourselves from something that seemed too good to be true. Diana did not push; she gave us a contract to read over. "Just let me know, after you've had a chance to think things through," she told us. Then she looked at my face and added presciently, "Don't worry, I won't show their pictures to anyone else until you have decided what you want to do."

Casey and I went to a restaurant to eat lunch but I wasn't very hungry. We talked about Diana's program and Nadia. But we felt unsure and didn't know why. What was the problem? After working on this for almost two years, why were we hesitating? We both trusted Diana. What were we waiting for? We talked some more and realized that we were waiting for another Maria. Nadia wasn't Maria. "That's *our* problem to work through," Casey said, *"Nadia's* our child. What more is there to think about?" He was absolutely right. We both felt relieved and sure of ourselves once again. We asked the restaurant manager to let us use the phone in back and called Diana excitedly. "Can we come back right now?" Casey asked. "We want to sign a contract and get the paperwork started for Nadia." We hugged delightedly and raced back to Diana's. We spent the rest of the day showing Nadia's picture off to anyone who would look, whether we knew them or not. Each time we told someone of our good fortune, we felt stronger that Nadia was indeed going to be the final hurrah in our story.

With Diana's support, paperwork that had taken us months to accomplish for the Colombian government took a matter of days for Russia. With Nadia's picture—a picture of a real child— in front of us, we were much more aggressive about moving along on fingerprints, paperwork, and doctors' appointments. We made a photo album of our home and family to be sent to the director of Nadia's orphanage.

We were invited to Diana's for brief lessons in Russian. We listened to Russian language tapes in the car. Even Meghan would listen attentively to the female voice over the speaker utter a Russian phrase and try with us to repeat it. (Meghan and I couldn't speak directly to anyone since there was something about the sounds that made both of us spit.) At first we could keep up—

the alphabet sounds were easy enough to repeat as long as we didn't have to remember what we had just said. Later, though, when the voice began expecting us to repeat longer, four-word sentences, we could only laugh.

"My husband is missing," the woman on the tape said in English and then repeated in Russian what sounded to me like *"Tioenr fkfdldoeorityehdkgflskdjhghf dlfkgjririeoririt didiekthtlrkejerjrkt."*

When she paused, I couldn't even remember what the first word sounded like, let alone pronounce it.

"You better be careful in Russia," I told Casey, "because I won't be able to let anyone know if you're missing!"

Three months after our first meeting with Diana we were given a date to travel: Friday, October 8. Diana gave us this news from Russia, where she would be staying until after our adoption was finished. She wanted to make sure there would be no problems or surprises once we got over there. We would be going to Russia with another couple who also lived in San Jose. They were adopting two boys from the same orphanage Nadia lived in. Their names were Steve and Frances Smith, and we often called them on the phone to compare notes as we prepared for our trip. What kind of coat are you bringing? What do you think the weather will be like? Are you going to bring bottled water? How will you carry your money? We kept our questions and conversations on the surface though, I suppose because we were each afraid to get too deeply involved in case something went wrong with either one of our plans. We knew firsthand that things could fall apart at the last minute. Still, it was fun having another couple just as confused and excited as we were to share shopping lists with.

After all our hard work getting our paperwork in order (we had been waiting so long that some of it had expired and we had to start over), we wanted and needed a time to be a family with Meghan. We went to Yosemite with my brother Chuck, his wife Penny, and their two boys, Anthony and Ashton. We spent a glorious weekend riding bikes, taking long walks, watching deer, and tuning out the outside world from inside our cozy cabin. Casey and I were dancing together again, moving to the same beat, no longer at arms' length. "Just think," I said to Casey, "the next time we're here, Meghan will have a sister."

We arrived home to discover that Russia was in political turmoil.

Chapter 6

RUSSIA

A traditional Russian doll.

~❧~

Newsweek

> *Twelve days after Boris Yeltsin had dissolved the hardline parliament, blood was flowing in the streets of Moscow. In response to the growing crisis, Yeltsin declared a state of emergency in Moscow on Sunday afternoon, hours after protesters had stormed police lines, smashing armored vehicle windshields and breaking onto the grounds of the White House parliament headquarters, where more than 100 deputies were still holed up. He called government troops out onto the streets, and seemed prepared to use force if necessary to put down the uprising.*

As we packed to leave for Russia, in early October 1993, we listened to the news of the *putch,* or coup, in Moscow. While we were buying gifts for the orphanage, Boris Yeltsin was dissolving the Russian parliament and calling for the early election of a new national assembly. While we were deciding how much bottled water to take, the White House in Moscow was under siege by troops with heavy artillery.

Diana was staying in a Moscow apartment close to the White House. We worried for her safety. Four days before we left, we received a notice from the U.S. State Department advising against travel to the Republic of Russia, but to wait any longer was unthinkable. If there was going to be trouble, we wanted to get Nadia out; and the doors to foreign adoption might be closed again at any time.

Our lives were crazy with last-minute preparations. You would think that after waiting almost two years for this event we wouldn't be running around like mad people, but we were. A million details and fears kept cropping up. We had shots, visas, gifts, and travel supplies to procure. We had work projects to finalize for clients. I wrote three pages of detailed instructions for friends who were going to care for Meghan while we were away. The day before we left, we were scrambling to get a document notarized stating that we would accept any medical problems Nadia may have—known and unknown. (We tried not to dwell on what that could mean.)

Meghan complained bitterly about not being able to go with us until she learned that anyone traveling to Russia had to get a shot in their butt. Then she had an immediate change of heart. "That's okay," she declared. "I'd rather stay home with my friends."

The night before we left, Diana's husband, Yephim, telephoned every hour or so with additional instructions from Diana. It was like a spy movie. We would be met at the airport by a tall, dark-haired woman named Natasha. Our driver would be with her. Around midnight Yephim told us that all our money, which we had to take in cash and totaled around $6,000, could not be dated before 1990 owing to problems in Russia with counterfeit bills. We had no choice but to carry so much money. All payments for orphanage fees, accommodations, transportation, translating fees, and other passport, embassy, and bureaucracy costs had to be paid personally in cash.

It was about this time I realized we didn't have a last will and testament—which seemed irresponsible—so I began writing one. There we were going through a huge stack of money and picking out the "old" bills, finishing up last-minute project changes for work, and writing up instructions for who would take care of Meghan in the event of our death and where to scatter the ashes (if a plane crash didn't do it for us, that is). A calm and blissful moment contemplating the joy of adding another life to our home? Definitely not!

When Meghan woke up that morning, we cuddled with her under our quilt. She was very brave about staying with friends while we were away but wondered how she would get along without her parents. We had never been away from each other for this amount of time. I felt as if I were leaving a part of myself behind. Earlier, we had considered taking Meghan with us—letting her be a part of our first meeting with Nadia—but Diana discouraged us. "This isn't a family vacation," she said. "Your schedule will be too exhausting for a child." When I thought about it, I also realized that we needed to focus all our attention, without distraction, on Nadia those first few days. I wasn't ready to submit her to possible sibling rivalry before she even got to know us. So the three of us stayed together, whispering I-love-yous, until it was time for Meghan to leave for school.

Then all hell broke loose. I ran to the bank to exchange our "old" money for "new." (The teller looked at me as if she was trying to discern whether this was some kind of new money-laundering scheme!) We couldn't fit all the supplies, clothes, and gifts into the suitcases so, at the last minute, Casey began taking everything out of their boxes and throwing aside bottles of water and my precious American snack food. We were supposed to leave the house at 12:00, and at 12:30 I realized I had forgotten to get the extra passport photos we needed for a new document requirement that I didn't fully understand. We struggled out of the house with all our baggage and loaded Penny's van. We raced into the Photo Drive-up and begged the saleswoman to take our pictures as quickly as possible. She used a blow dryer to speed up the developing.

When we arrived at the airport, I started trembling. I had been in a daze most of the week trying to get everything done. Now all my emotions were right at the surface. I had so many fears. Will the American Embassy close owing to the unrest? Is Diana in danger? Will they let Nadia out of the country? Will they let us in? Will Meghan be okay without us? What on earth are we doing? Penny noticed my shaky hand and clasped it in hers. "Well, it's finally happening," she said, and we both laughed as tears filled our eyes. "I can't wait to meet my new niece."

"Thanks for everything," I said gratefully and gave her a hug. It *was* happening, our "adoptive water broke," and Casey and I were going to meet our new daughter.

We found the Smiths just before we boarded the plane. We all sat next to each other along with coats, backpacks, and several stuffed animals. We wanted to carry on everything we could, which didn't leave much room in our coach-class seats. I envied the Smiths. They looked so calm. I might have appeared calm to them too, but it was only by sheer will that I was holding my anxiety in check. I knew that if I didn't control my emotions now, I would be a basket case by the end of the trip. I breathed deeply and took out a book I had brought along. I read for most of the ten-hour flight across the Atlantic. Sleep was impossible—I was experiencing "preadoptive stress syndrome" and adrenaline was coursing through my system. We had a two-and-a-half-hour lay-over in Frankfurt, Germany, then, after another three hours in the air, we landed in Moscow.

Casey began a conversation with a passenger named Sergei. Casey asked him question after question while practicing his Russian pronunciation. Sergei was full of advice—some of it frightening. He told us the customs officials might want to count our money. "Sometimes officials give a signal to criminals outside when they find tourists carrying a lot of cash. Be careful."

"So, what does this mean?" I asked Casey when Sergei returned to his seat. "What are we supposed to do to avoid being targeted? Should we *not* declare our cash?"

"I have no idea, but I guess it's a good thing to be aware of."

"Oh, I feel much better. Now I don't have to *imagine* things that might go wrong; I have something *real* to worry about."

"Relax. What's the worst that could happen?"

The word *gulag* flashed into my mind.

Landing in Moscow was quite an experience. Not only were Sergei's friendly warnings still fresh in our minds, but it felt as if we had landed on another planet. Except for the stream of passengers flowing down the dimly lit, cement-walled hallways, I didn't see any people at first. Then we arrived at a line of booths with soldiers checking our passports and visas. Past the customs stations there was a mob of people waiting. We were separated from the Smiths and didn't know where they were. All the faces I saw looked solemn. I felt as though we had left, somewhere in the air, the Technicolor world I was accustomed to and had entered a world of gray. One bit of off-color did remain, however. Two businessmen from Texas were talking loudly and whooping it up, oblivious to the quiet people around them. They lit cigarettes and later ground them out on the floor with the toes of their boots. As strange as the surroundings seemed to me, I was more surprised by their disrespect. "Ugly Americans," I thought.

We were nervous about being questioned regarding our suit-cases full of children's clothes and gifts. I couldn't shake my cold war impressions of the "evil empire" from childhood. Would they think we were bringing in this stuff to sell? How did they feel about Americans coming over to adopt Russian children? After waiting in line for almost an hour, we finally stood before still another soldier at the customs station ready to give our rehearsed answers to any questions we thought he might pose. He didn't even look at us. He scribbled something on the form, and waved us through.

We found Natasha (or rather she found us in the sea of people). She was to be our primary contact while we were in Moscow, but Diana had arranged for us to stay with Russian families each night. The hotels in Moscow are very expensive, and Diana didn't want us to have to go out on our own for food. The people she found (highly recommended and interviewed at great length) were willing to house and feed us in their apartments for a nightly fee of around $40. At that time, $40 was roughly a month's salary for many Russian people, so it was a win-win situation. We were to pay our driver about $8 an hour.

Natasha welcomed us with a big smile that faded a little as she told us we must hurry. Since the imposition of martial law, Moscow had a curfew of 11:00 P.M.—it was important that we make it to our apartment early enough for the driver to get home. We didn't know what the consequence for being out past curfew was, but we certainly didn't want our driver sitting in a Moscow jail when we needed him to drive us around.

As our car left the airport, it was stopped at a checkpoint by soldiers with automatic weapons. Great, I thought, not even in the country two hours and already in trouble with the military! Our driver reached into his glove compartment for papers and got out to speak with the soldiers. Natasha, in another car with the Smiths, hadn't been stopped so we couldn't ask her what this was all about. Casey and I just looked at each other with wide eyes and waited. When the soldiers were satisfied with our driver's paperwork, he got back into the car and took off again. He spoke only a few words in English, *"Putch*—revolution. They want . . . passport for me, passport for car." We relaxed a bit. Just another hassle in the life of a Muscovite, it appeared.

Off we went along pothole-riddled roads, lights off or on, depending on the whim of the driver, passing in and out of traffic, toward the heart of Moscow. We saw no single-family homes, only gigantic concrete apartment complexes that stretched for blocks. There were box-like, brightly lit, kiosks along the road every few feet selling snacks, drinks, and trinkets—the 7-Elevens of Russia.

As we entered the central district and crossed the Moscow River, we saw the Kremlin. Brightly lit, it was lovely, surreal. Casey grilled the driver with questions consisting of one or two

Russian words and he got one- or two-word answers in English. He wanted to know everything about what we were passing— the buildings, the architecture, the history, the politics. It was amazing how much he was able to learn this way, but it was also exhausting. Besides, I could think only of Nadia. Her orphanage was in Kaliningrad, which is in a region of Russia next to the Baltic Sea, separated by Byelarus (White Russia) and Lithuania from the main bulk of the country. We were much closer to her, yet still so far away.

We met the Smiths at the flat around 10:00 and were greeted by an older lady who evidently had, for some time, been preparing a meal for us. There were plates of cold cuts, sausages, potatoes, and thick-sliced, brown bread. Two sweaty pitchers were placed in the middle of the table along with a pot of beet-colored soup. The table and chairs filled most of the living room. There was no dining room and the kitchen could hold only one person at a time, but the apartment was large by Russian standards: it had two bedrooms. We put our bags in one of them, which pretty much took care of any extra space.

Ana was the name of our new hostess and she didn't speak a word of English. As soon as our driver and Natasha left, we only saw Ana when she was scurrying back and forth from the kitchen with more food. (She was horrified when Frances and I later offered to help clean up. She looked as if we might report her to Diana for not being able to handle her job. Since we couldn't explain our motives, we didn't ask again.) There was also a young girl—Ana's granddaughter, we guessed—named Victoria. She was so shy that even in this small place I did not actually see her face until late the next day. When I first saw her in the kitchen, she was looking out the window and would not turn around. She seemed to be terrified of us American strangers. I wondered if Nadia would have a similar reaction when we met her.

Our room had two narrow twin beds, which lay end to end. We guessed that we were staying in Victoria's room because childlike, charcoal portraits were neatly pinned to the walls. Perhaps she shared it with her grandmother. It was hard to tell how many people actually lived in this flat when American visitors weren't about. I sank deep into the mattress the minute I lay down and pulled the thick comforter around me. I fell into a deep sleep immediately but woke up just a few hours later and couldn't fall back asleep. All the images of Nadia I had created over the past few weeks began replaying over and over in my mind. Meghan made an appearance too—I pictured her missing us; wishing she could call before leaving for school; mad at herself for not figuring out a way to reach us. I remembered a week that summer when she had visited my mother in Iowa. She was having a great time, but when my mother was occupied, Meghan stole into the guest room and called us long-distance. I thought the first call was very clever—my little girl was growing up. But after I got another call that same morning at work, I had to lay down some rules."I memorized all the numbers where you might be," she told me proudly. (The only way I could get her off the line was to play the "let's-see-who-can-hang-up first" game.) God forbid Meghan should get her hands on a Russian phone book. Diana had warned us that we might not be able to place any calls to the United States while we were in Russia, but I still wished I could hear Meghan's voice and tell her we were safe and well. Finally, around 4:00 A.M. I heard Casey tossing. "Are you awake?" I asked softly.

"Yeah, come on over," he whispered back.

I squeezed in beside him and we cuddled. "I can't believe Maggie and Casey Conroy are sleeping in a twin bed in the heart of Moscow," I giggled.

"I can't believe we *fit* in this twin bed." We both quieted and stared up at the ceiling. "I want to see everything while we're here," he said presently. "Maybe Diana could arrange for us to visit St. Petersburg."

"Not me, I only want to see Nadia. We'll come back later when our children are wealthy and pay for a month-long tour. I think we should throw in Paris and Berlin while we're at it."

"Sounds good to me."

"This really is amazing, isn't it?"

"Yes, it really is."

The next day we all purchased tickets for the flight to Kaliningrad. Whenever possible, we paid for our purchases ourselves with American currency. While buying our Aeroflot tickets, we discovered why we had to bring new, clean money. When I paid for the tickets, the clerk slid each bill into a scanning machine. One of the bills she fed into the slot shot back out. She handed it back mechanically saying, *"Nyet!"* With a frown, she held out her hand for a replacement bill that wasn't counterfeit. I was embarrassed and wanted to tell her that the money couldn't possibly be bad. Natasha gave me a don't-make-a-scene look and I quickly fumbled for more cash, making sure it was especially acceptable-looking.

After we bought the tickets, our driver took us to view the city. We drove past the White House, the Russian Parliament building that had recently been under siege. The bright sunlight reflected from the windows of the still-elegant lower half of the building. In sharp contrast, the top section was blackened with soot; the windows blown out from the bombing early in the month. It felt surreal to see people walking along the sidewalks with their packages and bundles, dressed in fall coats, stopping whenever one of the many soldiers motioned them over to be searched. Nearby was the American Embassy, a low, mustard-colored building that took up most of the block. Casey and Steve got out to take pictures—the driver began to look nervous.

As Casey climbed over concrete barricades, trying unsuccessfully to engage a guard in conversation, our driver began pointing to the surrounding buildings. "Ah . . . ah . . ." he stammered, trying to think of the right English term as he stabbed the air with his finger. Finally, between gestures, he thought of the word he needed. "Snipers," he said.

"Oh, snipers!" I said, happy that I could understand even if I didn't speak the same language. Then it sank in. He was trying to please us by taking us where we asked. We didn't know there were snipers!

"It's time to go—now!" I yelled to Casey, who reluctantly got back into the car.

Moscow's Aeroflot Airport is like a crummier version of big-city bus terminals in the United States. Building inspectors and litigation lawyers in the United States would have a field day with all the visible code violations and disrepair. Stairways were crumbling, doors wouldn't open, and everything seemed broken. Because the ticketing system wasn't computerized, all the tickets, receipts, and transactions had to be done by hand, so the check-in lines were long. Thank goodness Natasha was there to speak for us to a multitude of grouchy clerks who didn't seem happy about being disturbed by those wishing to fly on their airline. Whatever Natasha told us to do, we did; wherever she told us to go, we went.

The jet we boarded was old and didn't look very sturdy. As we climbed the steps, I noticed some yellow-green fluid dripping from underneath the wing—I tried to ignore it. It didn't look like the interior of the plane had been maintained or even touched since the mid-1950s. The wall coverings were yellowed and peeling, the overhead lights were dim, the cloth seats were worn, and many of the seat belts were either nonfunctional or missing. (Later Diana told me that the limited funds in Russia have to be spent on necessities. "Would you rather have the money spent on the engines and the mechanics of the plane, or on the interior and the seats?") We finally found some seats that looked promising. The stewardess was a large, dour-looking woman dressed in a faded, dark blue uniform. She walked up and down the aisle twice during the three-hour flight pushing a small metal cart. The wheels didn't match and squeaked as she walked. She evidently felt that eye contact and a smile were not part of her job description. *"Pazhaoolsta, pazhaoolsta,"* she chanted in a monotone. *Pazhaoolsta* is the Russian word for "please" or "thank-you." It was her way of asking if anyone wanted anything, but everyone pretty much ignored her. Most of the passengers had already begun passing out meat and cheese sandwiches and bottles of vodka they had brought from home. I watched this scene with curiosity, cringing with fear each time we hit an air pocket—which, it seemed to me, happened with alarming regularity. If nothing else, we felt the flight itself was proof of our willingness to go through anything to bring our child home. We felt proud and adventurous.

When we landed, Diana was at the airport to greet us with two women from the orphanage and two drivers. I gave her a big hug—I was so happy to see her. She was familiar and safe, and I felt that, with her there, any possible problems could be overcome. Casey and I were driven to a one-bedroom flat where an older woman named Alyeh lived with her husband, Vladimir. (Vladimir had been banished to their *"dacha,"* a small cabin and garden plot in the country. We wouldn't meet him until two days later.) Diana left to help get Steve and Frances settled into their flat.

Alyeh, like Ana, had a huge feast prepared. The living room table, covered in linen and lace, appeared to be set for a small wedding party. Unfortunately, I couldn't eat very much because I was so nervous. Alyeh stood there wringing her hands in frustration and concern. Her whole reason for being there was to make sure we were well fed and comfortable. She took her job seriously and my light appetite was standing in the way of her success. Lucky for me, Casey was able to eat for the two of us. Of course, she loved him instantly for appreciating her hard work. I would soon learn to wait until she was in the kitchen or looking the other way and then dump as much food on Casey's plate as I could. The night we had liver he looked at me after I transferred my share onto his plate and said, "You owe me big time now, Maggie."

After we ate, Diana called to tell us that she needed to discuss some new information about Nadia. When she arrived, we all sat around the table. Diana looked so serious that a bad feeling settled in the pit of my stomach.

"Evidently Nadia has gained weight," Diana began slowly. "Her mother was quite obese. She didn't even know she was pregnant until she gave birth. Nadia may have her same body type. The orphanage director is worried that you will not want her once you see her."

I stared at her in shock. What did they mean by overweight? If they were this concerned, was there more to this than just being overweight? Why were they worried about how much she weighed? Casey and I looked at each other, trying to read between the lines.

"The director of the orphanage feels strongly that Americans won't accept a child who is overweight," Diana explained to us. "Americans only want thin children. The director doesn't want to prepare Nadia or tell her that we are taking her until you see her and accept her."

I wish I could say that I jumped up immediately and told Diana that I was Nadia's mother no matter what she looked like or what problems she had. But I was tired and Diana's ominous manner was making me panicky. So instead, I just sat there, my eyes brimming with tears.

Diana explained that the director's doubts had come about because, recently, an adoption of an eight-year-old child named Anya had fallen through. The orphanage director thought the

American woman changed her mind because Anya was missing an ear. Everyone was terribly upset—especially Anya, whose stay had already been extended to keep her out of the orphanage for older children.

"These orphanages are dangerous," Diana reminded us. "The youngest girls are subject to abuse and even molestation and rape by the older boys. It is not a safe place. Children have little or no chance of being adopted once they move on."

I couldn't stop the tears from streaming down my face.

Thankfully, Casey kept his calm and said, "Of course we will accept Nadia. We already consider her our daughter. We'll just do our best to give her a healthy diet and lots of exercise."

So simple. Why had I had any doubts? Nadia *was* already our child. My fears stemmed from emotional overload and the ingrained feeling that our society *does* discriminate against people with a less-than-perfect body type. Isn't it human nature to want a child that everyone thinks is adorable? Those who had met Nadia had told us of her sweetness and intelligence—why should she need a "perfect" outside shell? Yet I had almost fallen into that trap. I could understand Diana's caution.

I looked over to Casey, silently saying thank you with my eyes. What I saw in his gaze startled me because I knew right away that he was thinking the same thing I was. We were sure about Nadia; that was settled. But Casey and I wanted to help the girl named Anya. She was a bit older than Meghan, which was something we had earlier ruled against. But we were moved by her story. We asked Diana if it was possible to consider adopting Anya too. Diana wiped her eyes—this was as emotional for her as it was for us. Alyeh peeked in, worried about all the sniffling. Then Diana said, "Don't even think about Anya until you meet both girls tomorrow. Let's take one step at a time. You will be able to observe both girls and then make your final decision regarding Nadia."

"We won't change our minds," we both assured her.

After Diana left, we went into our room exhausted. Alyeh made up our bed and then hers right outside our door in the living room. I didn't want her to hear me cry anymore. Russians tend to be fairly stoic and I wondered what she thought of this American woman who wouldn't eat and who cried all the time.

In the middle of the night, Casey began exhibiting his stress-related habit: talking in his sleep—loudly. (I don't eat. He yells in his sleep.)

"Yeah!" he cried with his arms raised. "I am a handsome wrangler, yesiree!" Then he laughed and started talking to his invisible dream friend who was, I gathered, another cowboy. I shushed him and even began smacking him on the face and shoulders trying to get him to wake up. I had heard Alyeh cough earlier so I knew the walls were far from being soundproof. I could only imagine the impressions of our habits and personalities she was gaining by the minute. All I could think was, "Thank goodness she doesn't understand English. And I hope she realizes he is asleep!"

We awoke at first light. As I looked out the window, it promised to be a crisp, sunny day. I wanted to leave that instant. I couldn't bear to wait another moment, I'd already waited too long. I wanted to meet my daughter. "I'm close, Nadia," I whispered. "I'm almost there."

Chapter 7

NADIA

Nadia wearing some of her new clothes.

October 11, 1993

It was a beautiful drive to Nadia's orphanage, which was two hours outside Kaliningrad in a small village named Slavsk. The road was lined with birch trees on either side, forming a tunnel of yellow, red, and orange.

To calm myself, I gazed out the car window and was soon mesmerized by the trees. Guarding, protecting, and shielding us from the rest of the countryside, they stood at attention just like the German soldiers who had planted them during World War II. At the time it was a German city known as Königsberg; had Nadia been born then, she would have been German instead of Russian. Soon she would have dual Russian/United States citizenship—her life completely changed from what it might have been. Those color-soaked trees seemed to be guiding us onward as we traveled to change the destiny of one child, a child officially known as *Nadezhda Leonidovna Dubinina*. The trees remain in my memory as a symbol of life's unknown even though they themselves have remained unchanged by the history and chaos surrounding them.

I played the scenario over and over in my head, trying to imagine my first meeting with Nadia. I would give her a bear hug and then gently cradle her in my arms, gazing into her eyes with joy. She would respond with a warm hug of her own and cuddle close. She would sense immediately that I was her mother. We would love each other at first sight.

Along the way we were told an interesting bit of news. Even though she was five years old, Nadia had never ridden in a car before. In fact, she had never been away from the orphanage. I hadn't thought of this possibility before and couldn't help making comparisons in my mind. Meghan had flown to Iowa at six months. She had gone to preschool with me at one year. She had friends all over San Jose and was invited to frequent overnights. We had taken her to Disneyland twice before she was five. She had taken gymnastics lessons at four and was now learning to play the piano. This was all normal stuff for an American kid. Nadia, on the other hand, had never walked down the street, let alone stayed overnight at a friend's home. Her world consisted only of the orphanage and their daily routine. The only people she had contact with were those who entered her controlled world. I had never really grasped the enormity of what we would be asking of this little girl. She was leaving the only environment she had ever known for a universe filled with chaos and over stimulation. Our lives stressed *me* out sometimes. What would it be like for her?

Finally, we pulled up to the orphanage. It was a large yellow building which looked like a run-down, possibly abandoned, house that had once been very nice. The fenced-in yard had a few pieces of well-worn playground equipment sticking up from a mound of grass.

Diana went in first and, after a few very long minutes, motioned for us to follow. As we got out of the car, we were met by the director of the orphanage. She was a small, energetic woman with hair the color of a ripe, red tomato. (Many Russian women, we noted, are bold with their choice of hair color.) We followed the director into the front hall, where she told us to wait. Many staff members were arriving and milling around—getting their first glimpses of Americans. I figured that they must have been able to hear my heart pounding from across the room. We were all so nervous! Suddenly two of the workers (beaming) brought out one of the Smiths' boys. He was so radiant and happy! They told him Frances was his mother and he ran and threw his arms around her, then did the same with his new father. It was my fantasy! His older brother soon appeared and followed his lead. It felt to us as if we were watching a slow-motion movie scene in which the long-lost children finally find their parents—always during the final moments—when everybody in the audience digs out a hankie because they're so happy. But where was Nadia?

Soon Diana motioned us to come inside another hallway that led to a large playroom. We didn't see Nadia right away. None of the children looked like the picture we'd had up on our refrigerator for the past three months. Then Casey recognized her and grabbed my arm just as a woman scooped her up and smiled in our direction. She looked puffy to me and certainly had a stocky build, but she was far from obese. Although she wore a sweet dress, it looked three sizes too small for her. She was not smiling. Diana had been with the director, assuring her that we wouldn't change our minds and did indeed want to adopt Nadia.

Now we were all hustled out of the playroom and back into the hallway. *Our* movie scene was moving in fast forward instead of slow motion. This wasn't at all like my fantasy. Nadia wouldn't even look at me. The women around us were telling Nadia that I was her mama. They prodded her into my arms and told her to sit on my lap, which meant that I had to sit down on the floor in the middle of the hall. "Give her a hug, give her a kiss," they ordered. She did all these things like a "Stepford child."

I can't honestly say that I bonded with Nadia during this first meeting, but as Casey and I held her—even as she stared at the floor blankly—I knew this child was meant to be a part of our family. I knew that she needed us very much. For a split second I felt a sense of peace that gave me faith that I would grow to love this child as I would a biological one.

I gave her the doll we had brought. She immediately held it close. The women surrounding us told her she was a mommy too and how much she should appreciate this fine gift. They told her to reprimand the doll since it was sucking its thumb (evidently not a good idea in this orphanage). Nadia went back into the playroom to show the other children her treasure. She seemed happy with the gift, but rather disappointed when she noticed that we were following.

When the director told the children to line up (we didn't know why), Nadia immediately ran to the line, elbowing her way to the front. The director told her she must stay. That's when it dawned on me: Nadia had no idea why this was all happening. The staff had not been able to prepare her for a mother and father if they weren't sure we would accept her. A doll and strange visitors to hug and kiss were not Nadia's only surprises for the day. She had no idea that we were actually taking her away forever!

Anya, the girl Diana had told us of the night before, also stayed in the room with us and was much less shy than Nadia. She ran to show me her favorite doll. Diana was translating for us and Anya turned to her and said, *"Gdye moe mama i papa?* [Where are *my* mother and father?] *Ti ich privezla?* [Did you bring them?]"

Even before Diana told me, I knew what she had said by the hopeful look on her face and the pleading tone of her voice. I wanted to tell her that I would be her mother, but of course I didn't know yet if it would be allowed. We had just done months of paperwork for Nadia; how could we expect the government to allow a child out of the country on a moment's notice? We had only been approved by the INS to adopt one child—we would need to complete a new home study to be considered for another. Maybe, just maybe, we could get around all the legal ramifications. Maybe this *one* time, a child's future would be more important than a ream of paperwork. But I couldn't give Anya false hope. Her plight only emphasized the existence of all the other children who would be left behind that day. I will always see their faces in my mind's eye. Both Casey and I would be forever changed by the experience of meeting these children.

Meanwhile, Nadia hadn't even looked at us once. Diana was able to coax a few words from her, but everyone else was so insistent that they just cowed her all the more. It was as if the staff members had a mission: they were going to get her to interact with us no matter what. At one point, a large woman pulled Nadia over to Casey, put Nadia's arms around his neck, and pushed them together, commanding in a rough voice, "This is your father! Love him! Love him!"

Casey laughed, but it was out of sheer embarrassment and frustration.

When they asked the children to leave so the adults could have lunch, Nadia was the first one to the door. I was numb, my moment of peace long gone. Casey hugged me and we both laughed nervously. "What's the matter here?" I thought. "I can't believe there isn't a better way to handle this transition. How can it ever work?" By the look on Casey's face, he was thinking the same thing. I've since learned that not all orphanages handle first meetings like this one. Most allow the parents to visit the child for a few days while they become familiar with each other before the child leaves the orphanage. Each orphanage has its own style depending on the local and regional directors. We took Nadia home right away partly because the orphanage was so far away from where we were staying.

Lunch was mystery meatloaf, soup, mashed potatoes, and tea.

I forced myself to eat everything on my plate but still managed to offend my hosts by not accepting seconds. Again, Diana had to explain that it wasn't that I didn't like the food but that I don't eat much. Becoming an instant mother must dampen the appetite. I sat there wishing for some other way to show my appreciation.

After lunch we went back to the playroom and found the children dutifully sitting on little chairs in the hall outside. They had been waiting patiently for us throughout our meal. I marveled at their discipline. "Stand up and come," barked one of the caregivers to the children. They immediately obeyed, marching off. Diana motioned for Casey to get our suitcases and for me to follow Nadia. We obeyed immediately—suddenly feeling five years old. We certainly didn't want to find out what would happen if we didn't!

The minute Casey brought in her suitcase, three women swooped in with Nadia and, without any explanation, began taking off all her clothes. One look from them and I began pulling out the clothing we had brought for her. The women grabbed each item I took out and tried it on her. They discarded some and asked for more. I couldn't follow the logic—not to mention the aesthetics—in their choices but I did as they instructed me to do. When it was all over, Nadia had on underwear, a black velvet dress, checked stirrup pants, yellow socks, a slip tucked into her pants, and a coat. The shoes were too big so they let her wear a pair of orphanage sandals (with heavy socks). Nadia left to look in the mirror while I tried to figure out what had just happened. Even though it was fall, it was about 80 degrees outside. I knew she must be roasting but she never said a word. Something about the way she skipped off to look in the mirror gave me a hint that she must be pleased with her new clothes. I found out later this was a first for her: at the orphanage all clothing is shared by everyone.

With Nadia making her new fashion statement, we were taken on an informal tour of the orphanage. Nadia showed us her little bed (I could bounce a quarter, military style, on any of the covers) and the child-size table where she ate her meals (not a crumb in sight). The bathroom had a long sink with a rack of toothbrushes and a drain with a pot by it. We surmised that the children were bathed by standing in a shallow "tub" while water was poured over them. Later, when we gave her a bath at Alyeh's apartment, it was obvious that Nadia had never been in a "sit-down" bathtub.

She seemed shocked by the contraption and seemed to think that other children would be joining her shortly.

I stayed behind the rest of the group to take pictures of everything I saw. I wanted to be able to remember where Nadia had spent so much of her childhood, and give an inkling of her past life when she was older. I wanted our family members to understand where she had come from. This definitely wasn't the orphanage of *Annie*. The rooms were sunny and there were many toys. Everything had a place and nothing was out of order. My house had never been as organized and only one child lived there. But it felt too perfect. Where was the clutter? How could they be children and not mess up anything? How did they maintain such cooperation from preschoolers?

As I was hurrying upstairs to join the others, I passed a small room and happened to glance inside. It had a few toys and a row of little chairs and there sat Anya all by herself. I said hello and she smiled a big smile. I took her picture, and she gave me a big hug. Then she began telling me something emphatically. She was so intent on making me understand that I went to find Diana to translate. "She's trying to tell me something really important," I told Diana as we walked back into the room. "Can you help me understand?"

Diana listened to Anya as she spoke with an animated voice. Then she smiled. "She's asking you to please come back and bring her a Barbie doll!" I laughed, held her shoulders, looked straight into her eyes, and said, "You've got it! A Barbie for Anya!"

I wanted to take Anya with us that day. We asked Diana if there was any way to adopt her too, but she confirmed our fear that the bureaucracy made it impossible. Although it was hard to leave Anya in that room, we had to focus on Nadia. If Anya was meant to be a part of our family, it would happen. We wouldn't forget her or the possibility of bringing her to the United States.

Diana, the Smiths, and Casey and I took pictures of our new children and the orphanage caregivers, a dozen women, on the front steps. The caregivers, even those who weren't on duty that day, were all on hand to say goodbye to Yuri, Slava, and Nadia. They also may have wanted to see more of us Americans and perhaps assuage their doubts about having foreigners adopt Russian children.

When it was time to leave, the director reached out her arms to hug Yuri.

"No!" he cried. "I'm going with Mama and Papa!"

Everyone thought this was adorable—a sign of success.

"Do you want to go or stay?" the director questioned Slava. "I'm going too!" he shouted and gave his new mother a hug. Everyone was happy.

"Nadia," the director said, "do you want to stay or go?"

Without a word, Nadia turned and ran back to the orphanage door as fast as she could.

"No, no, no, no," the director cried after her, "come back to your mommy." Two caregivers intercepted her, and reluctantly, Nadia obeyed. I was beginning to wonder if Nadia saw horns growing from the top of my head. My fantasy of our perfect first day was now completely shot.

Nadia gave the director one last hug and slowly climbed into the backseat of our car. It was her first time in new clothes, her first time in a car, her first time to be away from the orphanage, and her first time away from the only caregivers she had ever known. I could feel the confusion and misery radiating from her body. I couldn't blame her. But why did Yuri and Slava seem so delighted to go with the Smiths?

Sensing the difficulty of the situation, Diana rode with us in our car. Casey and I sat in the backseat with Nadia wedged in between. Nadia sat straight and rigid, looking at us as little as possible. Several times I tried to rest my arm or leg casually against her just to make some physical connection, but the instant she became aware of any contact she immediately stiffened. She still hadn't said a word to us.

I wanted to hold her and tell her it would be all right: that we would protect her and love her and make her happy. I wanted to say all the lovely things a mother can say to comfort a child— yet there I sat, mute, unable to speak her language. But what would I have said if I did? I suspected that even with a full command of Russian, I wouldn't be able to ease her pain. I ached at my ineffectiveness. I suddenly wanted someone to hold *me*, to comfort me, and to tell me that everything would work out fine. I needed the reassurance I couldn't give to her.

Casey pointed out the car window to some cows in a passing field and asked Nadia, "*Shto eta?* [What's that?]" Meghan had always loved seeing cows as a small child. After prompting by

Diana, Nadia whispered her answer: *"Dver machinye,"* the car door.

The only time she relaxed a bit was when Casey offered her an apple. It was so big I thought she couldn't possibly finish it, but she ate the whole thing, core and all. Nadia had been taught to finish everything and not waste a bit of food. She still hadn't smiled. Diana asked her the name of her new doll. "Masha," she whispered, hanging on to it with all her might.

"I'm glad Masha is a comfort," I thought, wishing it were me instead.

When we got back to the flat in Kaliningrad, I was not anxious to say goodbye to Diana. "Don't leave us!" I wanted to shout, but I knew the Smiths needed her help, too, and that Diana had meetings to arrange so we could get Nadia's passport the next day.

My concerns were nothing compared to Nadia's. She was stuck in a strange place with two grown-ups who, when they *did* speak Russian, did so with a two-year-old's vocabulary. She must have really wondered about me. Not only did I speak the same few Russian words every time I tried to communicate, but I pronounced them horribly! And the phrases that I had mastered just didn't take us very far in our relationship—yes and no, please and thank you, excuse me, I love you, hello, goodbye, give me a kiss, do you want to eat?—and my favorite, how much does that cost?

Although still silent, Nadia was obedient and did anything Alyeh asked of her. Before dinner, she washed her hands and face in her soon-to-be familiar and deliberate way and sat perfectly still at the table while Alyeh served her a large bowl of chicken soup and thick piece of bread. She ate precisely, like a robot, not looking at anyone. She finished every bit of food.

As she sat watching us try to finish our dinner, Nadia's reserve finally dropped and her chin began to quiver. Alyeh immediately began telling her not to cry, that everything was fine. I pulled Nadia onto my lap, and although she stiffened, she let me hold her. How could she believe that everything was fine? Everything wasn't fine, she needed to cry. She began to rock forward and back with her head down. But she didn't cry and I was secretly relieved; I was afraid of her tears, tears that I couldn't help or speak to. "Maybe giving her something routine would help," I thought. It was only around 5:30, but maybe getting ready for bed would be a good idea. I knew I was tired. She must be exhausted (kind of like the times when I was cold and so asked Meghan to put on a sweater).

After Nadia had put on her pajamas (which she seemed to prefer to do by herself), I took her to brush her teeth. I gave her a new toothbrush with toothpaste and she brushed her teeth in an exact way, the way, I was sure, she did every night in the orphanage. She would brush back and forth, dip the brush in a little cup, look at the toothbrush, brush again, and then look again. Because this was American toothpaste, it didn't dissolve as the orphanage paste must have. Soon I saw blood all over the toothpaste. But Nadia couldn't quit until the paste had been used up and she had done things "right." I took the brush and rinsed it. Only then could she finish and go to the couch that Alyeh had made up into a bed. Nadia got in immediately with Masha, and Alyeh covered her up with thick blankets. The temperature was still unseasonably warm but she had on enough blankets for a blizzard. For the second time that day I was sure Nadia was roasting like a martyr at the stake—and just as uncomplainingly.

While she lay in her little oven-bed, I gently placed my hand on her back to let her know silently that I loved her and would give her the best home and life I could. Casey sat on the floor next to me where Nadia could see that he was near. And that's when, without a sound, her tears finally began to fall. This time I didn't worry about the tears. They seemed to signal that she understood what I had been trying to tell her with my heart. She put Masha up to her face to hide the fact that she was sucking her thumb. She glanced at me anxiously to see if I'd noticed and was going to reprimand her. I stuck my thumb in my mouth, smiled, and told her it was okay to suck her thumb. She looked at me as if I were *gloopy* (Russian for "crazy" or "stupid").

Soon after, thank goodness, Diana came by to see how we were getting along. She looked worried and surprised at finding Nadia in bed covered in blankets, surrounded by a couple of dejected Americans. I knew she felt bad for us. She convinced Alyeh that Nadia could be up and about, pulled back the covers, and drew Nadia into her lap.

Diana asked her to count her fingers and quizzed her about colors. Nadia answered by rote as best she could, each time in a whisper. Then Diana asked, "Do you want anything? Is there anything I can get for you?"

With fresh tears in her eyes Nadia said, "I want a *machinye.*"

"Oh, you want a car," Diana replied, beaming at us with pleasure at finding something Nadia wanted. Casey and I smiled hopefully at each other. Maybe she enjoyed the car ride today and wanted a toy car. Hurrah, we just happened to have brought two little cars. I stood up to get them out of the suitcase.

"I want a car," she said again. "I want a car so it can take me home."

I stopped. Our smiles faded.

"Maybe she would like to watch TV," Alyeh said to Diana, who thought this was a splendid idea. TV, the universal tool for adults who don't know what else to do with their children. Nadia watched a children's show with Alyeh while Casey and I went into the kitchen to talk with Diana. All three of us were worried and upset. Since Diana's program had just started, she had no idea if Nadia's reaction was normal or not. The stories I had read about other adoptions spoke mainly to the issues of finding a child. I had certainly been more focused on finding a child than on what to do with her once we'd met. I hadn't thought of this particular reaction once we'd achieved our goal.

Diana explained that we had to make a decision about accepting or rejecting Nadia before the passport was obtained. We assured her Nadia was already our child and nothing could change that. We were scared but we weren't going to give up! Diana looked exhausted too. We reiterated that we did not want Anya to be left behind. "Concentrate on Nadia, and we will discuss Anya later," Diana answered. She had enough on her mind with the adoptions already in process to think about starting another one.

When Nadia's television program was over, Diana asked her if she wanted to sleep on the couch where she had been earlier, or with Mommy. She chose Mommy! I glowed at the compliment. We fixed up the bed and tucked her in. I fished out the little toy cars and handed them to Nadia. She wanted to bring Masha and her new cars into bed and seemed surprised when I didn't take them away. As Casey and I got ready for bed, she played quietly with them and didn't look at us at all. The bed wouldn't fit three, so Casey said good night and left for the couch while Alyeh spent the night with a neighbor. I got into bed and Nadia tensed up, waiting for me to take the toys. Again, she marveled at a mother who would allow such a thing. "Imagine, toys in bed," I could almost hear her say, relieved not to have to let them go. I finally turned off the light.

We both slept fitfully. At first Nadia didn't move; I couldn't even tell if she was breathing. Then she began rocking her head from side to side. She would rock, listen for a reaction, and then rock again. I kept very still. Then she began a continuous rocking of her head while humming in a gentle monotone. I had never seen a child fall asleep this way. (Later, I learned that it is common for children raised in an orphanage to rock themselves to sleep. Since they were not allowed to suck their thumbs and were not rocked by adults, they soothed themselves as best they could. Casey and I call it the "orphanage rock.") I listened until she finally fell into a restless sleep and then I dozed off too.

Later in the night, I was awakened by Nadia actually reaching for me. I held her close and felt such joy! I couldn't tell if she was awake or asleep but we lay together for an hour like that. I didn't sleep—wanting to protect her, willing her to understand that she was loved. I hoped that she would somehow realize in her sleep what seemed impossible to convey while she was awake. Finally, she rolled over, making sure that all the blankets were safely on her side of the bed. I discovered that my daughters had something in common. Like Meghan, Nadia stole all the covers.

Before sunrise, I could hear Casey tossing and turning (no cowboy dreams that night, thank goodness). I carefully maneuvered my way out of the bed and joined him.

"How are you?" I asked.

"Happy . . . and scared."

"This is big stuff, huh?"

"Oh yeah," he sighed. "This is definitely big stuff. Life will never be the same."

We talked as if we were back in Casey's dorm room, dissecting every part of the day and sharing our reactions to each element. We shared our hopes and fears. Hopes that Nadia would learn to *like* us and that she would speak to us before she went off to college. Fears that she wouldn't.

"She just needs some time," Casey said after a while.

"I know—time and lots of patience." We held each other until finally I said, "I'm goin' back in with the cover hog to see if I can get some sleep."

Chapter 8

LEARNING TO LOVE

Nadia could only draw scribbles when first given a crayon, but a few months later she was able to draw a picture of her new doma *(home).*

＊

Excerpt from Russian document received October 12, 1993

Information about Phisical Development of Dubinina
Nadezhda Leonidovna (born in April 29, 1988)
　　The girl was two months old when she was put into
Children's Home in Slavsk. The diagnosis was: trauma of
childbirth, syndrome of nervous-reflex excibility.
　　When put into the Children's Home the state of the child
came to normal, however as to her intellectual
development it was to slow. She put on weight evenly.
　　She was practically healthy, but some rare cases of
catching cold. She has been inoculating since the age of
1.7 years.
　　　—Specialist-in-Chief,
　　　Boarding-School and Rehabilitation Department
　　　N. Shimakovskya

I woke at 7:00 A.M. to Nadia once again humming softly and rocking back and forth. I said good morning and handed her her toys. I was rewarded with a hint of a smile. For the next hour we played happily, if cautiously. I took off the doll's clothes and she made sure the doll was dressed properly—not a stitch out of place. I held up the pillowcase to create a fabric slide, and she released her toy car down it over and over, each time looking at me a little longer and smiling—at first just a hint of a smile but growing each time. Progress—she can smile and feel safe with me.

"Casey," I exclaimed as I entered the living room. "Your daughter can actually smile!"

"This I've got to see," he answered, hurrying past me to the bedroom.

We played together until Diana arrived. "I have good news,"

I rushed to tell her. "Everything is going to be all right." But even as I said this, Nadia saw Diana and suddenly lowered her head to her chest and began to rock back and forth. She must have thought that Diana might create another change for her just as she was getting used to us. Each time Nadia felt uncomfortable, the rocking would begin again. It was only after Diana had been in the apartment for fifteen minutes without taking her away, and with us keeping close, that she calmed down.

After breakfast, Casey and I took Nadia for a *gulyet* (walk) to a nearby park. The neighborhood consisted of medium-sized apartment buildings surrounded by beautiful oak trees. Elderly women were out sweeping the sidewalks and streets with old-fashioned brooms made of twigs. In the past, under Communist rule, these women had been paid to clean the streets. Now, they swept out of habit and without a livelihood. We found the park and put Nadia on the swing, trying not to speak very much so we wouldn't stand out as foreigners (more than we already did, anyway). She seemed content but didn't show much emotion of any kind, other than to look up at us tentatively to see if we approved of her behavior. Unlike Meghan, she didn't go running around the playground but waited patiently for us to suggest a new activity. Swinging seemed to soothe her in much the way rocking did. Being in the park and doing something familiar, something we had done hundreds of times with Meghan, helped us experience our first feelings of "family" with Nadia. Being with her started to feel almost normal.

That afternoon Diana arranged for the Smiths and us to take the children to the zoo while we waited for the passport office to get documents ready for us to sign. It was good to see Frances and Steve and commiserate, since while we were dealing with a mute Nadia, they were having adjustment difficulties of their own. Unlike us, the Smiths were staying with an entire family who had a number of people visiting that first night. Slava, and especially Yuri, were outgoing children and knew how to charm any adult in sight to get as much attention and food as possible. The Smiths tried in vain to put limits on them, knowing that the excitement would be too much for them. But the boys found that they could easily sidestep their new parents for apples and treats from the sympathetic Russian women. Consequently, Frances spent most of the night in the tiny bathroom while the boys took turns sitting on the toilet, each with a bad case of diarrhea.

By the time we got to the zoo, the boys were feeling better. But as we were walking down a pathway just past the entrance, Yuri, and then Slava, raced over to a tree and pulled down their pants to relieve themselves. A Russian family walked past looking disgusted and muttered to each other. Our guide told us that they were saying, "That's not how we raise our children in Russia!"

The zoo was a special treat for all three children. While the Kaliningrad zoo is known as a good one in Russia, by American standards it was in poor shape. Still, to these children, the run-down condition of the buildings and grounds did not diminish the excitement of seeing exotic animals for the first time. It was heartwarming to watch Yuri and Slava delight over the antics of the monkeys and stare in awe at the tiger. Even Nadia enjoyed herself. We heard our first chuckle from her, and Casey and I just grinned at each other. We were so proud of that chuckle! Smiles were still in limited supply—each one felt like a hard-earned prize.

Finally it was time to go to the passport office. Frances and I were told to wait with the children in a hallway, while Steve and Casey went into a small office to provide signatures. Evidently, being women, our presence wasn't needed for signing these official documents. Frances and I were having two very different experiences with our children. Although I had shared my concerns with Frances over Nadia's constant rocking when fearful (much of the time) and her lack of emotion, I do believe that at that moment she longed for a child who wasn't climbing on everything in sight and running around like a kid who had just gobbled down ten Hershey bars. At the same time I was watching her boys with envy, wishing Nadia could show such joy in life.

We still had to sign a variety of documents each day, but we spent most of our time getting to know Nadia. Each day she opened up a little more. One day Casey and I hired a guide to show us the sights in Kaliningrad. We wanted to know more about Nadia's birthplace to share when she became curious about her "past life."

One evening, a friend of Alyeh's brought her granddaughter Olyeh to play with Nadia. She was the same age as Nadia but years apart in poise and intelligence. At her grandmother's urging she recited from memory a fairly long poem by Pushkin (who was a local hero in Kaliningrad). When we set out crayons for both girls, Nadia methodically made scribbles on the paper (she hadn't had many, if any, opportunities to draw at the orphanage), while Olyeh created interesting scenes with people and animals. With the grandmothers in the kitchen chatting, Casey and I played with the girls. Actually, Casey was the star of this show. He began playing silly peek-a-boo games with the girls. He had been doing this each night with Nadia and she had gradually been more receptive. This time, though, with another girl to lead the way, Nadia joined in with much less fear. While Olyeh shrieked with laughter, I was staring with joy at Nadia. She was laughing *out loud*. I had never heard her speak above a whisper—now she was jabbering away. Alyeh and her friend came out to see what was going on and stared in disbelief at a grown man rolling around on the floor—and actually enjoying it! We wondered if they thought we were being too wild but later Diana told me that the women had described the scene with tears in their eyes. They were touched by Casey's love for the children and his willingness to play. Diana told us that in Russia it was rare for men to be so involved with their children.

Our last day in Kaliningrad, Alyeh asked what we wanted for our last meal. I told her I had enjoyed her chicken dish very much and would love to have it again. She looked stricken. Had I made a social blunder? I tried to tell her I would be pleased with *any* dish she prepared but she was set on fulfilling my request, despite the fact that it clearly disturbed her.

"Diana," I asked later that day, "have I offended Alyeh? I thought my request for chicken would make her happy—she's finally gotten me interested in food. What have I done?"

Diana talked with Alyeh and reported back to me. "Alyeh is worried because the chicken she prepared before was slaughtered and cooked that day at her *dacha*. She's afraid that even if she stands in line all morning she won't be able to buy a fresh chicken at the market. She doesn't want to disappoint you."

I hadn't realized what the abundance of food had been costing Alyeh in time, not just in preparing it, but also in rounding up the ingredients. In her eyes, my innocent request for chicken could stand to ruin her reputation as an ideal hostess and cook! I felt a great appreciation for this woman who was trying desperately to keep us content during this emotional time, sharing her tiny apartment without complaint and working so hard on every meal.

Earlier in the week Alyeh had gone to the library to get a Russian-English dictionary. After dinner each night we would beg her to sit down with us and rest, which she would do only after every single sweet and baked good was on the table and we all had a steaming cup of *chai* (tea)—even Nadia, since all Russian children drink tea with every meal. Our conversations were a mix of gossip, theology, political insights, and child-rearing advice. We would gesture wildly, page through our dictionary, and then laugh at our attempts to get our point across correctly. I sometimes wonder what we told her during those evening talks.

That last evening, Alyeh's husband Vladimir, back from their *dacha*, joined us for our nightly discussion. Casey had noticed a guitar leaning against the wall behind a chair and asked if he could sing for them. Casey has a beautiful Irish tenor voice and sang "Bring Him Home"—a song about a man pleading to God to spare the life of his daughter's true love—from the musical, *Les Miserables*. Alyeh and Vladimir listened intently. Soon Alyeh was in tears. Perhaps she understood a few key words in the song such as "God," "home," "live," and "die." Perhaps it was just the music itself. Casey's singing communicated our thankfulness in a way our words couldn't.

Nadia was curled up in my lap mesmerized. Although still guarded and rocking a great deal, it was amazing to see the trust that she was now able to show. It was obvious to me that she was capable of great affection when she felt safe. Each day she revealed another glimpse of her loving personality that was tucked safely behind layers of trepidation. I knew it would only be a matter of time before she was brave enough to come out of her shell for good. I marveled at how she accepted us as a part of her life even though we had only known one another for a few days. I knew that I would love Nadia no less than Meghan. The maternal instinct is truly a mysterious, soul-wrenching, and powerful force.

The next day we left early in the morning for the airport. As we said goodbye to Alyeh and Vladimir outside the apartment building, Casey gave them a note that he had spent the previous afternoon creating word by word in Russian. I gave Alyeh a big hug and thanked her in my limited Russian and then more profusely in English, knowing that she would understand my sentiments. Meanwhile, Nadia was quiet, wondering what was going to happen to her next.

What happened next, of course, was her first airplane flight. I was nervous, waiting for Nadia to get scared and start rocking back and forth, but to my amazement, she wanted to look out the window! When we landed in Moscow three hours later, Nadia turned to me and said something excitedly which Diana translated: "I want to go again!"

In Kaliningrad it had been impossible to call overseas. Now back in Moscow, we happily called everyone with the news about Nadia and our impending arrival home. Nadia sat and watched as I talked to my mother in Iowa. I motioned to the phone to see if she wanted to speak to her new *babushka* (grandmother). She was delighted and had obviously played with a toy phone at the orphanage. She must have thought that I had a very vivid imagination and was good at the telephone game because she took the phone and began talking right away. But when my mother said hello to her newest granddaughter, Nadia dropped the phone in shock. She had never experienced a phone that talked back! After a brief explanation to Mom, I held the phone to Nadia's ear and we both said, "*Dasvidanya* [goodbye]."

Through the window's lacy curtain, we could see the sun rise as we packed to leave the next morning. We had been in Russia for ten days. Since it was unclear how long it would take to get Nadia's physical and exit visa processed, it had been decided when Diana had planned our trip that Casey and I would go home once we got back to Moscow and wait for Nadia to be chaperoned to the United States by a regional adoption director. I wanted to stay with Nadia until we could bring her home ourselves and yet I longed to get back to Meghan. Nadia would stay with Natasha, who promised a trip to her *dacha* and many other special treats. We knew Nadia would be in good hands.

Casey and I tiptoed into Nadia's room and woke her up enough to say goodbye. She had accepted so many new things lately that I think she didn't have the energy to make a fuss about this latest development. "*Ya tibya lublu*—I love you," I whispered as I gave her one last kiss. "I'll see you soon." She gave me a hug and began rocking and humming to get back to sleep.

* * *

We were seated on a jet leaving Frankfurt, Germany, where we had a brief layover. In just a few minutes the plane would be flying, nonstop, to San Francisco, where Meghan, my brother Chuck, and his wife Penny would be waiting. Our lives were completely changed forever. We had another child—Nadia. What an incredible "birth" it had been (with almost a two-year gestation!). I sat back in my seat and took a deep breath. For the first time in a very long time, I relaxed. I missed Nadia already.

"Oh, Casey," I sighed. "Can you believe what we just accomplished?" Casey smiled and watched the last few passengers board and take their seats. "Just think," I said, getting more comfortable. "No more paperwork. No more forms to fill out. We've done it!"

Casey jerked up in his seat.

"What's wrong?" I asked, frightened by the panicked look on his face.

"The INS form!" he moaned, jumping up and reaching for his backpack. "You were supposed to sign it. I have it right here!" He fished out the form and waved it in the air. "Nadia can't leave Russia or enter the United States without this form!"

Chapter 9

LIFE WITH TWO CHILDREN

Meghan in her Halloween costume.

Journal entry, in flight, October 17, 1993

I can see the Hudson Bay from my window. While I'm sitting here writing and worrying, Casey is trying to call Moscow from the cockpit of the plane. I wonder if he could talk the pilots into turning around? I wish I could do something other than think about how badly Nadia's missing INS form might screw everything up! . . . Casey just got back. He says they couldn't get through to Moscow and there's nothing we can do until we get home, but seeing the cockpit was cool.

Meghan rushed into my arms the moment we cleared customs. I couldn't let go of her, I couldn't get enough of looking at her. We held each other all the way home. She was familiar and safe, and we loved each other unconditionally. What an exhilarating feeling; what a feeling we take for granted as parents. Her hugs held no doubts, and even when we were situating our luggage, she kept a hand on my back or leg, not wanting the connection to end for a moment. Could Nadia ever love me with such trust? I realized that this love is a gift and not something to be taken lightly.

Meghan's tenacious grip showed me how hard it must have been for her while we were not only away, but often unreachable—returning with another child to share her home. She had been a part of this adoption waiting game for the same two years we had, yet she still hadn't seen any tangible results. I don't think Nadia was completely real to her. She was still a phantom sister.

Chuck and Penny took us from the airport to their house for dinner. (Naturally, we stopped to drop off our film at a one-hour photo service—priorities!) When we walked in the door, the first thing we noticed was a wonderful dollhouse in the middle of the living room—a living room typically festooned with a wide variety of superheroes, intergalactic space stations, GI Joes, dinosaurs, and many implements of destruction, much as my brother had kept in his room when we were young. This pink and blue pastel-colored house, complete with matching pastel furniture and a pastel baby, was quite glaringly *not* part of their "all-boy" decor. "Surprise!" Meghan cried. "I bought this for Nadia, my new little sister."

I was astounded. Meghan's idea of a *long time* tends to be about a half-hour. So when she had saved her allowance *all summer*, it was a major undertaking; she intended to buy something BIG. She changed her mind daily as to what that special something would be: a new bike, videotapes, roller blades—always something she wanted for herself. Now she had spent all her saved money on something she thought Nadia would like. I felt such pride. Meghan had wanted to be a part of welcoming her sister in her own way.

Now we had to figure out the safest and fastest way to get our INS form to Diana. What should and would have been a week recovering from jet lag and preparing for Nadia's arrival was instead a time of urgent transatlantic telephone calls, letter writing, and trips to the airport. With the political environment in Moscow still shaky, Casey was on the phone researching all the options we had for our document delivery. All the express shipping companies would take too long. Finally, he went to the San Francisco airport and talked to a group of Russian travelers departing on the next Lufthansa flight. A computer scientist agreed to carry our envelope to Natasha, who would meet him at the airport. As a backup, they exchanged the phone numbers of everyone involved. The delicacy of these arrangements was nerve-wracking. The next twenty hours were very long. We were getting calls from all our friends and family asking us *when* Nadia would arrive, and we were wondering *if*. When the phone rang late in the night, we jumped at it. It was Diana. Casey's character assessment and document transfer had been successful. Natasha had been in the right place at the right time, the paper was now in Diana's hands, and we would meet Nadia at the airport in four days.

"Just think," I told Meghan in my most isn't-this-going-to-be-great voice that night while I tucked her in bed. "You're going to be the oldest. The queen of sisters. Nadia is going to admire you and want to be just like you."

My mind flashed back to a memory of my older sister chasing me through the house with a broom. "Witch, witch, you look like a witch," I remember chanting just before the broom handle crashed down on my head. I didn't share this with Meghan. "You guys are going to have *so much fun!*" I said instead.

We were all holding our breath, waiting for the first sight of Nadia, Yuri, Slava, and Ludmilla, their escort, to walk through the arrival gate at the airport. Nadia smiled weakly at the sight of us and gave us a hug. She looked tired and had dark circles under her eyes. We soon discovered that none of them had slept at all on the flight, which meant that she had been awake for at least thirty hours—no wonder she looked exhausted. Penny documented the entire reunion on video. Now we have a complete record of Nadia as deluged and as confused as she had ever been (and will hopefully ever be) in her life. This was also the beginning of a juggling act, giving Nadia the reassurance she needed while Meghan watched with an eagle eye.

Ludmilla, the Russian official in charge of international adoptions in the Kaliningrad region, did not say very much during the ride back to our house. (Who would have the energy to speak after taking three preschool children on a flight across the world?) Of course, we were nervous around her. This woman was seeing America for the first time and spoke very little English. She would also be observing—and reporting back to her superiors—what kind of people were adopting Russian children. Let's face it, we were intimidated by her, and we couldn't communicate with her.

On the ride home I realized something else. It was late October—almost Halloween. As we exited the freeway and entered suburbia, most of the houses we passed had ghosts, skeletons, pumpkins, and gravestones in the yards. What must Ludmilla be thinking of our society? Surely any propaganda she had learned in school about evil Americans must be flooding back. We didn't have the words to explain Halloween, but we kept repeating the word "holiday." Holiday. Holiday! She just smiled, nodded her head, and glanced out the window at a witch hung from a rope by its neck, with glowing eyes and blood splattered down its black dress.

When we arrived home, everyone piled out of the van and headed into the house. Meghan was excited. The dollhouse was set up on the dining room rug, ready to be bestowed upon her new sister. Nadia was as shocked and surprised as I would have been if someone had parked a new, cherry-red Miata in my driveway and handed me the keys. Then she did what I would have done. She looked around the room with a quizzical look that asked, "Is this really for me? What's the catch?"

We all nodded our heads: "Yes, yes, this is yours, go ahead and look at it." Nadia didn't need any further encouragement. She examined every feature and furnishing. Over the next few weeks especially she rearranged every movable part, with incredible concentration, for hours. She would escape inside that special dollhouse. Meghan had chosen the perfect gift and it was Nadia's treasure. Her first real possession as a United States citizen.

That night while I was unpacking Nadia's things, I found an envelope addressed to Casey and me. It was from Natasha:

Dear Casey and Megi!

Tomorrow Nadia will go to new life in her family and I keep her in my heart forever. I am very glad that we did our best to help Nadia and you to do it. I had a case to be with Nadia more closely and to know her more better. So I want to say you some words about her. She is a very clever and sensitive girl. The years which she spent in child house forced her to have a defense inside because of distrust. Even she is smiling her eyes full of this defense. But I am sure that your love to her will kill this distrust. Just now she believe in it very much by her instinct. I understand it through our talkings. Just now in her mind father (Casey) has a role of master. Father bought, father said, father called. . . . Mother—as a source of love (doll, sing . . .) Sister Meghan—she asked me, "Is she more oldest than I?" On my reply she said "This is okay. We shall be friends." When I said to her about [her Aunt Molly Anne] she said me, "I'll remember it." As you see Nadia in her five years has a very good mind. By the way she has a very good memory and hear. I checked up it. You can develop it and the main feature—it is her independence in everything. Take care about it and don't lose it. I had never before met such a child.

Finally, I want to say that I love you and Nadia and Meghan very much. And I am sure that now you will be more happier. I wish you it by all my heart and hope that with time I can see it by my own eyes. Be happy!!!

With Love,
Sincerely yours,
Natasha

My throat and chest felt tight with emotion. What effort must have gone into writing this letter in a completely different language and alphabet? It reassured me that Nadia had been well cared for during her separation from us. We had all participated in something very fine.

Introducing a five-year-old with little life experience to a new country and culture is hard enough. Introducing that same five-year-old, who speaks no English, to the complexities of family life is even harder. But accomplishing these introductions while entertaining a Russian government official in your home is downright unnerving. Nadia was in turn grateful, confused, curious, tired, and generally anxious. She kept one eye on Ludmilla, as though waiting for her to tell her, "Time's up! Back to Russia now!" If Nadia hesitated in following any directions I gave, one word from Ludmilla would render Nadia immediately compliant.

I wanted only to burrow into our home and not leave for at least a month, but I didn't think that would be fair to Ludmilla. So instead of making our introductions to Nadia slowly, we did what any host in the Bay Area does, we went sightseeing. (And of course we couldn't very well leave Nadia with a sitter, and Meghan certainly wasn't going to school with *all this going on,* so we all went sightseeing together.)

Ludmilla lived with us for four days before moving in with the Smiths for the remainder of her stay. For her last evening with us, we thought she might enjoy an extended American family get-together. We assembled as many family members as we could at Chuck and Penny's house. Along with various aunts and uncles, there were twelve cousins and their friends, all under the age of ten, running around screaming and chasing each other with those same implements of destruction I mentioned earlier. Penny and

I stood in the living room, grinning like fools, watching Nadia screaming with delight as her new cousin Anthony chased her up the stairs with a plastic godzilla that spit real sparks from its mouth. We were filled with satisfaction that Nadia was joining in so readily, her shyness dissipating by the second. I glanced over at Ludmilla to share the moment, and saw her lips set in a thin line, frowning; her eyes glaring with disapproval. What we considered a major victory for Nadia, she quite possibly thought of as the ruination of a young soul. From my limited experience, the Russian people love a good party, but children aren't usually a part of the celebration (or if they are, they are sitting politely with their hands folded in their laps on the sidelines). Oh well, I wasn't going to spoil Nadia's fun for the sake of appearances. (Who am I kidding? I couldn't have stopped that wild crowd with tear gas.)

Ludmilla was *really* horrified about an hour later when Nadia learned an important lesson in suburban architecture. The children had been running in and out of the backyard via the back patio door. As it got cooler in the house, some wise adult closed the door. The other kids knew the difference between an open door and a closed one by the smudges and sweaty fingerprints. Nadia didn't. She came running into the house and—WHAM!—ran right into the door. Thankfully she wasn't hurt, but she looked as if aliens had beamed down a special force field while she was at play. She couldn't understand what had happened and was going to try her luck again when we opened the door and rushed out to her. I held her and cooed my incomprehensible Russian phrases, Casey got some ice, Penny showed Nadia how to work the door, and Chuck grabbed the masking tape to differentiate open from closed. We had to start thinking of things from Nadia's point of view. We couldn't assume she would know what other five-year-olds know.

Finally we were on our own as a family. A major event for us each day was visiting the park. "Mama! Parrrrka!" she would cry when we drove up, wiggling around as much as the seat belt would allow. The swing was her favorite activity and she would have been happy to be pushed back and forth, from morning until night. I was starting to get seasick.

Similarly, she still could fall asleep only after rocking back and forth while singing her monotonous *la, la, la* for about twenty minutes. This drove Meghan crazy after a few nights, but there was little we could do about it. She would just have to learn that minor annoyances were part of the sibling package.

As Nadia felt safer, she slept more soundly, and soon she was wetting the bed every night. Her reaction the next day was to try to cover up any evidence and was shocked to realize that she wouldn't be punished for a wet bed. Unfortunately, this meant that she soon no longer worried about whether it was wet or dry.

I will never forget the first time Nadia broke something. She was playing with her dollhouse and accidentally pulled one of the furniture pieces apart. I had just walked into the room and saw what had happened. She immediately crouched into the corner with her arms held up, protecting herself from anticipated blows. My heart went out to her. "Nadia," I said gently, "you don't have to be afraid. I won't hit you. Accidents happen. Let's see if we can fix your toy." She didn't understand my words but she knew what I was saying. Her eyes thanked me, and I held her while she rocked back and forth, trying to relieve her anxiety.

Meanwhile, Meghan was busy preparing for Halloween night. Her Grandmother Lois (Casey's mom) had made a cape—based on Meghan's detailed description—for her witch's costume. It was purple with a large silver medallion button at the neck. A graceful hood blossomed around her face as she walked. She and Casey had searched a thrift store for something to wear underneath and they had found an old black velvet dress with black sequined sleeves.

We had not been able to find a way to tell Nadia what was going on. Each time a translator, referred by well-meaning friends would speak to her, Nadia would begin rocking back and forth silently at the first Russian word. As soon as she learned English, Nadia refused to speak Russian at all, even with Diana, whom she adored. Someday, I hope she will be able to unlock her native language, but when she first arrived, it wasn't worth the stress becoming bilingual created in her mind.

Nadia watched as Meghan put on her outfit and purple face makeup and left for school. Later, Nadia and I went to the school parade to take pictures. Here, not only was her sister looking strange, but there were hundreds of other children in weird, frightening costumes. I could almost hear the thoughts in Nadia's head when we first arrived. "Where are these creatures' parents? Why would my new mother expose me to these bizarre beings?" Then a kind teacher offered her a Halloween cupcake and juice, and she began to like this holiday much more.

That night we went trick-or-treating with friends. I didn't dress Nadia up because she seemed much more comfortable watching and trying to understand what was happening around her. I gave her a bag and we went up to the first house. Nadia hung back, holding on to my hand and waiting as Meghan and the other children rang the bell. She stood on her tiptoes trying to see what was happening at the door. When Meghan rushed back to us, she opened her bag to show Nadia the candy she had received. Nadia's eyes grew large. She went up to the next house behind the others, but held out her bag. Running back she squeaked, "Mama!" and opened her bag for me to see. Her face was beaming. After a few more houses it was Nadia who was first to ring the bell. She was grinning from ear to ear. She didn't understand a word anyone said, but whenever she rang a bell, whoever answered the door gave her candy. *What a great life!*

Nadia was a very disappointed girl when we wouldn't let her go door to door again the next night.

Marge had told us to expect a "honeymoon" period with Nadia. We had one: it lasted two weeks. It was *wonderful*. "So this is what it's like to have a child who obeys you completely," I thought. Every day Nadia made her bed and picked up her clothes without our asking (much to Meghan's dismay—I believe "suck up" was the word she used when we praised Nadia for her neatness). When it was time to get up, she was ready; when it was time for bed, she didn't argue. As nice as this was, I did feel a bit like the mother of an automaton. I couldn't tell what was going on inside her head unless she was extremely happy. So I had mixed feelings, about a week after Ludmilla left, when our honeymoon began winding down.

Nadia had come from a place of complete routine; day in and day out, everything ran on the same schedule. Now she was living with a totally spontaneous family. We tried to create more structure for her but couldn't match the Russian orphanage system by a long shot. Nadia started picking up more than just "kid slang" from Meghan; she discovered that she wouldn't be hit if she didn't comply with our wishes immediately. Once she saw that this home was much less strict than anything she had experienced, she began testing all the limits to see how much we would tolerate. She began saying *"da"* less and saying *"nyet"* more often. Soon she graduated to the English, "No!"

We were introduced to Nadia's stubborn side. She seemed to have learned how to dissolve every muscle in her body. Lifting her was like lifting a fifty-pound noodle. Since I couldn't move a fifty-pound noodle, we were often caught in a standoff of wills. I wanted her to leave so we could pick up Meghan from school; she wasn't going anywhere until she had colored *every* picture in her coloring book. When Meghan was younger and would throw a tantrum, I would sometimes insinuate that I might leave her to finish up her hysterics alone. She knew in her heart that I would never really leave her, but would often settle down a bit more quickly because of my implied threat. I couldn't use this tactic on Nadia, though, because she had, in fact, experienced both a biological mother who had given her up and an orphanage director who had shipped her ten thousand miles west with the first American family who visited. And if I said in my most patient Mommy voice, "Nadia, I don't like your behavior and will wait for you to get in control," she would have only heard, *"Nadia, al kfenv fdlb ksrlb aldknglfkbn kjasc lkjb npkiej fpbjag."*

In her mind I'm sure she felt that if so much in the United States was fun—just leaving the house each day to run errands was considered fun at this stage—why can't it all be fun? We made the new parent mistake of wanting her to be as happy as possible all the time.

As a result, she was falling apart at the end of each day. She cried every night for at least an hour. Not just tears, but a huge emotional release of energy. She would stomp. She would slam doors. And finally she would rock back and forth, sobbing. We couldn't ask her what she was upset about. I don't think she knew herself. Casey and I took turns holding her when we could get close enough. Amazingly she was very calm and relaxed after these episodes. We felt as if we had just sent the last kid home from a twelve-kid slumber party. Now I see that it's exhausting for a child to have too much fun. (Who would have guessed?)

One evening I took Meghan and Nadia, with their cousins Anthony and Ashton, to a local Burger King that had a special play area—the kind with tunnels and balls for kids to jump in and explore. Nadia had never seen such a thing. The play structure extravaganza was outside and three levels tall. After the children ate (in record time), they took Nadia out to play. At first she was hesitant and circumspect, but once she felt comfortable, she couldn't be stopped. Literally—I couldn't get her to leave. It had grown dark outside and it was time to go home, but Nadia *did not want this fun to end!* I coaxed all my other "charges" into their shoes and toward the door, but I finally had to haul Nadia out by force. I tried to explain that we would be back soon, but she was screaming too loudly to hear. All she knew was that she might never see this place again and she wasn't willing to give it up yet. I had to carry her "noodle body" to the car and strap her in with her seat belt. Meghan and the boys were wide-eyed, obedient, and quiet, watching warily to see what would happen next.

Nadia was still screaming as I turned into the main intersection of the six-lane thoroughfare and headed home. "It's Casey's turn now," I thought as I sped along at 45 mph with my ears ringing. It became quiet . . . then suddenly I heard the click of the car lock, the click of a seat belt, and the sound of the back car door opening. "NOOOO!" I heard myself yell as I reached back and grabbed the back of Nadia's sweater. Cars were whizzing by us, swerving to avoid her open door. As I pulled on Nadia to keep her in the car, Anthony reached over and grabbed the door. "Lock it!" I screamed. "Nadia! NYET!" The panic in my voice froze her. Somehow, although I was going slower, I was still driving. "Hold her, Anthony," I said, trying now to sound calm. "Talk to her."

"Na-dee-a," he mouthed carefully with his best "Russian" accent, "I don't want my newest cousin dead. Na-dee-a, stay in the car when it is moving. Na-dee-a, don't get dead."

Maybe it was the accent, or maybe it was his earnestness, but Nadia didn't move again until we got home. I couldn't speak because I knew I would burst into tears if I did. But I didn't have to. When we got inside the house, Meghan, Anthony, and Ashton were happy to retell the story to Casey in vivid detail. (According to Ashton, who was in the seat farthest from the action, he saved Nadia's life by throwing himself between her and the car door.) I went into my room and shut the door. I couldn't stop shaking. I could hear Casey as he flipped through our Russian/English dictionary, searching for key words that would make Nadia

understand the importance of his message. "Never." "Danger."
"Hurt." "Very hurt." "No matter how angry you are, never jump
out of a moving car!"

It was amid this mixed climate of joy and trauma that we got
a surprise call from our Colombian adoption contact. Colombia?
In the craziness that had been our lives for the last few months,
Colombia had disappeared from our minds and I had to think
for a minute before I could say, "Oh, right, hi. How are you?"
An excited staff member was on the line. "I'm great and have
wonderful news. We just received a referral for you. A little girl
named Ana Maria needs a home."

Chapter 10

ANA

A handmade Colombian doll.

Journal entry, November 8, 1993

Her name is Ana Maria. There's that name again:
Maria. Just like our first referral. Even though millions of
South American girls have some form of Maria in their
name, I consider this an excellent omen.

My first thought was, "You've got to be kidding. This is a joke,
right?" But I was also excited. After all our hard work with the
Colombian adoption process, we had a child! Of course, I knew
I should let the woman from the agency know immediately that
we had just gotten back from Russia with a child. In fact, I should
have let the agency know before we left the country. But I had
been afraid to burn any bridges and perhaps, as I look back on
it now, there was a small part of me that didn't want to give up
"our Colombian child." So instead of setting her straight, I said,
"Oh, please tell me about her!"

There wasn't a lot of information about her—not a big surprise
by now—but the agency did know that she was relatively
healthy—which we were smart enough to know was no assurance
of anything. Ana was thought to be four years old and had been
abandoned by her mother at around eighteen months of age. As
far as they knew, her mother had been a prostitute who abused
drugs and alcohol. One day Ana's mother left home and never
came back. Ana was left to fend for herself until she became so
malnourished that the neighbors took her to a local hospital. It
was in the hospital that Social Services became involved and found
a foster home for her. Now Ana was considered a hard-to-place
child—over the hill as far as easy adoptability.

"She was abandoned *around* eighteen months?" I asked. "So,
they don't even know what her birth date is?"

"All children in Colombia who are abandoned are given January first as a birth date," the agency staff person explained.

For some reason I was struck more by this news than by any of the rest. Nadia, who seemed to have so little in personal possessions, at *least* had her own birthday. By this time I could imagine children living without enough food, without shelter, or even without a parent's love, but the thought of a child without a birthday had never occurred to me. Ana's story was sad in so many ways. We never would know who her mother was. (Forget having a clue as to who her father was.) And to not know the day she came into the world ... Even now, I can't explain why this moved me so, but it did. For God's sake, Ana deserved her own birthday!

"Would you like to see a picture?"

Of course I wanted to see a picture. I wanted to take this child into our home and give her a birthday! Casey didn't want to see a picture. In fact, during the time when I was upset over our experience with Maria, he had requested that the agency only tell us of a referral through ACCEPT. He had wanted to protect us from another disappointment, and thought that Bee or Marge would be better equipped to discern whether or not the referral was a real possibility before we invested our emotions again. He knew how connected we could become once we saw a picture. But I didn't realize when we got the call that he had made this request. We did receive a fax—a fax of a Xeroxed copy of a photograph—of Ana Maria later that day. So, Casey was surprised for more than one reason when I told him the news.

We could barely distinguish a child on the page. We stared at this dark blurry picture, which looked almost like a sonogram of a fetus in utero. (The kind of fuzzy moonscape map image with arrows pointing to mountain terrain areas designating a head or a foot. "Oh, of course," viewers always say. "I see it now.") Still, I could make out two beautiful, large eyes through the black toner. They spoke volumes: "I need a home, I need a mother, I need a father." Casey's prediction had been right: Both he and I felt a connection with Ana right away.

Now that Nadia was a reality and safely home, I felt more confident in the adoption process. Anyone who is adopting a child for the first time gets to a point where they feel that, even though others have successfully completed the maze, *their* search will be futile. No matter how hard they try or how good their

Casey, Meghan, and I in 1991. We later submitted this photo to the Colombian and Russian governments along with our paperwork and home study to prove that we were real people.

This is our two-bedroom, one-bath house that seemed a lot bigger when we only had one child and a cat.

Our only picture of Nadia before we met her. We later found out the orphanage director hadn't told Nadia we would be adopting her because she thought we might decide she was too overweight. The director thought that Americans only wanted thin children.

Casey and Nadia outside the front door of her Kaliningrad orphanage minutes after we had first met. The orphanage director was behind me instructing Nadia to look up and smile as I took the picture. She is holding her new doll, whom she later named Masha.

Nadia with the dollhouse Meghan bought her as a welcome home present. Other relatives helped furnish this extravaganza, complete with a Barbie doll. Nadia loved it.

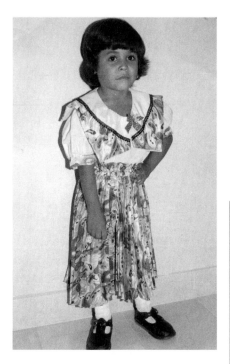

The photo we received of Ana soon after Nadia arrived home. We suspect Ana had been told not to smile because of her decayed teeth. I saw great strength and determination in her eyes.

Ana and I just after she came through the door and jumped into my arms. Little did I know that I would be holding her practically every minute for the next twelve days.

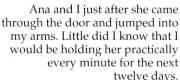

Ana and Nadia show off the snowman they built with the help of Lois and Eddie, Casey's parents, during a visit to Mount Hood. This was the first time Ana had ever seen snow. All the girls love visiting their grandparents in Oregon, and Lois came to our house to stay with the girls while Casey and I were in Colombia and Russia.

The first picture I saw of Alesia. Something about her face and the look in her eyes made me fall in love with her instantly. The child in front of the caregiver was adopted by another couple in the San Francisco Bay Area.

Thanks to another adoptive couple, Vickie and Rick Brummel, we were able to get a picture of Casey and me when we held Alesia for the first time. Her dress was embroidered with the words "I love Mummy." Although she appeared overwhelmed here, Alesia was soon showing us everything about *"her"* orphanage.

My mother, Ruth, gives me a hug shortly after we'd returned home with Alesia. Though she lives in Iowa, Mom spends a great deal of time in California giving us support and encouragement.

Meghan with our cat, Sylvia. Poor Sylvia ran away from home shortly after Alesia arrived—a fourth child in a two-bedroom house. We searched the neighborhood and posted flyers for her return. We all hope she found a less chaotic home and is safe and happy.

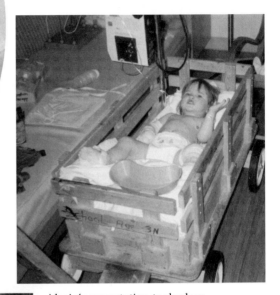

Alesia's amputation took place December 26, 1994. It was her second surgery in three weeks. This wagon, with the IV pole attached, traveled many miles around the Stanford children's hospital that first night in order to help soothe her pain.

The Conroy kids, fall 1995.

Nadia's first basketball photo. The first time she made a basket during warm-up, she was just as proud and excited as a kid making the tie-breaking shot during the game's final seconds.

Meghan and Ana posing together in our front yard. Although they often bicker, Meghan will protect any of her sisters from anyone outside the family who tries to pick on them.

Alesia, like Ana, loved to swim as soon as she tried it. Her missing foot and fingers didn't slow her down for an instant. When she jumped in, I would reach out to catch her but she would call to me, "Back up, farther, farther. I do it!"

Alesia playing at the park after receiving her first prosthesis. After having lived in Siberia, she insists on wearing a swimsuit as often as possible year-round.

The girls posing in our front yard. They each enjoyed playing the role of "fashion model" during my "photo shoot."

This recent family portrait took an amazing amount of patience on the part of the professional photographer. I don't think Casey and I will be up for another attempt for a while—we'll stick to individual shots. (Photo by Daniel S. Cocco)

intentions, somehow they will be the ones to fall through the adoption cracks. Now, for us, it was easier to want Ana to be a part of our family because we knew it really could happen. But there was another child to consider. What about Anya, the girl we had met in Nadia's orphanage? If there was a chance that we could adopt her, Casey and I had already decided that we would. We asked the Colombian agency for time to sort things out, and got an assurance that we could have the time we needed to decide.

We called Diana right away. "Is Anya available for adoption?" we asked after giving her a full account of Nadia's health and adjustment.

"No," she said, "she has been sent to another part of Russia for surgery to reconstruct her ear. The orphanage officials are hopeful that she will then be adopted by a Russian family."

I felt a mixture of relief that Anya was being taken care of and profound disappointment over the fact that we hadn't been given a real chance to adopt her. Maybe if we had been pushier and insisted on initiating the paperwork immediately, Anya wouldn't have been sent away.

"Should we wait to be sure she is adopted by a Russian family?" I asked.

"Forget about Anya," Diana answered. "She is in another region now and we will never know."

I knew I would never forget her. I prayed that she would somehow find a home . . . and a Barbie. Why, oh why hadn't I found a way to get her one as soon as we got home? Anya's voice saying, "Have you brought me a mother?" kept ringing in my ears.

What was happening? We had waited almost two years to adopt a child. Now, days after completing our first adoption, we had two other children we were ready to adopt too. What would adopting Ana Maria mean for us? We had our hands full with the adjustments Nadia and Meghan were going through. We had our hands full with the adjustments Casey and I were going through. We couldn't afford the travel costs of a mandatory trip by both parents to Colombia. We also had no way of knowing how long we would be in South America once we arrived. We had a two-bedroom house. Was there room for another child to live comfortably? How would Nadia react to our leaving her so soon, and for "who knows how long"? How would Meghan react to our absence and then the addition of yet another sister?

"We've worked so hard towards a Colombian adoption," Casey said. "I don't want to feel like we've wasted all that effort. Can we afford this?"

"No, not really," I answered. "But we didn't think we could afford the last one either. I'm sure we'll find a way." I had no idea how, but it sounded reassuring at the time. "I'm worried about Meghan and Nadia—is it too soon for them?"

"Kids are flexible. It's not like Nadia's set in her new routine, anyway. Maybe this is an okay time—before she gets too comfortable with her new parent-child ratio."

Around and around we went. How can anyone know how they will cope and afford and adjust to their future?

"We can do it."

"Somehow, we'll make it work."

There was one aspect of Ana's adoption that we couldn't ignore. Since her birth mother's history was one of drugs and prostitution, we wanted to have Ana tested for the presence of the HIV virus. With two other children, we didn't feel that we could give a child with AIDS the kind of attention she would need. So, even though we felt a bit guilty about it (realistic or not, I'd like to think our love has no prerequisites), we made a decision: We would adopt Ana Maria if she tested negative.

Soon we got the real photograph of Ana in the mail. She was beautiful. My first impression was of a very serious and stoic little woman/child. Her hand rested lightly on her hip as she looked out at the camera; without a smile, but with huge, brown, knowing eyes. She didn't have the fear in her eyes that Nadia had—Ana's was a defiant look. Clearly she was very stubborn, a fighter. She had on a white blouse with a floral skirt and a matching vest. Very feminine. Since she was standing against a white wall, we could not tell how big she was, but the look on her face made her appear bigger than the measurements and weight in the letter described.

Now that I know Ana, now that she is the real Ana in my mind and not a facsimile created from words and a single picture, I know that the photo is not of her at all. I look at the photograph now and wonder who that little girl is—it's certainly not the same child that is Ana today. She was putting on a mask of independence for us while at the same time seemingly daring us to become attached.

Along with the photo and measurements, the letter included a statement: Ana had tested negative for AIDS.

"Here we go again," Casey said.

Meanwhile, it was time for Nadia to begin school. I had looked into preschools earlier but made the mistake of taking Nadia with me to visit the final choices. We arrived at the first one during recess. The schoolyard was filled with play equipment and children. Play equipment similar to Nadia's orphanage. Children the same age as those in Nadia's orphanage. The teachers monitoring and interacting with the children were all women, like the caregivers in Nadia's orphanage. There were no other parents around. Yes, like Nadia's orphanage.

"Nadia," I said, bending down to eye level so she could see how excited I was about this great place, "would you like to join the other children?"

Nadia didn't answer or move other than to reach for my legs and hang on for dear life. I didn't understand her reluctance. "She must be shy today," I told the director. "I'm sure she will join in any minute. She loves the park and playing with other children. How long is the children's nap time?"

I was smiling, but by now my legs were starting to hurt where Nadia's fingers were digging in. "Please let go," I said. "Don't you want to play with the other children?" She looked at me with a combination of betrayal and resolve. It was a you-are-crazy-if-you-think-I-am-going-to-let-go-of-you look. I knew what she was trying to tell me: "There is no way I will stay here except attached to your leg!"

Then I was treated to a magnificent and truly artful display of temper in full tantrum form, all within inches of my legs so that she could reestablish her grip anytime I tried to move a foot in any direction. No amount of assurances could recast this scene. I looked at the director in disbelief, as if I'd never realized that children were capable of such behavior—or at least not my child. I couldn't understand what was wrong until . . .

I finally got it.

Now how to explain to Nadia that school was a place you visited? A place where you stayed only a few hours a day. A place where mothers and fathers always came for you at the end of the day. The director, the teachers, and the children all stared as I made my weak explanations. I finally got Nadia back into the car, where she flung herself into the seat.

We did manage to find a school for Nadia, though not that one, which I'm sure was a great relief to all who were there that day. The teachers took Nadia under their wings immediately. I could tell that they considered Nadia's special circumstances as gifts—they saw her as a child open to learning a whole new world.

Nadia loved school once she got there but hated any part of the goodbyes. I successfully resisted the urge to spy on her progress and risk detection but it was hard. Like so many mothers, I was torn between wanting my child to be independent and go willingly off with a teacher and also wanting that same child to need me more than anyone else. Since Meghan had attended preschool with me when she was young, I had only watched other mothers live out this paradox. I always wondered what their problem was, why they couldn't just say goodbye and leave—now I knew only too well. I must admit, though, that I was relieved to be able to get back to my graphic arts, grown-up, work routine. A routine in which people refrained from throwing tantrums for the most part.

Each day, for the first few weeks, Nadia would be on the swings when I arrived in the afternoon. Soon she was swinging beside her new friend Mimi. Mimi had recently arrived from Hong Kong with her parents and spoke very little English. She and Nadia would swing past each other, whooping each time they intersected, then giggling until they met again. I think Mimi made Nadia feel safe because she didn't speak the words everyone else did either. She became Nadia's first United States friend.

As I was tucking Nadia into bed one night during this time, she announced in Russian that she wasn't going to school tomorrow. I wanted to explain that she didn't have to because it was Saturday and children don't go to school on Saturday or Sunday. I'm sure that the weekends weren't much different from the weekdays in the orphanage. In my fragmented and limited Russian, I said, "Nadia, *neigh schola zaftra, da?* [No school tomorrow, okay?]"

Nadia nodded.

"No school tomorrow, tomorrow, okay. Then school. Understand?" She smiled and said yes as though I had finally figured out that I should give her what she wanted and do things her way.

When we decided to adopt an older child, I sometimes worried that I would be missing important "firsts" that make up a baby's initial years. The first smile, the first tooth, the first word (even if it is Dada instead of the much-coached Mama), the first wave, the first steps; and all the other firsts that are not so exciting but equally important, like the first serious diaper change that signals the end of a week's constipation, the first ear infection, the first scraped knee, the first nightmare. Sometimes I would see a little baby and think, "Oh, I'm going to miss that with an older child." But during those first months with Nadia we got to celebrate firsts just like any other parents, firsts that were sometimes even more special because Nadia was marveling in them as much as we were and didn't take them for granted as a tiny baby would. The first time Nadia called us Mama and Papa was just as thrilling at five as it would have been at eight months. For her to be able to identify two adults as "Mama" and "Papa" was an amazing feat. She loved it too! Her first time in a grocery store was a thrill in ways that children who grow up in the United States will never experience. Her eyes glowed with excitement over the shelves filled with food. She was awestruck as she watched me put bread, soup, milk, cereal—item after item—into our cart. I could tell she had never seen so much food in her life. She looked at me with wonder the entire time we were shopping. "What a great country!"

We not only got the normal firsts that other parents have, but we got other firsts as well; firsts that could only come about in a child who has gone without and is discovering things thought unobtainable. We got our firsts. We got our special firsts, and more.

I remember when we took Nadia to the mall to see Santa for the first time. She was now using English words more and more. The holiday decorations thrilled her. Other children her age were looking around but had seen it all before. Nadia was truly enchanted. When she came to the magical house, where Santa had children sitting on his knee, she looked at me with wide eyes.

"So *this* is where Father Winter has been!" she shouted, jumping up and down. Nadia had grown up hearing stories of Father Winter (the Russian equivalent to Santa Claus) from her caregivers in Russia. But no one ever *saw* him. "Wow!" her facial expression told us. "All this time he had been living in a shopping mall in San Jose, California. Amazing!"

Christmas was glorious that year. Casey and I had finished up most of our INS paperwork and travel preparations for our trip to Colombia. Family members came to visit from Oregon, Iowa, and New York. I'm sure Nadia thought each day from Thanksgiving to New Year's was Christmas day. We all took great delight in introducing her to more aunts, uncles, grandmothers, grandfathers, and cousins. Meghan was enjoying the attention too, as everyone applauded her role as instructor of her non-English-speaking sibling, and acknowledged her achievements in being an older sister. Nadia didn't really understand that we were preparing to adopt another child even though we had discussed the matter often, and Meghan still considered Ana a future event, possibly taking as long as the first one had. She'd worry about it later and concentrate on all the presents and attention that streamed in each day. I can still picture Christmas day at my brother's house, with all our family gathered together, the newest member's face lit brighter than the Christmas tree. We were all surrounded by an obscene amount of presents, and more love than I'm sure Nadia had ever dreamed attainable.

Chapter 11

COLOMBIA

*Ana the first day we met, wearing the dress her
foster mother had made for her.*

Journal entry, January 13, 1994

First day in Colombia. Too tired to write.

The preparations for our trip to Colombia were at the same time easier and harder than for our trip to Russia, easier because we now had some experience traveling to a foreign country to adopt a child, and harder because we now had two children to leave behind—one who was just getting to know us, and the other who was getting used to not having us all to herself. Casey and I kept to a routine as best we could and enlisted the help of both our mothers so the girls could stay in their own house and continue with their lives in a normal way. First Grandma Ruth would come for a couple of weeks and then Grandma Lois would arrive. We did our best to convince our clients and vendors that, although we had no idea how long we would be away, we wanted to have work waiting for us when we returned. Since we deal mostly with high-tech firms in the Silicon Valley, where technology changes daily and information has to be obtained and disseminated on a constant basis, we knew that we were taking a business risk by putting everyone on hold. We weren't big enough for employees, so we didn't really have anyone holding down the business. We knew we would have to hustle when we returned to make up for lost time, and we worked as hard as we could before we left to get as much work done as possible. We were exhausted before we even left.

Once again we found ourselves staying up the entire night before we left for Colombia, finishing up last-minute details. Around 4:00 A.M. Nadia, awakened by our preparations but too sleepy to be concerned, wandered into our room and I held her until she fell asleep. Later, Meghan got up too and began to cry. I gathered her into my arms.

"I'm afraid you're going to die," she sniffed when she could talk. I knew that this newest trip was weighing on Meghan's mind but I was surprised by her worry for our safety. Had she overheard us discussing the traveler's advisory we had received from the INS warning us that Colombia wasn't on their list of "safe" countries? What else did she hear and interpret in her own way? What else must she be worried about?

"Your dad and I will be safe, but I would certainly feel better if you said a prayer for us each night," I answered, my eyes filling with tears.

"I'll really miss you."

"I'll miss you too."

"I wish you didn't have to go."

"I do too. But we have to go to bring Ana home."

"What if I don't like her?"

"You may not at first and that's okay, but I think we'll all grow to love her."

"What if I need help with my homework?"

"Your grandma can help you with your homework, and your dad and I will call as often as we can."

"You mean Grandma knows how to do multiplication?"

"Yes, believe it or not, Grandma had multiplication during prehistoric times when she was in school."

"Okay . . . Mom?"

"Yes."

"I love you."

"I love you too."

Then it was Casey's turn to hold Meghan and answer the same questions in the same way.

Finally, again, we were on a plane, flying off to meet daughter number three.

The flight was long, and Casey and I spent most of the time reading. I had brought along a Barbara Kingsolver novel. Casey was engrossed in *A Tourist's Guide to Colombia*. Every once in a while he would read aloud passages about how to be aware of and avoid hazards such as drug dealers, pickpockets, disease-carrying insects, and contaminated food and water. "Please don't share any more with me," I finally said. "I'd rather be surprised."

I got my first surprise as soon as we landed in Barranquilla.

"Where is everyone?" we wondered, looking around at the deserted airport. We cleared customs and looked for signs of life. We were supposed to be met by a translator named Helena, but when the few passengers and the flight crew left, she was nowhere to be found. We went outside but we saw only two stern-looking soldiers guarding the steps. We sat down to wait. It was dark and we felt very vulnerable sitting there with our mound of luggage waiting for Helena to rescue us. We had been awake now for thirty-six hours and our travel high had begun to wane. It was now obvious to us that something had been miscommunicated. Unfortunately, there were no longer any taxis in the area and the hotel was about a forty-five-minute drive from the airport. We ended up hitching a ride with a Continental Airline staff shuttle van when the airport closed for the night.

We reached our hotel around 2:00 A.M. and Casey and I looked at each other with relief. We hadn't known what to expect. If our information was wrong about someone meeting us at the airport, would we have reservations when we got to the hotel? Would it be deserted at this early hour? The Hotel Majestic was true to its name as far as we were concerned. The desk clerk had been waiting for us to arrive, with a neatly written message that we would be met by Doctora Rosa Barbosa, a Barranquilla lawyer, in the lobby at 8:00 the next morning. Little did we know that soon we would feel as if this were our second home and know all the Majestic staff on a first-name basis. That night, though, we were busy noticing all the intricate tile and woodwork in the hallways and foyer. Huge vases of flowers filled the lobby. A winding staircase stretched to the second floor with a gleaming wooden banister. Our room was comfortable and we couldn't wait to collapse into sleep, but we both woke up early in anticipation of meeting Ana for the first time.

We took a cold shower (there was no hot water) and dressed quickly. We went down to the lobby to wait for Doctora Barbosa. When she arrived, we introduced ourselves and realized that she didn't speak a word of English. Casey had his first test of speaking Spanish for something other than ordering dinner. She brought out legal forms and indicated that we must sign them, but they were written in Spanish and we had no idea what they said. Although this worried Casey and me, it didn't seem to bother her in the least. Cheerfully, she handed us a pen. Luckily, we were saved by the desk clerk, who translated for us until it was time to leave the hotel. If only we had thought to ask him to find out what our schedule would be for the rest of the day, but we just assumed that we would be going to see Ana as we had with Nadia. Instead, we spent the rest of the morning following Doctora Barbosa around from a court house clerk's office, to a judge's chamber, and finally to the Social Services offices. We were so nervous. Every time I entered a building, I expected to see Ana. I studied every child I saw, thinking that it could be her. I wondered whether she would like us, if she would be with her foster mother, if she would be afraid of us like Nadia.

We waited in lines and signed more papers that we didn't fully understand. It wasn't until we arrived at the Social Services waiting room that we met Helena, who had gotten the time wrong of our flight but who was now here to explain the Colombian adoption process to us and to translate. She began to explain the things that we had already done and signed that morning.

"You are very lucky," she told us with a smile. "The judge you got is very fast. The last family who had him was processed after just a month's time."

A MONTH—four weeks—thirty-one days! How could we afford to miss that much work? How could we stay away from our other children for such a long time? A month seemed like forever.

"Of course, I can't guarantee that yours will be so smooth because you never know."

Casey and I stared at each other.

We were taken into a small room in the Social Services building to speak with a psychologist who had examined Ana and told us more of her history. Evidently, Ana had been cared for by a foster mother after she was released from the hospital for malnutrition. When her foster mother decided to leave the area, Ana was moved to yet another foster family. She had been with them for about two years. A boy, eleven, and a girl, five, also lived in the home. It wasn't clear to me whether there was a father in the home or not. If there was, it sounded as if he barely saw the children. We tried to ask more questions about Ana's personality but the psychologist didn't really know much about her other than her circumstances. Her answers were not very specific and, we learned, not even accurate. She said that Ana was shy (wrong), that she didn't talk very much (wrong), and that she needed help with her fine motor skills (not as much as her large motor skills). When the psychologist was finished, someone was sent to buy us juice and cake for a snack. We continued our wait.

Suddenly there was a flurry of activity in the hallway and the door to the room we were waiting in opened. In flew a tiny little girl who immediately reached out her arms to me to be held. It was Ana! She was grinning from ear to ear. Was this really the girl in the photo who needed a smile? She saw our juice containers and her eyes brightened. Casey gave her some of his cake. She immediately stuffed part of it into her mouth. She hugged us and kissed us and we were all excited, relieved, and happy!

Ana had on a pink and white ruffled dress with little pearl buttons. Her white anklets were trimmed in delicate lace. Her hair was combed neatly, partially pulled back with two large pink balls attached to a rubber band to create a small pigtail that stuck out from the top of her head. She was smiling so wide that her eyes looked like little crescent moons, almost disappearing in her delight. And best of all, she wasn't going to budge from my arms. I was thrilled! What a charmer. We were totally smitten.

Helena told us this was only the second time she had seen a child not cry when making a transition from foster mother to adoptive mother. I radiated with pride, feeling that surely much of the credit belonged to us for being such wonderful parents and the rest to Ana for being clever and bright enough to realize how wonderful we were. We silently thanked the foster mother for loving her enough to make a smooth transition—we assumed Ana must have been well prepared for this day. Sadly, we were wrong. Soon we were to learn only too well that Ana's charm and instant attachment to strangers was her way of survival. She knew that charming little girls were given food and attention.

"Isn't she beautiful? Isn't she brilliant?" I wanted to ask everyone. It was as if she had known us forever. How could it be so perfect? My fantasy had come true, or so I thought at the time. As we were leaving the office, everyone was smiling, smiling, smiling. "Ana loves us already and she doesn't even know us," I thought. "We are the luckiest people in the world!" But our ignorance was our bliss and we floated on our cloud of relief and joy for those first few hours. It turns out that we were the luckiest people in the world, but not for the reasons I thought at the time. I thought our luck was in adopting a child who seemed to love us from the moment she saw us. Even though this "love" we first witnessed was actually Ana's protective facade, the deeper levels of Ana's ability to trust and truly love others, those aspects of herself she kept safely buried, were intense and beautiful. We *were* the luckiest people in the world because we would eventually share this largess—all the more valuable because we had to "mine for it" over the coming years.

We were given a paper stating that we had the right to have Ana with us. We scoffed at the formality but would be thankful for it later.

We took a taxi back to the Hotel Majestic with Helena and proudly showed Ana off to the hotel staff. They were surprised to see a four-year-old child because everyone who had come before us from the United States and Canada had adopted only infants. A maid ran to trade the crib they had assembled during our absence for a child's bed.

We began to see that the solemn, resigned child of our photograph was actually a busy "monkey" who never stopped moving. At first, we attributed it to nervousness and excitement. We had lunch in the hotel restaurant, and although we thought she seemed active then, we would soon learn after several future meals with our perpetual-motion child and countless spilled water glasses, that she was exhibiting great restraint. We had been together for only a couple of hours but between her energy and my lack of sleep I was ready for a nap. Casey volunteered to take Ana swimming in the hotel pool out in the courtyard. While undressing her, I felt something in her sock. It was a note from her foster mother. At the top was her address and telephone number. Trying to make out the flowery handwriting I read:

> *Por favor euviorme fotos de lat niña para saber couuo se encueutra. Gracias.*

She was asking us to send her pictures and tell her that Ana was all right. We had been told that Ana's dress had been made by her foster mother. I'm sure it took hours to make with all the ruffles and buttons. I wished I could have met her and thanked her in person for caring for Ana. I wondered how she was feeling, whether her arms felt empty today.

We spent the rest of the day playing games, exploring the neighborhood, and watching Ana try on every stitch of clothing we had brought for her. That evening I took a photo of Casey and Ana and he said, "Be sure it shows how tired her new papa is!" It did. She wasn't the least bit tired though.

Before finally falling asleep that first night, Ana did cry—not sobs but more a whimper with big tears. Both Casey and I rested a hand on her back and tried to let her know that it was okay to cry and to feel sad. She fell asleep after about fifteen minutes. Except for the brief tears before bed, we couldn't help but be awestruck by the differences between this day and our first-day experience with Nadia. What other major divergences were in store?

The next morning Helena escorted us back to Social Services. Ana was very skittish. She didn't want to leave my lap but didn't want to sit either. I became a human jungle gym to this child, who was so flexible and wiggly that she seemed only muscles and skin—no bones whatsoever. She reminded me of the Gumby toy I had as a child, the one that could bend in any direction but couldn't stand up on its own. Doctora Barbosa reprimanded her twice for climbing on me and I'm sure that she thought I should be telling her to sit still and behave, but I felt that Ana needed comfort, not scolding. She had every right to be nervous. No one was explaining to her why she was there. For all she knew, we were rejecting her and sending her back. Or worse, maybe she thought she would be given away to another set of strangers. I soothed her as best I could and Casey tried to explain what was happening with the Spanish words he knew. We soon discovered, though, that Ana didn't take an adult's word for any situation. She would be nervous until she got solid proof—like going home for a swim.

We were interviewed by the Spanish-speaking director as Helena translated and a secretary slowly pounded out our responses on an old manual typewriter. How did the night go? Would we accept Ana? Did we want her still? Would we make her a U.S. citizen? We answered all the questions and signed all the copies. It took over an hour.

Ana got more and more restless. We had been told that she was on thyroid medication. We asked if we should continue the medication—maybe it was contributing to her hyperactivity. They assured us that Ana didn't need it anymore. We also asked about her teeth. "We noticed a lot of fillings in her back teeth," we said. "Has she had a lot of dental work?"

"Oh, no," the director answered, "she did have some teeth pulled but she hasn't had any fillings."

We looked again, trying not to make Ana feel like a horse on a trading block. All her top front teeth were missing and two on the bottom. The rest of her teeth looked dark, so we thought they must be filled. We looked again. They were rotted. Oh my. So this is why she wasn't smiling in her first picture.

We asked more questions about Ana's early history. Did they have any more information about Ana's mother or father? Did they have any idea whether or not Ana had been abused or molested as a young child? We tried to understand her timeline. Why did the first foster mother leave the area? Was Ana close to her? How did she react to the transition? How long was she in the hospital when she first came to Social Services?

The director and psychologist nodded their heads through Helena's translation of our questions. Their answers remained vague. "Is this really important?" they wanted to know. "What does it matter what happened before?"

I couldn't understand why they didn't think this information was important for us to know. "We'd like to know, so we can help Ana. Someday she may want to know her history."

"Ana's life began yesterday when you accepted her. She was born yesterday. Forget the past, it can't be changed and is best left alone."

These two Colombian women smiled sympathetically at our American need-to-know-everything attitude, our inability to forget the past and move forward. We were told that, if we insisted, we could meet the foster mother. Unfortunately, our request was not met.

I still find myself wishing that I knew more details of Ana's situation before she met us. Sometimes today, she will cry in a deep and heartbreaking way and I know in my soul that she is crying over past demons and hardships that we can never fully understand. I long to be able to at least name her sorrows. Although it might not do any practical good to know Ana's detailed past, I can't help feeling it would be easier to deal with a known evil than a shadowy, unknown one that gets triggered when we, and often Ana, least expect it.

We were sent back to our hotel to wait for the next round of paper signatures. Helena told us that it might be several days and asked if we would like to visit Cartagena, a coastal city about an hour's drive from Barranquilla. A vacation—"Sure," we answered excitedly. This was our chance to see part of Colombia. We went "home" to pack for our trip. (We had only been in Colombia three days and already we were calling the Hotel Majestic "home.")

Before we left for Cartagena, we ventured out to a local department store to buy a better-fitting swimsuit for Ana. I couldn't believe how heavy and tiring Ana could become on a simple trip to the store. She wanted to be held constantly, only by me, and yet squirmed and wiggled the entire time. If she did let me put her down, she immediately went limp onto the floor or ran off giggling to the nearest stranger who would hold her. The shoppers looked at us with what I imagined could only be disdain. Obviously, we could not control this tiny, sweet child ourselves. Casey tried to help but Ana wouldn't let him touch her in public—and sometimes even in our room. Ah, but when I got to the end of my rope and was ready to give up, Ana turned on her most luminous smile, wrapped herself around my legs, and we began the cycle again.

While Casey paid for our purchases, I got Ana and myself something to eat at a cafeteria just outside the store. It was a trick trying to carry a tray filled with food and pay for it, while balancing a squirming Ana who threatened to scream if I let her down. When we got settled at an outside table, a young girl approached us and stared at me with big brown eyes. She was disheveled and filthy but had a big smile on her face. Where had I seen that smile? She asked me something in Spanish while slapping a steel pipe into the palm of her hand, like a policeman with a billyclub. People around our table stared, waiting to see what I would do next. I was very uncomfortable. I also felt guilty because I didn't want to be around her begging eyes—they scared me. She was a tiny child, just a few years older than Ana, and yet I felt that she could inflict great harm on my body. She continued to smile and plead at the same time. She didn't get that I had no idea what she was saying. When Casey found us, I immediately hopped up, telling him I needed to get napkins. Before Ana could protest, I was back inside the cafeteria trying to regain my composure. When I returned, Casey was talking to the girl. When he asked her why she had the pipe, she just grinned. I asked if we should offer her some food but Casey had been told by the desk clerk not to give street children food because you could become a target. (I wasn't sure what kind of target, but I knew that I didn't want to become one.) What happened to my noble spirit and goodwill toward the less fortunate? It flew out the window at the sight of that pipe. I couldn't help but think that this girl's history probably paralleled Ana's except for the intervention of the Colombian Social Services. I added her to my growing list of children's faces that still roam my mind.

We thought our visit to Cartagena would be a pleasant side trip—a diversion while we waited. It turned out to be a constant struggle to be civil. Ana was in perpetual motion and had no idea why we were in this strange city. Rather than enjoy the new surroundings, she seemed more fearful. My arms ached but she wouldn't let Casey hold her at all.

She also began to show signs of having the smallest bladder in the entire country of Colombia. We couldn't decide whether she was uneasy, punishing us, or marking her territory for future adopted children. We found ourselves on a "rest room tour" of the city. We memorized the location of every bathroom within a five-mile radius of our Cartagena hotel. Ana wasn't particular, though; bathrooms were fine but she was just as content to pee outdoors behind trees and shops, or in an alleyway. She was especially fond of going pee in front of large groups of tourists. Ana couldn't wait a moment longer! She had to GO NOW! Then she would HAVE TO GO NOW a minute later. We worried about a bladder infection but she was not in any pain and, interestingly, rarely had to go when we were in our hotel room.

"It's your turn to take her," I would say to Casey. "I've taken her three times in the last half hour."

"Okay, I'll try," he would answer, reaching to take Ana by the hand.

"No!" she would scream and begin to cry.

We drew crowds.

"Never mind, I'll go!"

"Let her cry. She has to get used to me."

Casey would drag her away and I would smile weakly at the crowd. Someone would ask me something in Spanish, but I wouldn't be able to respond. We could all hear Ana screaming from the bathroom. I began to interpret strangers' looks with my "guilty mother" imagination. "What's happening in there?" said these looks. "Why isn't the mother helping? How can she be her real mother with that light skin? Why won't she take her little girl to the bathroom herself?"

"Because I've been holding her for three days straight!" I wanted to yell. Instead, I saved it for Casey. "Why did you leave me alone?" I hissed.

Minutes later Ana would cross her legs and begin to whimper. This became our routine.

There were some happy times too. Since I grew up in land-locked Iowa, the ocean has always been a powerful and mysterious force to me. Here the ocean was a deep blue color with consistently gentle waves moving in along the shore. Ana and I spent an entire morning together in the water. I held her in my arms letting the waist-deep water help support her weight. We would move up and down with the incoming waves and laugh at our sudden buoyancy when the larger waves would lift me up and deposit us gently a bit closer to the shore. The water soothed us both and helped wash away some of the strain that was building. Regrettably, the relief didn't last for long.

One night in particular was the hardest for our little family in Cartagena. We had called home and talked with Nadia and Meghan. Meghan was feeling especially hurt and lonely for us. She complained about having to be without her parents, and we were just as unhappy about being away from home. Ana sensed the tension and began jumping around on the beds. She wouldn't settle down.

Suddenly Casey's patience evaporated—burned up from exhaustion, stress, and the hot Cartagena sun. *"Ananita!"* he shouted sternly. He lifted her up and tossed her onto the bed—something he had done a hundred times in the last week. Tossing her onto the bed was usually accompanied by giggles and pleading for more. But the tone of his voice and the tension in the air on this night frightened her. She looked up at us with genuine fear. Her mouth moved silently at first. Then came a slow whine. Then she caught her breath and a huge sob came out of her, all in slow motion.

She cried louder. Tears streamed down her face and snot came pouring out of her nose. Casey was embarrassed and confused. Contritely, he apologized and reached out to try to comfort her but she wouldn't let him touch her. I took her in my arms and rocked her shaking body back and forth. I sang every soothing song I knew and then began again. I could understand Casey's frustration. He hadn't meant to be rough—only stern—but it came out stronger than he had intended. Still, I was furious.

Finally she settled down and fell into a labored sleep. But she was asleep for just a short time when she was awakened by what must have been a bad dream. Casey jumped up, wanting to help her, but when she saw him, all her panic returned and she began to scream again, more loudly than the first time. Ana was inconsolable. I carried her back and forth across the floor of the room, trying to calm her and trying not to cry myself.

When Ana had finally fallen asleep again, I wanted to call Marge.

"I want to ask her what to do with this child," I told Casey. "I can't tell what she wants or needs. One minute she's happy, the next, she blows up. We never know if she's going to let you near her or not. We need some help."

"Maggie, let's wait until morning," Casey said.

"Sure, you don't mind waiting because I'm the one who's going to have to deal with her screaming when she wakes up again." I didn't know if I could get through one more wailing scene with Ana that night.

"Do you think it's easy watching you and knowing I can't do anything to help? I'm scared too."

If I hadn't been so tired, I might have been able to see his point. But I was way past tired and heading toward collapse. I was angry with Casey because he was the only person in the room I *could* be angry with. Neither one of us had the energy to fight anymore. I finally fell asleep with the depressing thought that if we couldn't handle this child in paradise, where we had no other responsibilities, what nightmare did we face when we got home to two other children and full-time jobs? Everything looked dark and depressing.

The next day Ana woke up smiling, as if she had been cleansed by the previous night's tears. Maybe it will be all right after all, I thought. How things can change with the light of day and a little sleep.

* * *

We traveled back to Barranquilla and were truly glad to see our hotel room and the now familiar faces of the hotel staff. Eating around the table in our room felt like having a home-cooked meal in a safe place. Even Ana seemed more comfortable in this little room than in the bigger hotel in Cartagena. The next days were filled with errands for Ana's adoption paperwork.

Foreign adoption creates a kind of time warp. A day seems like twenty-four hours (or sometimes less) when you go about your daily routine at home, but my two weeks in Colombia felt like two years. Each day seemed longer than the one before. I just wanted to *go* home, I just wanted to *be* home. I know it sounds like whining to complain about two weeks out of my life, but those two weeks went by in slow motion. Everything felt like a major effort that I couldn't escape for a minute. I wanted desperately to be able to jump into a car and drive to a grocery store, or the dry cleaners, or a friend's house (a friend who wouldn't ask me to sign any papers). I was tired of being exotic and adventurous. I wanted to have my entire family in our own house being boring, being lazy, being normal. Poor me, I was pathetic, and I was thankful when the day came that Casey and I had finished the legal requirements that called for the presence of both parents, and one of us could return home. Since Casey spoke some Spanish, we had already decided he should stay and I should go back to Meghan and Nadia. I tried to at least put up a front for Casey— to pretend I wished I was the one who got to stay behind and finish up the final paperwork—but I never could have convinced him for a second. While I felt sorry for him, I counted the minutes until I could climb aboard the plane and fly home. My only wish was that we were leaving together. I couldn't imagine how Ana would cope without me to carry her everywhere. *Sure, I'm going to be your mother forever, but just now I have to leave you with this man that you aren't real sure you like yet. Don't worry, you'll be joining me soon, even though we don't know when soon will be.* It was a recipe for disaster.

For all my longing to return home, I felt frantic inside when Casey and Ana said goodbye to me at the gate. We explained to Ana that I was going home to get her room ready and to be with her sisters while Daddy was going to stay with her until it was time to come home. We described her room, clothes, and all the marvelous toys that would be waiting when she arrived. Casey and I smiled as if this were no big deal, but I was feeling heartsick with guilt at leaving, Casey was feeling heartsick with apprehension, and Ana was just plain heartsick. Would she ever feel secure?

As I made my way to the gate, Ana reached her arms out for me crying; begging me to stay with her. As I walked down the boarding ramp, I could hear her call to me. I dissolved into tears the second I sat in my seat. Casey told me later that Ana cried and screamed during the entire hour-long taxi ride back to the hotel. Casey paid the driver double his fare to cover the ear damage that he was sure to have sustained. While Ana had allowed me to hold her whenever she was upset, she wouldn't give Casey the chance. She wouldn't let him come near her. If her new mother would leave, how could she trust her new father?

Chapter 12

❧

MORE WORK AND MORE JOY

Nadia, Meghan, and Ana learning the art of being sisters.

Journal entry, February 3, 1994

It's been fourteen days since I got home from Colombia. The girls and I talked with Casey over the phone today. He's depressed. Doctora Barbosa told him that he and Ana will either leave for Bogota tomorrow or they will have to wait two more weeks before they can travel. Thank you, thank you, thank you it's him and not me alone in Colombia with Ana, the human dynamo. I hope he never reads this.

Casey and Ana arrived at the San Francisco International Airport on February 5—sixteen days after I'd left them. Our exhausted travelers!

I had ordered a bright green banner with WELCOME HOME CASEY AND ANA in large white block lettering. I had pastel-colored helium balloons with matching ribbons to brighten their arrival. Penny had curled Nadia's hair and put Meghan's into a stylish twist on top of her head. I wanted to welcome our travelers in style but my timing was off. Getting everything exactly the way I wanted it for Ana's first glimpse of her new family, and getting all the people who wanted to be there organized, didn't work out quite as I had expected: our welcome party was still in the parking garage when Casey and Ana stepped off the plane. I imagined them searching the faces of the people who had managed to get to the airport in plenty of time to meet their loved ones, yearning for hugs and kisses, and seeing only strangers. When we finally caught up with them in baggage claim, Casey didn't really care about banners or balloons or visitors. He just wanted to be home. His first words to me after a brief, not-too-heartfelt hug were, "I've been through hell and you aren't even at the gate to meet me?" Ana's expression was blank, mirroring her father's displeasure as she looked at the crowd that had gathered to welcome her. But when my eyes met Ana's, I was rewarded with a radiant smile. I reached out to her—safer than dealing with Casey, I reasoned—and she immediately settled into my arms.

"Nadia and Meghan, meet your new sister, Ana," I said proudly, surveying all three of my beautiful daughters—together at last.

Casey translated. Nadia glowed, while Meghan looked a little leery. She didn't seem as eager to admit this newest sister into her heart. She was, however, thrilled to see her father again. This was the longest time they had ever been apart and she wanted to concentrate all her attention on him. Her hugs helped Casey get over his disappointment about our earlier tardiness.

Finally, Ana spoke. Her first words in America—we were all excited to hear them. Casey translated, but he needn't have. I knew this request only too well.

"I have to pee."

I untangled myself from her arms and legs and set her down. "Let's find a bathroom," I said, looking around for the nearest one. "Over here, let's go, sweetie."

Nadia raced up and grabbed Ana by the hand. "I'll take her, Mama," she said in her newly acquired English. "I'll take care of Ana."

Ana looked at Nadia and her outstretched hand and, with a wide grin, grabbed hold. Off they skipped to the bathroom.

Our timid, insecure Nadia was now the older, savvy sister. Ana gazed up at her in awe. They couldn't look more mismatched. Ana, thin and still teetering from poor muscle tone as she walked, her skin a milk chocolate color, her hair dark and wavy. Nadia, thick-boned and sturdy, with pale Russian skin and blond hair. Ana, with her large brown cow-eyes, gazed up into Nadia's small almond-shaped eyes, an intense blue that now sparkled. They spoke no common words, yet each knew that Nadia was to be Ana's protector. Nadia knew what it was like being the new kid in the family and both knew instinctively that they were sisters.

As soon as we got back home, Casey began telling us tales from his "captivity" in Colombia. He told us that he probably would have had irreversible emotional damage if it hadn't been for a couple who checked into the Hotel Majestic soon after I left. Casey was unable to alleviate Ana's sorrow over what she must have viewed as her latest abandonment. He was at his wits' end and desperate for a way to stop her tears. One afternoon, as he was dragging Ana away from one of the cleaning crew, whom she was trying to convince to spirit her away, he met a family checking into a room down the hall—a minister named Carlos, his wife Katherine, and their daughter Melissa, who were in Barranquilla to attend a week-long Christian revival meeting. (They might have thought God had sent them for a revival, but Casey is convinced they were there so Melissa could help calm Ana.) The girls played in the room and out by the pool for hours at a time, giving Casey a chance to regroup for his many visits to one official or another.

One evening several days later, Katherine offered to take Ana over to the coliseum for one of their meetings. "She can play behind the stage with Melissa," she said. "Just pick her up when it's her bedtime." Casey assumed there must be a children's play area behind the stage, and since the coliseum was within walking distance, took her up on her offer. When it was time to pick Ana up, Casey followed the directions to the coliseum, where he was greeted by volunteer guards with ID badges. "I've come to pick up my daughter," he told them in Spanish as best he could. Then he gave them Carlos's name.

"*Es Christiano?* (Are you Christian?)" the guard asked severely.

"*Sí,*" he answered, trying to look pious. There was no way he would have told him anything else. Casey was sent from guard to guard, and had to pass through several checkpoints and a maze of stark corridors lit by single lightbulbs, which cast ominous shadows against the concrete walls. Still another guard took him down a ramp to the stage, where he was told to wait. It was dark and there were no seats, just tiered steps that were filled with people. He felt as if he were in a different time. Another man, who looked quite official, appeared and asked, "*Que pasa?* [What's going on here?]" in a condescending voice. Casey explained once again that he was there to pick up his daughter, who was with the minister's daughter. "Is there an area where the children are?" Casey asked.

"Just a minute," he replied and started to walk toward the stage. Just then Casey saw Melissa and Ana peek their heads from behind the podium. They were playing *on* the stage, not behind it. He pointed to Ana and said, "That's my daughter." Immediately, Ana looked away as if she didn't know who this man was, and even if she did, didn't want anything to do with him. This didn't help Casey's cause. The man looked at Casey, then looked at this brown girl. Casey explained as best he could that she was adopted and really was his daughter. He stood there hoping that, if he waited long enough, Ana might feel more comfortable leaving with him and he could get out of there without too much of a scene.

The last sermon was over and the crowd began singing songs. Casey decided to wait until Carlos was ready to leave and then go home with them, but he finally realized that these songs would continue until the last person left. He could see that there were some die-hards who weren't nearly ready to have this religious experience end. To make matters worse, Carlos had begun playing the piano for the hymns and Casey couldn't get his attention. He knew he was going to have to somehow get Ana off the stage if they wanted to get home anytime soon. This wouldn't be easy. Sure enough, when he tried to get her to go with him, she struggled—filling the coliseum with her screams. Everyone began turning toward them wondering why this *gringo* was carrying away this Colombian child who obviously wanted nothing to do with him. Thankfully, no one stopped him as he struggled through the crowd to get back outside. He bought Ana a popsicle to quiet her for the trip down the street to the hotel. Later that night, he thanked God, in his own way, for giving him such a keen lesson in patience and perseverance.

The mornings proved to be the time that Ana gradually, out of necessity, began to trust her new father. During the time between waking up and when Melissa was ready to play, they would talk and color pictures together. Ana liked him to tickle her, and throwing her on the bed was fun again. When I got home, I asked Marge if she would call him in Colombia and give him some encouragement. "This may be hard, Casey," she told him gently. "But what a marvelous chance for you to bond with Ana."

"It doesn't feel marvelous," was his reply.

"I know, but trust me, the confidence you'll earn now while you're alone with Ana is far greater than if you were at home with the entire family. It often takes months for a girl who hasn't known nurturing men to accept their adoptive father. Most are terrified of men. You're going to have a great head start on a solid relationship together."

Leave it to Marge to think of the positive.

The hardest aspect of the time alone with Ana was waiting for word from Doctora Barbosa that he could travel to Bogotá for a final meeting with the American Embassy. Having a definite date, even if it proved to be farther in the future, would have been easier than the hope and despair he faced each day wondering if the phone would ring. It was a very lonely and trying time for him, but the day came when he and Ana flew to Bogotá, and of course, eventually home.

His other trials included driving through the largest hailstorm to hit Bogotá in years to obtain Ana's exit visa before the office closed. He had reserved tickets for the next day's flight to the United States and would have to wait over the weekend if they didn't get there by 4:00. The hail came down in pebble-size chunks with such ferocity that roofs collapsed, many areas were flooded, and traffic ground to a halt. "Please hurry," Casey pleaded with his Bogotá translator and driver. "I'm sure we can make it." When they finally arrived, the office window was closed and Casey slumped against the wall in defeat. Just then, a guardian angel in the form of a clerk walked out another door and agreed to let Señor Conroy pick up the visa that had already been prepared in anticipation of his arrival that day. It may have been the fact that Casey looked ready to explode that opened the clerk's heart and allowed this special treatment.

"Well, as grueling as these weeks were, they make a great story," I told Casey. Everyone around the table agreed, still glad it hadn't been them. "I'm sure they'll sound even better next year," I added.

As we passed around pictures of our trip to Colombia to family and friends, Ana stayed as far away as possible. Each of our children had trouble looking at pictures of their "past lives" when they first arrived. We decided not to push her but not to hide things from her either.

Although Casey spoke Spanish to Ana as much as possible, she, too, wanted only to speak English, the official language of the household. Because Nadia and Ana were inseparable, Nadia ended up as Ana's default English tutor. Soon Ana was speaking English with a Russian accent. Nadia was even picking up some Spanish words. Spanish, Russian, and English of various proficiencies were spoken daily. When we were upset or in a hurry, we never knew which words would come out of our mouths. *"Nyet, don't put your zappatos on la couch!"*

With all the discussion of our most recent trip, Nadia began to become a little curious regarding her own past. I kept a photo album out on a table in the living room. One day I found Nadia curled up on the couch looking through pictures we had taken at the orphanage during our first meeting with her.

"Hi," I said, "do you remember the children's home in Russia?"

"Yes," she answered softly, "but I don't know who these people are."

They were the people she had lived her whole life with until six months ago.

"Would you like for me to help you remember who they are?"

"No."

"Okay. Can I look at the pictures with you?"

"Yes."

We both sat quietly as Nadia turned the pages of the photo album, studying each page intently. Her face was set with a pensive expression as if she were trying to figure out a riddle.

"Mom?"

"Yes."

"Why you take so long to get me?"

"What?" I asked, surprised yet not surprised, knowing and yet not knowing what she was asking.

"Why you take so long to come get me in Russia?"

My eyes filled with tears as I tried to think of what to say. What is the right answer? Why should she have had to wait for her mother? Was she wondering what kind of mother wouldn't know where her own child was for five years? Was this the time to explain the concept of birth mother/adoptive mother? How much information was needed . . . desired . . . necessary?

Nadia stared at the picture of Casey and me holding her in front of the orphanage on the day we first met her.

"We didn't know we *could* come get you," I said, "but as soon as we knew where you were, we came as soon as we could."

"Okay, Mom," she said, and gave me a hug. There were no more questions that day.

Our house felt smaller—and louder—as the days passed. With one mom, one dad, three children, a cat, and many visitors each day, our house literally shook with activity. The features that had seemed cute and quaint when Casey and I first bought our house, with two children at the most in our minds, became cramped and breakable with all the commotion our brood now generated. Limited storage space became no storage space. After seeing the cramped living quarters in Russia and Colombia, I had sworn that I would always be thankful for our American standard of living. But the *idea* of one more person in a two-bedroom, one-bath house and the *reality* were very different. Ana wasn't very big but her incredible energy consumed a lot of space. Meghan had always had her own room. Now in a period of six months she was sharing her space with two other children. She liked to remind us that none of her friends shared a room with two sisters. Their homes began to loom palatial in Meghan's mind.

The girls' room was divided by an archway. We set up bunk beds on the one side for Nadia and Ana, who would have shared a bed if they could (sometimes we would find them in the same bed in the morning), and created a loft bed for Meghan on the other side. This left room for dressers but little else.

Meghan was becoming more and more aware that her stuff was being appropriated for group use. She didn't like it. Toys that she wouldn't have been caught dead playing with six months before were suddenly her favorites.

"Where's my doll?" Meghan demanded.

"You mean the one you never play with?" I asked.

"Well, it's still mine and I might want to play with it someday."

"Honey, you didn't play with it the day you got it for your birthday three years ago."

"But I want to now."

"You mean now that Nadia and Ana are playing with it?"

"They can't just take my stuff whenever they feel like it. Even if I don't use something, they still have to *ask* me. It's still mine!"

"I know it's hard. And you're right. They should ask, but I also need for you to understand that they have never had toys or have at least had to share their whole lives. Give them a break. We'll set up some special places for you to put your important things that you don't want them to touch."

"Can I get a padlock?"

"We'll see."

"Couldn't they just live in the garage and give me back my room?"

"No."

I did try to explain to Nadia and Ana the difference between

Nadia's things, Ana's things, and Meghan's things. As hard as it was for Meghan to understand how it had been for them, it was equally difficult for them to fathom that one child could have so many possessions. In Nadia's orphanage, all the toys were community toys; the children didn't even have clothing of their own. Each morning, whatever clothes were set out for you were put on, whether you liked them or not. The next day someone else would be wearing them. Ana had had her own things but she never got to take them with her when she left, possessions came with the family of the moment. It was a confusing concept. Unfortunately, both Nadia and Ana grasped the concept of "mine" long before they grasped the concept of "not mine."

Ana adored Sylvia, our cat, and couldn't leave her alone. At times Sylvia thrived on the attention; other times she hid as much as possible. Luckily for her, Nadia was still afraid of animals at that point in her life. She stayed a safe distance away from the cat but was paralyzed with fear over the sight of a dog. Well, I shouldn't say paralyzed because, if she spotted a dog, she would jump into my arms, ready or not, and try to climb as high as possible, hoping to end up on my head and out of range of any teeth. Ana had no such qualms and never saw a dog that she didn't want to hug and pet. When we would go to the park, I coaxed Ana away from dogs of unknown origin while I balanced a terrified Nadia on my shoulders. Nadia was convinced that we would all end up as dog food; Ana was convinced that every dog she met, the bigger the better, needed to come home with us.

One of the biggest problems we had with Ana when she first arrived was her desire to be held by any stranger she encountered. The more I tried to give her my love, the more she needed from other people—preferably ones she had never set eyes on before. Most people thought it was charming, although some were embarrassed by the extreme attention of a child they had never met. I thought it was dangerous—not to mention how much it hurt my feelings. If we were at the park and I turned my attention away from Ana for even a moment, I would find her sitting on some strange man's lap giving him coy little looks with her big brown eyes. She was not the least bit shy about searching through his pockets for anything she might find interesting.

"I'm so sorry," I would say, sweeping Ana into my arms. Then she would give me a look that could kill, as if I were the cruel mother she had tried to escape, and reach out her arms to the man as if I were taking her away from her only friend in the world.

Usually, the men were flattered by her attention. I knew how they felt—the same way I had when I'd first met her at the Social Services office in Colombia. When I'd thought she was attached to me because I was special!

Sometimes Ana wouldn't give up easily and would soon be back with the stranger. If I scolded her and tried to take her back, I looked like a wicked witch denying her child attention from another loving adult. "Surely, she wouldn't need so much attention from strangers if her parents gave her enough at home," they must have thought. But the truth was that no amount of love was enough for her. What I gradually came to understand was that Ana didn't trust that we would keep her and so she wanted to keep her options open. It was much safer to get affection from strangers on her terms than to fall in love with a mother and father who would surely send her away after a while.

Ana went through the same period of crying each night as Nadia did, but there was a difference. After the first day, Nadia had let us hold and comfort her; Ana wouldn't. Casey and I took turns sitting next to her as she cried—a deep sobbing that would last up to an hour at a time. We wanted her to understand that we loved her no matter how miserable she was, no matter how much she rejected our comfort. It sounds odd, having to convince a child to accept your comfort, but that is what we found ourselves doing those first few months.

Nadia, on the other hand, was crying less and less each night. She had learned that she could get comfort by asking for it. "Mom, will you hold me?" usually worked just as well as breaking into tears. Meghan, who had started to outgrow her desire to be held and cuddled, suddenly needed just as much touching and holding as the other two. I couldn't blame her. My lap was seldom empty in the evening, and as much as I loved all my children, their constant need took its toll. "When I asked you to close the bathroom door, the idea was for you to be *outside*."

Once again, Casey and I had very different ways of dealing

with this stress. He began to set strict limits regarding his free time. He would use a stern voice to announce to the girls when he wanted to be left alone and refused to carry anyone capable of walking on her own. He actually enjoyed sitting in a chair by himself—imagine that. He would sometimes speak up for me: "Leave your mother alone. Give her a break."

I knew he was trying to help, but it made me exasperated that he wasn't being more charitable. "Please don't tell the girls when I can and can't hold them," I told him.

"Well, it seems that you're unable to tell them yourself and then you wind up overwhelmed."

"They need the attention. Maybe if you were more available, they wouldn't need it all from me."

"Maggie, all the attention in the world wouldn't be enough for these kids right now. They have to learn to soothe themselves. They have to—"

"They have to be held as much as possible, that's what. If I can't handle it, then I'll tell them myself. I don't need you telling them what my limits are." I was angry. The truth was that I *was* feeling overwhelmed. Unfortunately, I was only able to set limits with Casey. All day long I was pulled between three very needy youngsters fighting for my attention. Then Meghan would beg us to let her stay up at night after Nadia and Ana had been put to bed so she could have us all to herself again, even if only for an hour. By the time she went to bed, the last thing I wanted to do was cuddle with my husband.

"I need some attention too," he would say.

"I don't have any left," I would answer. I didn't, and I felt guilty.

When Meghan was born, I felt similarly, but since my body was a hormonal battlefield, I didn't care as much what Casey thought. Besides, most women I knew concentrated more on their babies than their husbands just after they gave birth; it was normal. Adoption seemed the same in emotional intensity to me, but I didn't have a standard to gauge what was normal and what wasn't. Most people agree that you can't spoil an infant. What if your "infant" is four years old?

All I knew was that after being needed and clung to all day, I was exhausted. I didn't want to be touched. If touching was out, then sex was certainly the last thing I had in mind. Casey, though, wanted something to show that our marriage hadn't been completely taken over by our children. Casey was exhausted too, but not that exhausted, never *that* exhausted. I didn't want to have to *prove* my love to Casey. In fact, I couldn't understand why he didn't see this as a short-term challenge and not as a permanent loss of our personal time. I was insulted that he didn't seem to trust my love for him even if I couldn't always show it in the moment.

So we bickered, felt bad, apologized, and continued on each day. We finally instigated a "10:00 P.M. rule," an agreement not to talk about any controversial issue that might start a fight after 10:00 at night. Many times this meant not saying very much at all.

With three children to take care of, our lives were busier than they had ever been since we had been married, and the stress extended to our finances. We had taken out loans to pay for Ana's adoption. What we thought would be a cheaper adoption through the Colombian government turned out to be just as expensive, if not more so, than the Russian adoption because we had to stay in Colombia so long, missing work and paying our expenses both at home and in a foreign country. Those expenses added up fast. When we first started down this path, I had figured that we would work hard for another year or two and then we would be caught up. Well, we were working hard, but instead of catching up, we were actually falling farther behind.

Then came Ana's medical bills.

Chapter 13

❧

NEW EXPERIENCES

*Ana's drawing of herself with her
new mom and dad.*

Pediatric Dental Sedation Information, April 1994

Most patients do quite well during their appointment. However, do not be overly concerned should you hear crying. The patient is simply saying they would rather be home playing. Forty percent of the time patients receiving premedication may cry and resist during treatment. Therefore no guarantee can be made concerning patient behavior. I usually recommend that we proceed with the appointment in spite of resistance by the patient.

"I'm sorry but I don't know what this is, Mrs. Conroy," Dr. Morgan said. I had taken Ana in after finding her bed sheet stained with blood each morning for about ten days. I even brought that morning's sheet along as proof, which got several looks in the waiting room.

This was one of many doctor's visits we made the first months Ana was with us. Stool samples had been taken to check for parasites, a common malady among internationally adopted children. She was treated for an intestinal parasite called giardia.

Blood work had shown that Ana was anemic and also had several vitamin deficiencies. We had already guessed these results by her eating habits—or should I say, compulsions. She downed bananas as if she couldn't get enough. She craved meat so intensely, she would have eaten a whole cow if we had given her the opportunity. Once, when our family was invited by friends for dinner, the adults were served immense New York cut steaks. The kids were given a few small bites but most turned up their noses and requested peanut butter sandwiches. Not Ana. She ate her portion and asked for more. She kept asking until she had eaten one entire steak and half of mine. She declared in her pigeon English/Spanish that this was the best chicken she had ever had!

She also begged for beans and any other source of protein she could put into her mouth. After a while, her cravings lessened and now she will often refuse to eat even bananas. (She's certainly eaten enough to last a lifetime.)

The doctor also suggested taking an X-ray of Ana's hand to see if her age could be determined by the bone growth. (Not really, it turned out. According to her X-ray, she was a year younger than she could be. The only part of her history we were sure of wouldn't have fit into the three years that her bone age specified. "Well, they can be off," said the technician.)

We never did discover the reason for the bloodstains. Dr. Morgan thought it might have come from her gums, but we hadn't noticed any blood on them. "Keep feeding her nutritious foods. If it's serious, there will soon be other symptoms," she assured us. Thank goodness there never were. Whatever the real cause, the bleeding soon disappeared.

We also made frequent visits to the dentist. I'm sure her mouth was quite different from what he was used to seeing in his suburban practice. He rarely—if ever—saw decay of Ana's level in San Jose, California. The dentist, who was known by all as Dr. Jim, told us Ana would need oral surgery to pull several teeth and cap the rest. The work was so extensive, in fact, that he would have to split it into two procedures. As wonderful as our dentist is, as you might imagine, he was not becoming one of Ana's favorite people. There was certainly no flirting going on between Ana and Dr. Jim! By the time it was all over, Ana was left with no front teeth top or bottom and silver caps on all of her back teeth. We all hoped that with this surgery, a proper diet, and proper brushing, her permanent teeth would eventually come in healthy and strong. In a few years we'll find out!

As we began filling out postadoption papers, we decided that we needed to come up with a birthday for Ana. We didn't want to keep January 1 because it signified to us and to the Colombian Social Services that Ana's birth date was unknown. It was important to us to find a day that would be special to her, and as accurate as possible. We were beginning to narrow the time down to June or July as appropriate months. This was partly because many people thought her energetic and strong personality suited the sign of Cancer (as good an indicator as any, we figured).

Okay, now for a date. Casey's birthday is the twenty-sixth of January so, partially in honor of their time spent together in Colombia, we chose his "half birthday": July 26, 1989, was Ana's new official birthday.

Part of the urgency to pick a date was because birthdays were such an important topic around our house. Nadia's is April 29, and we were getting ready to throw her a birthday party, the very first she had ever had.

During this time adjusting to our new family, people would ask us, "How are you handling everything?" Casey's answer captured the feeling best: "This has been more work and more joy than I've ever experienced." We were happy (yes, even without a lot of sex) but tired, feeling alternately as if we could achieve any goal we desired and as if we would never get to do anything other than child care and drudgery again. The work was hard but the joys were well worth it. One of those joys during that spring was Nadia's birthday.

We explained to Nadia that she got to invite guests to a party that would be held in honor of her special birth day. She invited two friends from school, all her cousins and aunts and uncles in the area, Yuri and Slava (now Daniel and Tyler), and—her first request—Diana. She and Ana dressed in their finest Sunday dresses and were ready to begin the party around 6:30 A.M.

"I'm afraid your guests won't be here for at least a few more hours," I said sleepily as they stood beside my bed. (Ana and Nadia had a habit of not wanting to disturb me, even in the middle of the night, and would stand there waiting for me to sense their presence. The funny thing was that I did sense them even when I hadn't heard a sound. I would open my eyes and there would be one face, or sometimes two, right there next to me, staring with large unblinking eyes. I was used to Meghan calling me from the safety and comfort of her bed knowing that I would stumble in the minute I heard her call.)

"Can we go outside and play then?"

"Please . . . let's wait until at least seven-thirty, okay?"

Later that morning, both Nadia and Ana were in awe as the decorations went up, the cake was brought home (with my lackluster cooking skills, I wasn't going to risk making the cake myself), and balloons began to fill the room. Brilliant hues flashed everywhere. Each place setting was a different color combination and the cake was sprinkled with bright confetti and topped with blue, yellow, and red candles and loopy frosting letters spelling out "Happy 6th Birthday Nadia." We had goodie bags with the tackiest-but-most-popular toys I could find, each one tied up with a primary-color ribbon.

As the first guests arrived, Nadia immediately took on the role of hostess. "You brought a present too!" she would squeal. "Wow, so did Anthony and Ashton!" It was about this time that Ana began to realize this day was going to be a bit more special for Nadia than for her. She had yet to have anyone give *her* a present. "Where's mine?" she whimpered.

"Don't worry, your birthday is next."

"You mean it's tomorrow?"

"No, your birthday is in July."

"Is that tomorrow?"

"No, July is still a little more than two months away."

"Is that after tomorrow then?"

"It's quite a few tomorrows after."

"Why?"

"Here's a goodie bag."

Diana arrived bearing gifts that would make any American girl who had ever watched a single TV show dance with glee. The house was filled with screaming children, happy adults, and one very excited Nadia.

This was Meghan's first birthday party given at our house that didn't have her as the center of attention, but she couldn't help getting swept up in the fun. She took on the role of "birthday expert" for Nadia and Ana, letting them know the birthday routine. "Aren't you ever going to open your presents? It's time to eat the cake and ice cream—you can't just play all day, you know."

By the end of the afternoon the girls were completely spent. The house was a disaster area with puddles of melted ice cream trailing down the hallway, cake crumbs in every room of the house, streamers drooping from the walls, partial goodie bag remnants, and wrapping paper and presents strewn everywhere. My cheeks ached from grinning. I was proud and happy and honored to be a part of Nadia's life. Our family felt complete. We were doing an ordinary family thing: celebrating Nadia's birthday—not because she was adopted or different, but because she was our daughter. I didn't quit smiling until everyone began whining about bedtime. Then cleaning up the kitchen actually looked like an appealing option.

When all the girls were tucked in and quiet, Casey and I gave Nadia one last birthday hug. "You're the best mom and dad," she sighed. "Thank you for my special day. I love you!"

"We love you all, girls." we said together as we turned out the light.

"Is it my birthday tomorrow?" Ana asked sleepily one last time, just in case the answer might be different. "The next day then?"

While special days like Nadia's birthday were fun, the daily grind was becoming unbearable. Casey and I were both playing "catch-up" with our business. I'd get up, get the girls ready for and off to school, go in to the office, work in a doctor's appointment or two, come home with the girls for dinner, homework with Meghan, bath time, bedtime, and then work until midnight at home. In between all that, I did my best to squeeze in laundry (which seemed to grow exponentially with each child) and housework. Forget gourmet, or even well-balanced lunches, I threw whatever I could into brown paper bags and put their names on them. Luckily, Meghan was the only one who knew better. Nadia and Ana thought that catch-as-catch-can was a normal American lunch. Often Casey or I would go to the supermarket after midnight because it was the only time we could get there. "Can't we wait one more day?" he would often ask.

"Well, there's no milk, no bread, no lunch meat, no fruit, no cereal, no juice, and no soup. I fixed graham crackers and jelly for breakfast and mystery peanut butter tortilla wraps for lunch. I found a bag of raisins in the back of the kitchen drawer that I divided up but I can't expect a windfall like that again. Yes, somebody has to go to the grocery store—*tonight!*"

Casey then pointed out that whenever I said somebody, I meant him. I couldn't argue with that.

"We need some help," I told Casey.

"That sounds good, but can we afford it right now?" Mr. Practical asked as he always did in these situations.

"Compared to a month in the hospital recovering from a nervous breakdown, getting some help will be a bargain."

"You're right. Let's get some help."

What many people probably know, but Casey and I didn't, is that finding the perfect someone to come in and care for your children and home, even for a few hours a day, isn't as easy as it seems. We wanted someone who would love our children as much as we did and be understanding of their unique situations. She had to drive and she had to speak English well since Ana and Nadia were still perfecting their pronunciation. We wanted someone who was mature, yet young enough to keep up with three "live wires." Basically, we were looking for an aerobically fit Mary Poppins. Because we were used to going through agencies, we did what came naturally: we called a "nanny agency."

"I can't hire a nanny," I told Casey. "Nannies are for rich people. What if they laugh when they see our teeny home? Can we at least call whoever applies a 'babysitter'? I can handle hiring a babysitter."

"You can call them whatever you like, but let's hurry." He was starting to warm to the idea.

I called several nanny agencies listed in a local parenting magazine and selected the one I thought sounded best. I filled out all their forms, which were only slightly less complex than the INS forms, and waited for a referral. Four days later, the referral came.

We all sat in the living room during that first awkward interview staring at each other. I had a long list of questions but didn't know where to begin. With her long, straight, California blond hair, tanned skin, and tiny size three physique, Marnie Morrison looked fourteen, but was actually twenty-two. She was a college student, studying to become a first grade teacher. Great. Our desire for someone to work from three to six, four days a week, fit well with her school schedule. Fantastic. She had a great deal of experience babysitting other children. Perfect. A babysitter, not a nanny. Marnie looked promising. The agency told us she was an excellent driver, had wonderful references and experience, and had a much better credit history than we did.

We explained to Marnie that we didn't want our crazy work schedules to adversely affect our three girls. They were getting involved in activities such as swimming and dance, and not only needed to be driven hither and yon but also needed an after-school routine, a consistency we hoped a sitter could provide. We explained a little about how our family had grown in less than a year. The bottom line for us was—would Marnie like our children, and would our children like Marnie? (And would she demand combat pay after she met them?)

Luckily, the girls came through for us that day. They were charmed by Marnie, who was quiet and sweet—dare I say, the opposite of their mother—and they charmed her right back. Experience has taught me that no matter how well I think I know my kids, I can never predict how they're going to react in social situations. They had all offered valuable lessons in public humiliation. Therefore, I was surprised as well as pleased to see Meghan, Nadia, and Ana all making a concerted group effort to win Marnie's heart.

"When can you start?" we all asked.

It takes a lot of organization and preparation to ask someone else to help run your life. It means knowing what you want to happen hours ahead of time. As far as scheduling, I always knew what had to happen in my head, but I would often figure out the logistics on my way from one appointment to the next. Now I had to convey what an entire day would look like to someone else, which meant keeping to a schedule. We did develop a program of sorts, but each day had its unique exceptions. I would call Marnie every day at noon.

"Marnie, today is a typical Monday except that Ana has a doctor's appointment at three o'clock. I will take her before you pick the other girls up from school. Meghan has a project due at school tomorrow and will need to stop at the store to pick up some more pipe cleaners on the way home. I forgot to put out the chicken from the freezer this morning so disregard the menu I wrote out and fix soup instead. Oh, we probably don't have any milk so you might want to get some before dinner. Also, Nadia needs to put lotion on her rash five times a day so please help her put some on around four-thirty. Yes, this should be a typical Monday."

It was even better when Marnie got to listen to my explanations on her answering machine.

Beep—"Marnie, this is Maggie again. Disregard my last two messages, there's something I just remembered . . ."

Marnie became our rock—our bit of stability. She was always

willing to pitch in, drive around, clean up, or do anything else we asked her to do that day. Sometimes I will hear a long pause from Marnie after I've given her some especially intricate daily instructions, and I wait for her to question my sanity, or at least my organizational style, but she never has. Marnie takes it all in stride. I like to believe that she finds life with us an adventure. We are giving her the opportunity to experience motherhood firsthand, in the trenches, so-to-speak. We think of ourselves as the best form of birth control for today's young adults. If you're careless, all this can be yours for much more than just three hours a day!

I would soon be testing Marnie's stamina, though, with news of a two-year-old girl named Alesia.

Chapter 14

ALESIA

Alesia wearing a typical Russian bow—usually
bigger than the child's head.

~❧~

June 20, 1994

I enjoy the idea of helping other people through the same adoption bureaucratic mazes that Casey and I struggled with. What I've discovered during the last four months is that it's impossible to take the stress out of adopting a child. The ``easiest'' adoption is hard by any standards, and the easier I try to make things, the more people expect of me. Maybe the uncertainty is an important part of adopting; learning to live through a period of time when you have absolutely no control over the outcome of events. I think adoption is like a natural disaster; it brings out the best and the worst in people.

I first heard about Alesia (A-lay-see-yuh) when Diana called from Russia with news that she had found a girl who would be a great match for a woman in Berkeley named Lisa, who wanted to adopt a special needs child. "She's smart and beautiful," Diana told me. "She has three fingers missing on her right hand and her left foot has no toes. Her left leg is a little shorter than her right, but she's strong and doing everything the other children her age are doing. Maggie—she even dances," she told me with a laugh. "She's always smiling and has brown hair and eyes. She is two years and two months old. Another couple will bring pictures back with them."

She sounded wonderful, as do all the children that Diana tells me about. I had been working part-time for Diana, in addition to my design work, since I got back from Colombia. It wasn't that I needed more work, but that I was enamored by the idea of learning the mechanics of adoption from the inside. My assignment was to help hopeful adoptive parents through the initial steps of finding a child once their home study was completed.

Diana would give me photos and birth dates of children who were available for adoption and I would meet with the parents, answer their questions as best I could, and get them started on the Russian paperwork after they had made a commitment to a child. The work was addicting. I loved the excitement of sharing our story with prospective parents. I loved listening to their stories. I felt like a midwife helping with the delivery of miracles. As much as I loved it, though, it often created a great deal of angst. Casey thought I was becoming a magnet for stressful circumstances.

"But this is *good* stress. *Worthwhile* stress," I reasoned.

"Stress is stress whether it's good or bad," he said. "And we're all affected by the stress you bring into the home."

I knew he was right. But there aren't any 12-step programs for adoption addicts. Yes, it was stressful, but I felt exhilarated whenever I received a photograph of a child looking out, grinning and content, with a baseball cap on his head and a parent on either side, remembering the same child whose demeanor and appearance had, only a few months earlier, looked like that of a lonely inmate from the local jail. I wanted Casey to enjoy my newfound mission too. But while he often enjoyed hearing the stories, he soon began to get jealous of the time I spent on the phone with distressed prospective parents.

Each parent wanted my undivided attention, just as we had wanted during our adoptions. Each couple thought *their* adoption should be the top priority. I began to learn the ups and downs of adoption work from the other side of the fence, and it wasn't always pretty. Some people approach adoption like a supermarket shopping experience, seeking perfect, name-brand children with this kind of hair or that color eyes. Some are still grieving over their inability to conceive a child, and see adoption as an unwelcome, last-resort option after years of failed infertility treatments. These people often bring the effects of years of frustration and fear to their attempt to adopt a child, and working with them can be an emotional challenge.

But the vast majority of adoptive parents are loving, intelligent, vibrant people whom I feel honored to have worked with. I am still very close to many of the parents I got to know during this time, and our children will grow up together. Casey's worries over stress, while warranted, weren't the entire story.

I was very excited and anxious to tell Lisa that Diana had

found a child for her. We didn't often receive requests for special needs children so this adoption was especially dear to me. When I called with the news, I didn't get the response I had hoped for. After listening to my version of Alesia's health and personality, Lisa wasn't sure this child was right for her. She had seen a videotape of a different child with a cleft palate from another agency whom she felt drawn to and felt needed her more. I wasn't worried. I was certain I could place Alesia with another family. Who wouldn't want a child as alive and wonderful as Diana described? I'd wait for the pictures to arrive. Surely I would find a home for her then.

A couple of days later the photos of Alesia arrived via a couple who had just been to Alesia's orphanage to bring home their new son. Nina described her as a child who led the pack and demanded hugs and attention from all new visitors. She hadn't even noticed her "differentness" until much later in their stay. I invited Nina to sit down. I took the photos out of their envelope and placed them on the table. "She's wonderful," I gasped as I looked at her chubby, cherry-cheeked face. She stood by a small table staring directly into the camera lens demanding to know what the photographer was up to. She listed to one side because of her leg, but other than that she looked the picture of health. She had on a plain dress but was wearing a gigantic bow on top of her head. Maybe it was the bow and not her leg that was putting her off balance.

I have now seen pictures of hundreds of children needing homes. Boys and girls of all different ages, all gazing out from the photo willing someone to find them a future in a place other than where they now are. Some are orphaned, some taken by officials from abusive homes, most given up by mothers who cannot see a way to raise them in their current circumstances.

Certain pictures jump out at you for different reasons. Maybe it's a child with an uncanny resemblance to a family member. Maybe there's a spark of hope in his eyes. Maybe it's the personality conjured up for you by a smile or a tilt of the head. Whatever the reason, a connection is formed, for better or for worse. I will always be thankful that I didn't have more choices when we adopted our children. Choosing between Nadia and Ruta was a hard enough challenge. I have seen many people burst into tears when faced with a group of children to choose from. Now that I was working with Diana, I came into contact with many little faces, and naturally, some of them reached out to me with their compelling stories and engaging poses, begging for my attention. But Alesia was different. I can't explain the spark I somehow recognized in her determined countenance. I loved the fact that she didn't have all her fingers and toes and still ran around and led the other children in games. I sensed a strength in her that didn't come from the photograph directly but from some unknown place deep inside of me. Some things cannot be explained. My feelings regarding Alesia are one of those things. I vowed to do everything within my power to find her a home.

I showed Alesia's picture to another couple. I gave them all the information I had on her and showed them the pictures. They smiled politely but said that in truth they'd been through so much grief in trying to conceive a child that they didn't want their first child to have special needs. I understood; hadn't Casey and I discussed into the night our decision to adopt Maria because of her health problems? But by this point I was feeling like Alesia didn't *have* special needs. Compared to my affection toward her, missing fingers and a deformed foot seemed insignificant.

I called several other couples and each one said they weren't interested in considering Alesia. I couldn't understand why others weren't having the same intense feelings I was having. When I next spoke to Diana to deliver the bad news, she wasn't surprised. "Two agencies have already tried—unsuccessfully—to place her," she told me. "The director didn't even show her to me when I first arrived because she didn't think I would want to place a less-than-perfect child. It was the caregivers who came to me and begged me to try to find a home for Alesia."

"I know we can place her," I told Diana. "If no one else wants her, I'll adopt her!" Somehow the words popped out of my mouth.

Diana laughed. "Well, I'll tell them, but I think your husband will hope you find another home quickly for her."

Of course, I was joking. (Wasn't I?) At that time I honestly felt I'd find a home for Alesia. I showed her picture to everyone. But the odds were stacking up against her. Diana had been working hard in Russia to create relationships with orphanage officials and she was increasingly able to find orphanages willing to release babies and very young children for adoption in the United States. With this knowledge, most of the families we were working with chose to wait for a healthy infant to begin their family. With so many children to be placed, Alesia was low-girl-on-the-totem-pole.

Meanwhile, I was falling in love with her. I had her picture up in my office. I began talking about her to family members, and to Casey. Finally, one day after yet one more couple chose another child over her, I approached Casey. "You know the child Alesia with the missing fingers and toes," I asked.

"You mean the one you talk about all the time?" he said.

"Yes ... well ... what if *we* adopted her?"

"Well, Maggie, it's going to be pretty hard to raise four girls *on your own.*"

I got the hint, but I couldn't get Alesia out of my mind. Yet all my logical faculties were telling me it was a losing proposition. Just last month, Casey and I had had a conference with Marge, about the issues and challenges we were facing with Meghan, Ana, and Nadia. Although they were all adjusting, wasn't it too soon to add a new member to our family? Especially one who might require special medical attention? Not to mention, we were looking for new health coverage—not an ideal time to add another child with unknown needs. Speaking of attention, how could Casey and I both work and give the attention we needed to four young children, three who were adjusting to a new life, culture, and language?! It was ludicrous, it was impossible—but Alesia still tugged at my heart and I wouldn't let her go without a struggle.

I decided to talk to Bee. At first she simply thought I was out of my mind. When I assured her I was serious, she brought up all the problems we would face. But Bee's role is to give out information and make sure people have the knowledge they need to make intelligent decisions. What might be crazy for one person might be fine for another. Besides, she has five children and has been a working mother too. She assured me that missing fingers and toes were not really special needs, that they wouldn't neces-sarily cause any more stress than anything else. So, although she was guarded in her enthusiasm, I felt she understood my attachment to this photo-child. Since I respect Bee, and know she's always honest and forthright when asked her opinion, her support made me more determined than ever.

Marge, on the other hand, had another valid perspective. She knew what we had been going through firsthand with Ana and Nadia. She had counseled us through our entire adoption experience and had spent countless hours on the phone assuring us things would get easier. She was worried that we weren't considering the financial ramifications of adding another child. She was uneasy about the effect it would have on Meghan, Nadia, and Ana and whether or not we could give both them and this new child the attention they would need without overextending ourselves emotionally (not to mention giving Casey and my relationship the attention it needed).

From personal experience, she knew how easy it is to be drawn to rescue a single child, who has touched you in some way, instead of seeing the global picture. "You can adopt this child or continue your work with Diana and help hundreds of children. Which is the better path?" she asked.

It was a good question.

I felt very calm talking with Marge. She was concerned because she cared about our family. She didn't make me feel as if I were stupid for considering another adoption so soon and was only raising the same issues I'd been thinking about for the past weeks. I knew that it would be financially hard. I knew that we might not be able to pay for expensive colleges for the girls. I knew our house was very small, and that if we adopted Alesia, our plans for a bigger house would have to wait.

I didn't feel threatened by her worries (even if I did have a moment of doubt that our glowing home study could be stretched to include another child). I knew that we could overcome the hardships, I just didn't know the details of how. There were two basic things that I had to do to make a smart decision. First, I had to be honest with myself and with Casey as to what might be in store for us. Second, I had to be patient, more patient than my personality usually allowed.

Early in our marriage I had pushed for my way in major decisions and Casey had gone along to avoid a conflict. For example, I had insisted that we try to get pregnant soon after we were married. "It took my mother seven years to conceive her first child," I reasoned. "My sister tried for three years before Beth was born. What if it takes us that long? I'll be in my *thirties* soon. Please let's not wait too long."

Three *weeks* later, I was pregnant. Casey tried to act as thrilled as he knew I was with the news, but he wasn't thrilled. He was scared. On our first wedding anniversary I was five months pregnant. Things had happened too quickly for him. He loves Meghan with all his heart, but he has often told me he wishes we had been married longer before we had kids.

I didn't want to make the same mistake now after we had worked so hard to break that pattern. I was trying to accept the fact that, if adopting Alesia wasn't right for Casey, it couldn't happen. It had to be both of us who wanted to raise this child. It couldn't be me talking him into it. But I wasn't sure how to plead my case regarding Alesia without trying to convince him and "get my way."

In mid-July I finally felt as if I had sorted things out in my mind enough to broach the subject again with Casey. The girls were with Marnie, and he and I were standing in our kitchen. "I have something I need to talk to you about," I said, trying to keep my emotions in check. "I want to talk about Alesia—about her becoming a part of our family."

Casey sighed, and sat down heavily in a nearby chair. He listened silently as I explained all the effort I had put into examining my motives regarding Alesia. I told him of the powerful pull that she still had over me. He began to understand that I was truly serious about this child. "Maggie, I know you. When you have an idea, it happens," Casey said, throwing up his hands in frustration. "There is too much going on right now for us to even *contemplate* adding another child to our household."

He was right, I knew that, but I had to finish. "You know that there have been other children who I've had a special feeling for, Casey, but I can honestly say that none of them have spoken to me as this child has." I was choking on each word. "Please consider Alesia. I feel that we have a lot to give her but—just as significant—that she has important things to teach us. I can't explain it but I have such a strong feeling about this girl. Please take me seriously. Please don't discount the possibility of bringing her into our home. At least let me tell you her story before you say no."

The whole house was still. I held my breath. Then Casey looked into my eyes and said the words that I will always remember and be grateful for.

"Maggie, if there's one thing I've learned in our eleven years together, it's that when you have this strong a feeling for something, it's usually been the best path for us to take. I don't always like your timing, and even though it drives me crazy, it's one of the reasons I love you. If you're willing to look into the ramifications of adopting this child, and let me get through July, I'm willing to consider Alesia."

I was thrilled. I reached out and held his hands tightly. "Thank you," I whispered. "Thank you so much."

Now my task was to figure out a way to curb my intense urge to mention Alesia to Casey every five minutes.

I talked to Marnie, who was shocked, and to Diana, who was not shocked in the least. In fact, Diana was very supportive and offered to help in any way she could. She got as much information as possible and asked a family who was in Ekaterinburg (where Alesia's orphanage was) to observe Alesia so I could ask them questions about her. I let Diana know that I would have to reduce my workload if I adopted Alesia, and even though it would be in her interest to put her agency first, she was completely understanding. Diana is in love with these children too.

On August 3, we put the girls on a plane to visit their grandparents in Portland. They were thrilled at the trip and the wonderful plans of baking and swimming at Grandma and Grandpa's house. Casey and I were ecstatic at the thought of five days alone. Five days alone! I asked Casey if he wanted to go to Diana's house to discuss new families interested in adoption. "Then you and I could go to San Francisco for dinner," I suggested.

On the drive up, we began to discuss Alesia in more detail. I told Casey the stories I had heard about her always getting into every picture that was taken, of being a leader, an independent little soul who would run to greet the parents when they came to visit. One mother told me of a day when she had arrived at potty time. In this particular orphanage the children all sit on their potty chairs at the same time and must wait until everyone has gone before they can get up. Alesia saw this mom and started to get up to run to her. She quickly sat down again, though, remembering that she didn't have permission to get up off the potty yet. The mother turned her back for a moment and the next thing she knew, little Alesia had scooted her potty chair across the room and held out her arms for a hug. She hadn't broken the rule but had gotten what she wanted!

As we sped down the interstate, Casey chuckled. We reminisced about our last year and all that had happened with the girls. Remember when Meghan talked Nadia into sitting on the Easter Bunny's lap and she almost pulled his head off? Remember when Ana tasted grapefruit for the first time? Her rubber face had become a character of disgust! We both laughed as the memories stacked up one after another. "We've had some pretty good times, huh?" I asked, leaning back into my seat. It was definitely easier to feel good about our girls when they were safely at Grandma and Grandpa's house and five days of relaxation stretched out ahead of us. After a while I asked Casey something else that was on my mind. "If we adopted Alesia, would you mind not raising a boy?"

Casey talked openly about his fears—and there were many for both of us—but having four girls was not one of them.

"I'm satisfied raising girls," he said. "In fact, I think I'm getting pretty good at it. If I want to be around boys, I have my nephews."

"Who knows, the future might hold a boy or two in it," I sighed, but quickly dropped that line of thought when I saw the panicked look on his face.

I still couldn't give him a specific, rational explanation as to why Alesia meant so much to me, but he admitted he was beginning to feel a connection with her too. How that admission thrilled me! He felt it too. It wasn't just me anymore. I leaned over to give his arm a squeeze, and we switched topics to our dinner plans.

When we arrived at Diana's, Casey was full of questions about Alesia, but he reminded both of us that we must not speak of the adoption as final—that we still needed to work out the financial details and give him a little more time to think things through. But as we were saying goodbye, Casey wondered aloud where we would stay when we were in Moscow. "That sounds pretty final to me," I teased. Diana just laughed. Casey was caught.

It was August 5 when Casey formally agreed that we should adopt Alesia. We were getting ready to go out with friends when he told me with the most radiant of expressions. "Now, we'll have to cut back on our expenses," he said. "And this summer may be our last vacation before the millennium. We'll have to make lots of changes."

His words were all harsh but his face was all smiles.

"That sounds awful! Why are you smiling?" I demanded.

"Because we're going to do it! We're really going to do it!"

"I love you."

"I love you too."

Our friends helped us celebrate our good news. The next day we called Diana and Marge and gleefully told them our plans.

We called all our relatives. This was becoming a familiar, but still exciting, routine.

The next night we picked the girls up at the airport. After we had gotten over the first joy of seeing each other again after five whole days apart, things began to break down in the car. The girls were arguing over who was sitting in whose space. Nadia was imitating whatever Meghan said. Meghan was mad at Nadia for imitating her. Ana had to go to the bathroom and couldn't wait another second! Then somebody hit somebody who hit somebody else who yelled and who still had to go to the bathroom NOW. Casey and I looked at each other with terror in our eyes. What had we done?

As usual, dinner helped everyone feel more civilized toward one another, and we told the girls about their new sister. Nadia said, "Okay" and resumed eating.

Ana asked, "Will I be in charge now?"

They didn't mention Alesia again for the rest of the evening. Apparently, a new sister wasn't big news for them. Meghan, on the other hand, was much more animated about this newest adoption. I think she had felt left out by Nadia and Ana's instant attachment to each other and hoped to have a partner of her own. Plus, she had followed my efforts to find a home for Alesia and, like me, had been smitten by her picture.

Now that Casey and I had agreed on the decision to adopt Alesia, my fears resurfaced. "What if my instincts about her are wrong?" I wondered. "What if everything becomes too much to handle? What if the girls hate each other? What if having a two-year-old takes away any free time we have? What if it turns out badly and Casey blames *me?*"

Then I thought, "I can't wait to see her dance!"

Chapter 15

GROWING

Nadia's family portrait.
(Mickey Mouse is third from the right.)

~❧~

August 7, 1994

> *I feel like I've been filling out paperwork forever. I
> should be getting better at it. I'm not, I'm getting worse.
> I don't want to fill in another blank for as long as I live.
> Today I had to document all our expenses from the last
> adoption. How depressing.*

As we began the paperwork for our third adoption in less than
a year, we were also completing post-placement paperwork for
Nadia and Ana. We were required to fill out several reports on
their progress and submit various documents that would lead to
a day in court to obtain legal U.S. citizenship status. Nadia's court
date was August 9, 1994.

In our usual disorganized fashion, we found out the week
before that there were still more court documents that had to be
filled out before we went before the judge. I found these valuable
papers after a search of the basement, and had the weekend to
get them organized and properly typed up. We picked up the
finished court documents Monday night and Tuesday morning
tried to get everybody ready for our 10:00 A. M. session with the
judge. Even as we waited for our turn and I tried to keep the
girls from bickering, Casey filled out one last form!

Ana was having a tough time. She seemed worried and a bit
confused as to why we were doing this for Nadia and not for her.
We explained to Ana that her day would come in November and
assured her that she would always be our daughter. "A judge
doesn't have to tell us you are our daughter, we already know
it's true. This is just a ceremony."

She looked at us blankly. She was just learning English. She
had no idea what a ceremony was.

Meghan was jealous that she wouldn't have a special day to

be legal. We reminded her of her christening, held when she was six months old. "We invited all our friends and had a special day just to honor your arrival into our family."

"Well, I don't remember that at all," she huffed.

Nadia had her own worries. "Am I going to get a shot?" she finally asked.

"No, judges never give shots," Casey answered.

Even while we were explaining the day and trying to get our papers in order, we still had the pressure of preserving this historic family moment on film. The bailiff was a wonderful woman who seemed to love having people in court for adoptions. She told us we could get our pictures taken in the judge's enormous black leather chair. Meghan loved the idea of "sitting in judgment" over us and we had to agree that it suited her. Nadia whimpered about what she was going to have to do since this was her court day—and by the way, since it was *her* day, how come we weren't doing everything *she* wanted? Ana got angry because I was consoling Nadia.

The first picture shows Meghan in a regal pose, with me holding a worried Nadia in my arms as I try to smile into the camera. Ana is not in sight because she is hiding under the judge's desk, sulking, and Casey is absent—still finishing up that final form. Another picture shows Casey and a reluctant Ana (now in my arms so she can't escape). Nadia looks happier but Meghan is frowning because Ana "looked at her *that way!*" And still another picture includes the smiling bailiff whom Ana is asking why she has a gun and if she could play with it. I look as if I need a tranquilizer and another set of arms.

Finally we were called into the judge's chamber. Thankfully, she was used to disorganized parents with curious children. She read what she needed to read and said what she needed to say to satisfy the letter of the law. She asked if the financial figures we had provided on the forms were correct. Casey and I were both so disoriented by that time we just nodded our heads. "I can't proceed unless you answer me out loud," she told us. We both said "yes." Then she asked if we were willing to assume all the rights—something, something, something, I was trying to control the children—and were willing to—something, something, something—in adopting our child and we said a resounding "Yes!" We signed the papers, the judge signed the papers, her assistant took our picture, and we were done. It took less than five minutes. "We promise to be better organized next time," I told her. "We'll be back in a few months for Ana's day." (I didn't want to press our luck by mentioning Alesia. After this performance, the judge might rule that we couldn't possibly handle another child.)

Next, we had to go down to get the clerk's stamp (whatever that was). We waited in line with the girls, who were all pulling on me and trying to get any scrap of attention possible. The shoeshine man approached us and asked if we were here for an adoption. He wanted to shine my shoes free for the occasion. It sounded good to me, so I took off my shoes and Meghan and Ana followed him out into the hallway.

When it was our turn with the clerk, Nadia got to use his stamp on a special certificate the judge had signed earlier. Even though we weren't very good with the other forms, we had created our own, complete with Nadia's drawing of our family—which also included Mickey Mouse. It had space for our signatures by the judge's, welcoming Nadia into our family forever and ever. When Meghan and Ana came back in with my newly polished shoes, we all signed on the dotted lines and took more photos of Nadia proudly holding her original and "family official" certificate. Finally, we were out the door with three active, hungry, and grouchy sisters.

We walked to a soda shop in an extravagant downtown hotel. Even though it was a soda shop, it was very elegant, with white linen napkins and china place settings. The meal began with bickering, but when everyone had had something to eat, we began to have a wonderful time. For the next thirty minutes, we were a "Leave-it-to-Beaver-only-with-girls" ideal family. We told our waitress that this was a special day, so she brought out a round of ice cream on the house. Nadia's even had a candle in it, which she blew out with great flair, as befit her queen-for-the-day status.

While Casey and Ana went to get the car, Meghan, Nadia, and I waited across the street at a fountain where water shoots up from the cement in little geysers. Nadia took off her shoes and socks and had a great time playing around the fountain, squealing with delight and making no attempt to stay dry. I thought of the first few weeks Nadia was with us and how she would never have felt free enough to take off her shoes and socks and play in her nice clothes. She had come a long way.

Still, that evening when she was getting ready for bed, Nadia burst into tears. She was inconsolable. I held her for a long time while she cried and asked her what was wrong. Through her tears she said, "I don't want it over." I asked her what she meant. She said, "I'm not ever gonna have a day this good again. I don't want it be over." Then I told her that Marnie was planning to take them swimming the next day. "Really?" she sniffed. "We goin' swimming? Oh boy! That'll be great!" The tears evaporated. She was sound asleep in a matter of minutes.

Eventually, all our girls loved swimming, but for Nadia this wasn't always the case. Meghan had been an accomplished swimmer for quite some time. Ana was like a fish, but had more bravado than proficiency. Nadia had never seen a body of water larger than a washtub when she first arrived in our home. Soon after we adopted Ana, we decided that swimming lessons were in order for the younger two girls. I found a wonderful swim school that held classes from January through October. The pool was small and covered with a dome in the winter months. The first day of class, as we walked through the entrance to the dome, Ana's eyes immediately brightened with happiness. She was returning to her favorite element: the water. She couldn't wait to begin. I laughed out loud at her enthusiasm, but then noticed that Nadia was still standing at the entrance. Her eyes were also bright—but with panic. "Too much water, Mommy!" she cried. "Too much water here."

"But Nadia, this is a swimming pool, it's supposed to have lots of water. That's the fun of it. You get to swim and play in all this water. Isn't that great?"

She looked at me doubtfully. "I don't know about this," she said.

While Ana raced to meet her new swimming instructor, Nadia had to be coaxed into getting her feet wet—literally. Her first lesson consisted of being convinced that it was a good idea to put her body in "too much water." Watching Ana swim gleefully on the other side of the pool helped ease Nadia's mind in ways my words never could. In hindsight (which is where I do my very best parenting) I wish I had insisted that I be in the water with Nadia for her first few lessons. But the pool policy was that mothers only swam with their children when they were very young—a policy I'm sure made perfect sense in most cases. But their policy had never come up against a child who, at six years of age, had never even seen a swimming pool—who hadn't even been in a bathtub until recently.

It was Nadia's third lesson. She was playing in the shallow part of the pool where she could easily stand. Ana's free play consisted of somersaults underwater, kicking, and splashing across the area. Nadia's consisted of hanging on to the side and watching Ana. Although Nadia wasn't keen on going to these lessons, she did seem to enjoy herself once she got in the water. I think she was trying to figure out why Ana liked the pool so much. Nadia certainly didn't want to miss out on anything fun. On this day Nadia was feeling more confident and she let go of the side and took several steps. "Hurray!" I called, clapping my hands. Nadia grinned. Even though she could easily stand, this was a major accomplishment. Ana cheered too. Nadia took a few more steps, looking at me for encouragement. All of a sudden, maybe because Ana was splashing, or maybe because she took a larger step, Nadia slipped underwater. As I watched, she slowly sank to the bottom. "Stand up!" I cried even though I knew she couldn't hear me. "Why doesn't she stand up?" She became completely disoriented and reached out in slow motion with her hands as if searching for solid ground. The teachers were in the other part of the pool teaching their next students. They were close—but not close enough. I stood there, still waiting for her to *just stand up*. "Go get her!" another mother yelled. So, in my jeans, my dry-clean-only sweater, and brand-new wool vest I hopped into the waist-deep water, reached down, and scooped up my daughter. Though not the most heroic of rescues, it was certainly one of the most appreciated. Nadia looked up at me and smiled gratefully. "Why you take so long?" she asked calmly. "Are you gonna play now too?"

"I prefer to swim in a swimming suit," I answered, feeling my heart beat fast and hard in my chest, and feeling the water slosh through my leather shoes. "I need to get out now."

"Keep her in the water," the instructor said. "We want her to know it's safe. You can borrow a pair of my sweats. Good job, Mrs. Conroy."

Nadia stayed in swimming lessons just long enough to be safe in the water. Now she looks forward to going to the pool for fun but still prefers to stay where she can use the skill she has completely mastered—standing up in shallow water.

A few months later, Nadia took up dance lessons, which she thoroughly enjoys. She commented to me once that she likes to be able to "feel the floor underneath me all the time." I have yet to be asked to rescue her from a grand jeté or a split leap. I like that a lot.

As September approached, the girls got ready to enter public school. Casey and I successfully enrolled all the children in the same elementary school. This meant that Meghan would have to change schools because the one she attended didn't have classes for children under third grade. We knew changing schools might be hard for her with all the other changes, but we hoped the pluses of having all the girls together and being in a neighborhood school would outweigh the additional minuses for Meghan.

The first day of school all the girls were on edge, but Meghan was more nervous than Nadia and Ana. She already missed her friends from her old school and she was worried she wouldn't fit in at her new school. Ana didn't seem to care what was going on—ready for whatever adventure was going to happen next. Nadia, as usual, was cautious, but willing to go along with things.

Casey and I have always been good about making an effort to be with our children on their first day of school. When Meghan started first grade and rode the school bus for the first time, Casey and I waited at the bus stop, waved goodbye to her, raced to the school in our car, and were waiting to greet her when she arrived. Then we walked her to her classroom.

We went with both Nadia and Ana on their first days at preschool. When Nadia began, I made an extra effort to help ease her adjustment. When Ana started preschool, she had me and Nadia for support. But this situation was different. We now had three children in three new situations. How were we going to pull this off? There were only two of us.

Meghan wanted us to make sure she found her room but didn't want to be seen with her mom and dad. It's tricky to be helpful but unnoticeable at the same time.

Nadia was fine until she got into the classroom and then she didn't want me to leave. I had my own misgivings and was nervous for her. All of a sudden these first graders looked so . . .

competent. They looked as if they had been reading since they were three—obviously first grade was a review for them all. They all greeted each other and sat down happily in front of their new teacher. Nadia clung to me and didn't want me going anywhere. Maybe we shouldn't have skipped kindergarten, I worried. The teacher was very understanding and allowed me to stay until Nadia felt comfortable enough for me to leave. I was proud that my beautiful Russian daughter spoke English so well. But as the teacher began talking to the children about room monitors, lunch money, tardy slips, and taking attendance, Nadia turned to me and said, "I hear the words she is sayin', but I don't know anything she is talking about!" She strained forward to listen, but all the concepts the other children took for granted were new for her. She had just learned to write her name but couldn't recognize it when told to get her name tag—who ever heard of a *name tag* anyway? She looked at me as if asking why on earth had I sent her to such a foreign school. Only ten months earlier she had never even seen the English alphabet. Now she knew the alphabet song but could only identify some letters separately and then she referred to them as numbers. My heart ached for her as she strained to understand what was expected. But Nadia had made a lot of progress. Even though she was visibly upset, she didn't revert to rocking and humming. Instead, she hung in there—trying her best.

She cried when I left. So did I, as soon as I got out of the room. I felt guilty and wondered if we had made a terrible mistake by not sending her to kindergarten, but Marge had warned us that children who are put in with younger children will only reach their level. As hard as it may be, she advised, we should give Nadia the chance to learn with her peers. "Act as if you have a foreign exchange student for a year," she advised. "If it doesn't work out, you can always change later."

I knew that Marge's recommendation was based on solid experience but it didn't make that first day any easier. That night Nadia was exhausted. Concentrating on figuring out what was expected of her took a lot of energy.

Ana's experience was quite different. She was pleased to have a new audience. If she didn't understand, she simply smiled radiantly at her teacher. But in the afternoon when I attended her kindergarten briefing, I realized that this kindergarten stuff wasn't what it was when I was young. Gone were nap time and cookies.

There would be homework each night and we were given an information sheet to pretest Ana's academic skills. Ana was anxious to go back the next day. Who cares about letters and numbers? She liked the monkey bars on the playground.

When I gave Ana her kindergarten pretest that night, I was clued in to her amazing adaptability. Ana had seemed to learn English effortlessly. But now I realized she didn't understand nearly the amount of English we had all assumed. In fact, Ana was such a master at fitting in, she had fooled us into thinking that she knew much more about *everything* than she actually did. We had been much more worried about Nadia's readiness for first grade because we knew exactly what she did and didn't know. She never tried to hide the fact that she didn't understand. I soon discovered, though, that Ana was missing as much if not more of the core knowledge she needed for her age group.

"What is this color?" I asked, pointing to her bright red T-shirt.

"Green," she answered.

When I asked her to count, she could only reach three and that was with help. She couldn't write her name, say her phone number, and when I read the story of "Goldilocks and the Three Bears," she couldn't tell me what it was about or who was in it.

"Ana, what was the story I just read about?"

Flashing a big smile: "I don't know."

"What do you think 'Goldilocks and the Three *Bears*' was about?"

Flashing a big smile: "I don't know."

"Was it about *bears*?"

Flashing a big smile: "Okay."

"Yes, it was about bears. How many bears were there in the story 'Goldilocks and the *Three* Bears'?"

Flashing a big smile: "I don't know."

I went back to colors, but every answer was green.

This didn't seem to bother Ana at all. Since I just went on to another question, she was content whether I corrected her or not. If I told her what the correct answer was and then repeated the question, she still couldn't tell me the answer. I got a little worried. "Doesn't my smile make you happy, Mommy," she seemed to be saying. "Isn't that enough?"

*   *   *

All the girls had to get used to the homework routine. We were still working on establishing a general sense of family routine. I knew how the girls felt. Just filling out all the emergency forms, getting the correct vaccinations, and figuring out how on earth I could help in each classroom, seemed like a monumental task. Of course this was all happening when we were in the midst of doing the continued paperwork for Alesia and pulling together documents for Ana's adoption finalization court appointment.

Nadia's homework one night consisted of writing her name ten times. This seemed simple enough. But by the evening, Nadia was worn out. After working very hard for thirty minutes, she had written her name only three times. Fortunately, her teacher was very helpful and explained that in first grade children are only expected to do what they can. This was a relief, but I didn't want Nadia to feel that she would never be able to accomplish what was assigned to her.

I didn't have to worry. Nadia was very proud of her accomplishments, much more so than most children. She loved to tell her grandmother or aunt and uncle about even the smallest achievement. She didn't dwell on whether or not she was doing better or as well as other children. One night while doing her homework, Nadia looked at me and said, "I am really smart!"

"Oh yes, Nadia," I answered, "you really are." It took time for her to care about how she stacked up in the class. Meghan had always been aware and concerned about how well she was doing in school even though we had always tried hard to minimize that aspect of learning. It was refreshing to witness a child so unspoiled by competition. Nadia was truly happy for anyone who did well, while other children worried that it might make them look stupid. Unfortunately, she has now lost much of that innocence. The awareness that there is a social and academic pecking order crept up on her slowly, but what a gift her naiveté was to her in that first public school year.

Toward the end of October, it became clear to Ana's teacher and to us that although she enjoyed school a great deal, she wasn't quite ready to be in a kindergarten classroom. She was charming, she was sweet with the other children, but she couldn't sit still (she really couldn't—she could not hold her body in a sitting position for longer than a minute at a time). Ana's large muscles and her attention span had to be strengthened. Consequently, she wasn't ready to learn the materials being presented.

We decided Ana would do better going to preschool for an additional year, where she could learn at her own pace and in an environment with less sitting and more children of varying skill levels. Luckily, the staff at the preschool were supportive of our decision and glad to have Ana return. Even though she enjoyed her kindergarten teacher, Ana was thrilled to discover that her other school had "opened again."

"Don't worry," she said to her kindergarten teacher, "I'll see you next year."

"I'll wait for you," her teacher answered with a smile.

Chapter 16

❧

RETURN TO RUSSIA

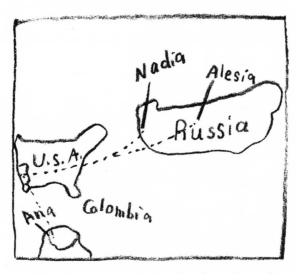

Meghan drew a map for her fourth grade teacher to show where her parents had been and where they were off to next.

November 6, 1994

> *In Moscow once more—hard to believe that we were*
> *here just about one year ago to adopt Nadia. This trip is*
> *different in many ways and yet it feels as if we were here*
> *only a week ago. This time I was much more nervous than*
> *I was last time before we left—dreading everything,*
> *remembering only the hard aspects of our previous trip.*
> *But once we were on our way to the airport, everything*
> *seemed natural and I have been feeling calm ever since.*
> *I'll enjoy this feeling while I can.*

The kids were adjusting to their schools; Marnie was her steady self; our business was going well; our lives were beginning to calm down: Time to adopt another child. We got our travel date in late October. We would leave for Russia on November 4.

As usual, our departure from home was crazy and hectic. No matter how well prepared I thought we would be, the week before we left for Russia was frantic. We didn't know if we would receive our final clearance from INS until the afternoon before we left. Talk about last minute. The man at the INS office told Casey he would cable acceptance to adopt that day, but if any criminal activities showed up from the last six months, he would cancel it. I wasn't worried; with three kids and a growing business, who has time for felonies!

Friends brought us care packages Friday night—for Casey, sunflower seeds, granola, and healthy snacks; for me, chocolate.

By 10:00 P.M. we had made our last phone calls, gotten the girls in bed (Meghan shed many tears), and were trying to finish packing when all the lights went dim. Minutes later, we had no electricity at all. We packed in the dark, using flashlights.

Casey's sister took us to the airport at 6:00 A.M. Before we left, we woke Ana and Nadia to say goodbye, and received "soggy" hugs and kisses. We had tried to prepare them for our departure as much as possible during the previous weeks, but there were so many other activities going on with school starting, new friendships being formed, Halloween, and now Grandma Lois coming to stay with them, that they hadn't really had time to worry about their new sister. Nadia seemed to accept the fact that adopting a child was something Casey and I did every six months. Ana seemed to be having a difficult time understanding what was going on. This was partly because it was a first experience for her, and partly because she still had inner doubts regarding how long we would be her parents. We reassured them we'd be back as soon as possible and tried to be cheerful about the whole event. The fact that our final goodbyes were made so early in the morning helped keep them calm. They were back to sleep before we stepped out of the room. Meghan asked to come along, though, and I held her in the backseat until we arrived at the airport.

Our flight to Moscow seemed much shorter than the last flight. Knowing what to expect helped take the edge off our newest adoption travel. Since we were already familiar with Russian customs procedure, we breezed through with only one minor hitch. Casey had written that he was bringing in allergy medication and the customs official wanted to know why he was bringing drugs into the country. Casey had to pantomime sneezing and various allergy symptoms for the official, who conferred at length with a colleague and finally said with a scowl, "Just write no drugs!"

We were met by Natasha, who was filled with hugs and stories. She couldn't believe we were back already for another child (we were still getting used to the idea ourselves).

Our driver, Andre, was also our host. He and his wife, mother-in-law, and four-year-old son lived together in a two-bedroom flat. Their boy was very shy at first but warmed up by late afternoon when we were proudly shown all his baby pictures.

Because we couldn't travel to Alesia's orphanage in Ekaterinburg, which is located in Siberia, until the next day, we were able to do some sightseeing in Moscow. We visited Red Square. We visited a cathedral where we lit a candle for Casey's grandmother Bertoli. We toured St. Basil's, saw the eternal flame for World War II soldiers, and walked past the Kremlin. By then we were both worn out and freezing. When we left San Jose, it had been a balmy 75 degrees; here in Moscow, the temperature was hovering around 0 degrees with a strong wind blowing in from the north. I didn't want to imagine how cold it would be in Siberia.

That night after dinner we toasted to friendship, to our newest child, to Russia, to the United States, and to life in general. Andre teased that we wouldn't have to worry about translating English and Russian if we just kept drinking!

The next morning we got up to a breakfast of soft-boiled eggs, salami, cheese, bread, and tea. Both Casey and I were glad that we had only "sipped" our vodka the night before. We distributed gifts—a calculator, a lipstick with a case, a decorated hand towel, and for Andre's son, some gum and a bottle of bubbles. Whenever I had given a Russian a gift, I couldn't tell if he liked it or even cared what it was. I wondered if it was a cultural thing or if we were missing the mark with our choices. Later, Diana told me that, as a rule, Russians do not make a big production over a gift but accept it quietly, without much comment. Often, she said, they will not open a present until after the giver has left. No wonder our Russian friends had always seemed a bit surprised whenever they gave us a gift and we immediately opened it, told them that it was wonderful and how it would be used in our household, and then gave them a big hug in thanks.

On the way to the airport in the morning, Natasha kept us entertained with stories of the past year's adoptions. It was interesting for me to hear the Russian side of the same adoptions I had helped with in the United States.

We arrived at an airport outside Moscow we hadn't seen in our past travels. Evidently, Moscow has four different airports depending on where you are going. We waited outside in the icy wind for twenty minutes for a bus to shuttle us to the main terminal. Finally we gave up and decided to walk. All my winter clothes were meeting the coldness challenge except my boots. They were "California-weather" thin. I vowed that from then on I would wear the hiking boots with liners that a friend had loaned me, and thick wool socks. In the meantime, the cold traveled from my feet, throughout my body, and lodged in my bones. My muscles ached from shivering. As we waited, we were too cold to speak and so my mind kept wandering, mainly playing scenes from *Dr. Zhivago*.

Since it served as protection from the cold, this Aeroflot airplane looked much better to me than the last one we'd ridden in. The plane was old and as decrepit inside as I remembered, but with the benefit of our previous experiences, I wasn't nearly as fearful as I might have been. Ah, we were seasoned travelers.

When we landed, we met Leda, our new translator. As we waited for our luggage, she told us that our paperwork was almost finished and that we would be seeing Alesia the next day. While I wanted to see her immediately, this was so similar to our routine during our other adoptions that I wasn't nearly as disappointed as I might have been—I knew what to expect. We were taken to an empty flat whose owners were holding on to it until their son and his family could move in. A woman named Natalia would come in and cook. A place of our own. Yippee.

On the way, Leda told us about meeting Alesia. "She is a very *active* girl who is always smiling," she reported. Why was it that everyone used the word "active" accompanied by a chuckle and a small shake of the head when first describing Alesia? At first we made no reply. Then Casey and I looked at each other and said in unison, "But it couldn't be harder than Ana."

Then we were silent again, a pause which implied, "Could it?"

"She is very smart and very strong both physically and personality," Leda continued, but Casey and I were still thinking about the connotation of the word "active."

Natalia was very nervous because it was her first time hosting an American family and she didn't speak English. She was terrified at the prospect of feeding two Americans. Would we like the food? Would she be able to cook enough to make us happy? This was also very familiar.

It was a very comfortable home, with a kitchen, a bathroom, and two rooms. Natalia apologized for the old furniture—all beautiful, dark, rich wood antiques. We told her that in America this furniture would be very popular and valuable. She snorted and shook her head in disbelief as if saying, "Why would anyone like things so old?" Natalia's mother, who had lived there before she died, had sewn intricate sheets and pillow cases with embroidery, tatting, and crocheted inlays. They were exquisitely beautiful, but Natalia couldn't imagine why we would admire things done by hand and not purchased from a store.

That night, after Natalia had left, Casey and I looked at our sleeping arrangements. Our excitement over a place of our own was short-lived when we discovered that there was one thin bed in one room and an even smaller cot set up in the living room. "Well, at least we can visit for a while before we move on to our separate beds," I said, sitting on the edge of the cot. We talked about our foreboding over dealing with an "active" 2 1/2-year-old. In the past few months, I had been reluctant to voice my fears. I didn't want Casey to change his mind about Alesia; I was worried that if I showed any hesitation, we wouldn't go through with the adoption. Besides, after the initial decision had been made, we'd been so busy preparing for Alesia, we didn't have time to discuss much of anything except what needed to be done the next day. Now that we were only a few miles and hours away from meeting her, I finally felt safe voicing my concerns, and it was good to get it off my chest. I discovered that it's possible to know *absolutely* that you are on the right path and still be terrified of the direction you're headed.

It is interesting to me that we weren't concerned at all about dealing with Alesia's birth defects. Other than hoping we had brought the right kind of shoes she needed, we gave her imperfections no thought. We were both much more afraid of having a busy toddler in the family. How could a two-year-old generate this much trepidation? Extra physical and emotional problems aside, any two-year-old has to be carried and chased and watched constantly. "Active" two-year-olds don't sit still, and while they like to say "no," they don't like to hear it. Casey seemed relieved to know that, as strongly as I felt pulled to this child, I was also fearful. It had actually been hard on him to see me so certain and confident. He hadn't liked thinking that he was the only one who was afraid. Now that he knew we had common misgivings, he felt much better. We held each other and I marveled that admitting our fears had brought us even closer together.

Quietly, and with much reverence, Casey told me he felt that Alesia was going to make an impact not only on our family but also on the world. He didn't know quite how or when, but he felt this strongly. We were united in following our hearts, knowing that, even without having seen her in person, Alesia was already our child. Somehow by faith we knew that this adoption was meant to be.

In that small, warm Ekaterinburg apartment in the middle of the night, with the cold Siberian wind whistling outside the windows, we both acknowledged the hard work, the adjustments, the expense, and the effort we would need to parent this child. The blessing and the curse of our experience was to know how hard it would be, but to also understand the incredible joys that awaited us. We couldn't wait to meet her, but we indulged ourselves with one final night of reflection on the unknown.

Chapter 17

❧

MEETING ALESIA

Alesia and her friends at the orphanage.

Statement of Medical Risk Form, November 1994

I/WE have been informed fully about the risks inherent in the international adoption due to unknown birth parents and other lack of information or unreliable testing. This child/children has been referred to us with the expectation of good health based on available testing and information. . . . We acknowledge, understand and accept the medical policy of . . . and hold them harmless for diseases and conditions that cannot be diagnosed with reliability.

Meeting Alesia was extraordinary. Even though I had been through this twice in a year, in many ways, I was still a nervous "first-time" mom. We drove to the gate of a building surrounded by huge apartment complexes. Snow blanketed the small enclosed yard, and pieces of play equipment peeked out where the drifts were low.

We were ushered inside to the director's office and, to our surprise, were introduced to a child care worker—and a video photographer. Instead of taking us to see Alesia, they wanted us to see a video of her. The child we saw on the TV screen looked vaguely like our photographs of Alesia. She was held by a woman, set down, and immediately began to walk away, only to be turned around and brought back each time. She began to cry—evidently she was afraid of the cameraman. Then all we saw were close-ups of missing fingers and a misshapen foot. We got to see in great detail, and in full color, the extent of Alesia's deformities and her lung capability. It was maddening to watch a video of her when I knew she was waiting for us somewhere in the building. "I just want to see her in person," I wanted to tell them, but for some reason it was very important to them that we see the video first. At this point, we knew better than to offend our hosts.

Finally, we were escorted to a playroom, where Alesia was waiting. There she stood in a pretty pink dress with the words "I love Mummy" embroidered across the smocked front. There were other people gathered around but I wasn't aware of them. I saw only my daughter.

I stared at her. She stared back. Her large brown eyes said, "I know you. You are my mother." I knew her too. I had always known her. My heart felt as if it might explode with joy. I knelt down, she walked into my arms, and I held on to her as electricity coursed through each of us. Although I tried not to compare "meetings," I couldn't help but notice that Alesia wasn't as overtly affectionate as Ana had been. But she wasn't afraid of us as Nadia had been either. Alesia was comfortable with us from the first moment we walked into the room, and she wanted to show us everything in her domain. Casey and I spent the next half hour playing with her. Then, much too soon, she was taken away to change clothes and return to her group. (The dress was community property and worn only for meetings with new parents. Between adoptions, the dress went back into its boxed tissue nest.)

There were only boys left in Alesia's age group; all the girls had been adopted. My experience taught me that boys are much harder to find homes for than girls, especially boys over the age of two. I never did figure out exactly why. Perhaps an unknown boy personality is more daunting than an unknown girl personality. One man told me he thought that it was because women usually drive adoptions and they want their "little girl." We had felt more comfortable adopting a girl since she and Meghan would be sharing a room. After Nadia, the other adoptions just seemed to happen.

One boy looked at me and asked, "Would you bring me a mother?" I'd hoped I would never hear this question again—the pang that resulted was just as intense each time. This boy would probably never be adopted, we were told, because his father was in prison and wouldn't sign the papers relinquishing him. It is a terrible feeling of helplessness when confronted by the enormity of finding homes for all the children who have the need. For every child who is adopted, hundreds, maybe thousands, are left behind. It can be numbing. Once you become familiar with a history— however brief—of a child, that child becomes real. You have been given the opportunity to help him or her. Does *this* child need you more than *that* child? What will happen to the child left behind?

We didn't take Alesia with us that day. We were told to come back the next day to visit, and then Alesia would be able to go with us. Although it was hard for Casey and me to say goodbye, we both knew from our experience with Nadia that this was a much better alternative than whisking her away after an initial meeting. Alesia gave us each a strong hug but didn't seem at all concerned.

Even in this brief time, we could tell that Alesia was queen of her group. Again, unlike Nadia's experience, the caregivers here seemed to dote on Alesia and gave her much more leeway in expressing herself than we had previously seen. (This was by Russian orphanage standards, though, and not to be confused with leniency.) We were told that many of the caregivers would bring Alesia into the staff room with them to play with their hairbrushes and lipsticks, and keep them company while they prepared to go home after their shift.

The next day the children were outside playing when we arrived. Even in the bitter cold the children are sent out to play. (If they waited for warm weather, they would rarely see the outdoors.) Each one was bundled in so many layers of clothing that we couldn't tell which one was Alesia. Only their eyes were visible in the mass of wool and cloth. One boy fell over and was so weighed down with winter wear that he couldn't stand up again on his own. "Help me," he cried out in squeaky Russian, and immediately a caregiver raced over to stand him on his feet. Off he waddled to join his friends. I don't know how they managed the stairs up to their classroom when they went inside. Off came all the layers and on to their potty bowls they went. After each had finished, they washed their hands and sat down for their midday meal of soup and bread. Alesia kept glancing over at us and slurping up her food as quickly as possible—she didn't want to miss a thing. After lunch the boys went in to the sleeping room for their afternoon nap.

After all the boys were in their beds, Alesia went to each one to say goodbye. She went over to the first boy and gave him a big hug. Then she began telling him something in Russian while she wagged her finger at him. Then to our chagrin she smacked him soundly on the side of the head. The boy cringed but didn't complain. Then he smiled at her and she smiled back. The caregivers didn't seem phased by this action at all. In fact, Alesia repeated this farewell ritual with each and every child. A hug, a lecture, and a smack on the head. Then she marched out of the room without another look back—she was ready to go. The caregivers, on the other hand, looked distressed as they lined up for their goodbye hugs from Alesia. Once again, it was obvious that she was a favorite.

We changed Alesia into her new clothes and distributed our gifts. As was the custom at this orphanage, Leda brought champagne and chocolate and we toasted to Alesia's future happiness. We were given a certificate of stock from a local company that Alesia had received from the government upon entering the orphanage. Whether it was worth anything they could not say, but who knows? Casey and I can't wait until she is old enough to tell her she is a partial owner of a company in Siberia.

Once we arrived back at the flat, I put Alesia down for a nap in the crib. I found Natalia sitting at the kitchen table, crying silently. My heart went out to her and I motioned for her to come into the bedroom, where we both watched silently as Alesia slept. Natalia had tears running down her cheeks and I gave her a hug. She reached over and got the Russian-English dictionary and led me to the other room, sniffling the entire time. She tried to find the words that she wanted to convey but could not. Her powerful emotions seemed to fill the room and I wondered what was causing such a reaction. Was she thinking of another young child? Did she lose a child? Did she give up a child herself? Was she sad that Americans were taking a Russian child? I began to cry also. "I will take good care of her," I said in English even though I knew she couldn't understand my words.

Then she began to speak to me in Russian, both of us crying. I sat and listened and tried to understand her feelings since I didn't understand her words. After speaking for a long time she looked up a word and showed it to me—the word was "responsibility." She seemed to be telling me that Alesia was going to be a huge responsibility and that I must be a good mother for her. I must understand the responsibility involved with this child!

I showed her the word "special" and said "Alesia is a special child." She agreed. I showed her "lucky" and pointed to myself. I showed her the word "forget" and told her that Alesia would not forget Russia. Natalia seemed glad about this and I think she told me that Nadia would help keep the connection, that they would help each other. We cried some more and I told her in my broken Russian that I loved Alesia. Finally, I got some tissues and she got a handkerchief and we tried to dry our eyes. *"Harasho babushka,"* I told her. "You will make a good grandmother."

Later, Leda told us that Natalia was feeling as if she were a godparent sending a child out into the world—very happy for the child but feeling great sadness and loss at the same time. I still feel a sense of honor that Natalia would share such deep feelings with me, a stranger from a distant country.

Although soon to be overshadowed by our trip back to the States from Moscow, our flight from Ekaterinburg was the toughest plane trip I had ever experienced. Alesia didn't know what was going on and had, of course, never been on an airplane before. She didn't have the awe and curiosity that both Nadia and Ana had displayed. She just wanted to see for herself what a plane was all about. She couldn't understand why I insisted on holding her on my lap. Her love affair with having me as her mother was now history. By the time we were in the air, she did what two-years-olds do under such stress: She pooped in her pants. This was not ordinary poop. This was poop from bowels experiencing great change. Were we idiots? Why didn't we think of bringing along an extra set of clothes? As soon as I was able to, I took her into the tiny lavatory to see if I could clean her up. The toilet paper roll was empty. My little travel tissues were no match for this mess. I was starting to wear more of the mess than I was getting off. This wasn't a pleasant experience for Alesia either and she was quite vocal regarding her discomfort. Casey and I took turns trying our best to comfort and quiet her. We were left alone for the rest of the flight by crew and passengers alike. The Moscow Airport bathroom never looked as good as when I went in there with Alesia after landing and grabbed some fresh clothes out of our bags. Splendor is relative.

We spent the next few days back with Andre and his family, filling out paperwork and attending a physical for Alesia. It was during this time that I could finally take a closer look at her hand

and foot. The only whole finger on her right hand was her pinky finger, and it had a tight portion of skin at the base that looked as if it had been wrapped several times with a rubber band. She had a partial thumb and a bit of a ring finger but there were only mounds where her other fingers would have been. It seemed as if the fingers were hidden just under the skin, and that if I squeezed her hand, they would pop out and wave like a puppet. I also saw that not only was her left foot deformed—small, misshapen, covered with crusty calluses, and with no true ankle—but on her right foot she had only two toes; those farthest away from where her big toe should have been. I saw wide, embossed scar tissue which zigzagged around her lower left leg from a surgery, the orphanage director had told us, that was done to increase blood flow to her foot.

I have to admit that at first my skin crawled whenever I looked at Alesia's hands and feet. Because they were different, I felt they must be uncomfortable if not downright painful. It was hard for me to imagine that what looked odd to me might feel right to her. In watching her handle utensils, toys, and clothing, it was never apparent that she was compensating for anything. I was amazed once again by her agility and resourcefulness.

The Russian doctor who saw Alesia assured us that American doctors would be able to correct her foot through surgery. "They have the technology to do this," she repeated several times. "She is a very healthy little girl." Indeed, throughout the entire physical Alesia was cooperative and charming. "Thank goodness," we sighed, "we can give her the medical attention she needs."

Our every-time-we-travel-to-a-foreign-country-to-adopt-a-child-blow-out fight occurred two days before we left. It had been only a week since we'd arrived but it felt like forever. Casey and I were both feeling claustrophobic in our tiny room, which we were now sharing with Alesia. Getting her to sleep was the hardest part of the day. I wanted to lie down on our bed with her until she fell asleep, then transfer her to the crib. Casey wanted her to get used to falling asleep in the crib. I didn't want her to cry. He thought that by crying she would soothe herself. I'm sure the two Russian women of the household were biting their tongues trying to stay out of our nighttime struggle. I didn't have the Russian words to comfort Alesia as they did, but I was her mother and I wanted to care for her myself. Casey and I should have been supportive of each other. Instead, we rushed headlong into a fierce battle of the wills.

"You don't want me to comfort our child," I whispered in the meanest voice I could muster. "I can't believe you're this callous." Our host family was just behind the closed door and I didn't want them to hear us, even over Alesia's crying. "Do you want her to cry all night?"

"Do you think you'll want to hold her every night from now on?" he replied in his own nasty whisper. "I'm not going to let this child ruin our family."

"I can't believe you think an innocent two-year-old can ruin our family. What kind of family do we have if it can be ruined by my holding our child!"

"This child will take what little energy we have left!"

"Good, then she's welcome to it!"

"You're being unreasonable and hysterical!"

"You are unreasonable, and I wouldn't be hysterical if it weren't for you!"

"Well, I see that I can't talk to you right now."

"And I don't care to talk to you!"

"Fine!"

"Fine!"

I spent the rest of that night planning my divorce and how I would raise four children on my own.

It took a whole day before we were able to patch things up. Having released some of the steam of our pent-up emotions, we were able to remember that we were on the same team. Besides— Alesia had fallen asleep in the middle of our fight on her own.

Our last day in Russia included a trip to the United States Embassy for final permission to take Alesia home. The room was crowded with translators, adoption officials, parents, children, babies, and huge piles of winter coats, hats, and mittens. Each group of people represented an amazing story of persistence and courage—this was their final obstacle. We all wanted to be done and get out of there, but shared our stories as we waited.

We met a couple who had traveled to Russia to adopt one child and were leaving with eighteen-month-old triplets! Another woman held a baby with a huge cleft palate. When he grinned, his face opened from nose to chin. He was an extremely happy baby. She told us of a doctor who had volunteered to perform the needed facial surgery. "I know this sounds crazy," the woman told us, giving her baby a hug, "but I'm going to miss his big smile."

When we had finished, we celebrated the occasion with a trip to the Moscow McDonald's. That chocolate shake was the best one I will ever have. Later that night as Alesia sat on her potty with a slight case of loose stool, Galia and her mother tsk-tsked over the fact that we would feed this child American fast food.

Both women spent a great deal of time trying to show me the correct way to do things for Alesia. While Andre translated, they explained that I must buy my child only cotton nightclothes. They were appalled that I would try to dress Alesia in synthetic pajamas. I tried to explain that by law American pajamas had to be flame resistant and couldn't be plain cotton, but they didn't accept that flimsy excuse. They showed me the proper way to rinse out her clothes in the bathtub and hang them up to dry. I paid careful attention, though I knew that I would be using my washer and dryer as soon as we returned home. The morning we were to leave, I was called into the kitchen for instructions on the proper way to cook porridge, the only food Alesia should be fed for breakfast until she turned twenty-one. I was given a box to take home with me so I wouldn't get the wrong kind. "It must be hot! Only a hot breakfast for Alesia. Yes, yes, promise—a hot breakfast." I lowered my eyes, thinking of the microwave oatmeal that awaited this child when she was finally in my exclusive care.

We were on our way home. That sounds so simple. It was agony. Negotiating the airport with Alesia and all our luggage wasn't easy (although we did feel a little bit luckier when we spied the couple with the eighteen-month-old triplets trying to check their bags while holding on to their children). We thought we were home free when we sat in our seats but our real ride had just begun. Our beautiful daughter was about to turn into "monster child." Our flight from Ekaterinburg to Moscow should have been a clue that the flight home would not be easy, but we weren't prepared for the enormity of the emotional test that awaited. Upon takeoff, Alesia was suddenly transformed into a writhing, screaming demon of incredible strength. We were experiencing raw, primal panic manifesting itself in a thirty-pound body. All of Alesia's instincts for survival rose to the surface. She was terrified. She wanted to get away from us but wanted to be held by us. When we tried to comfort her, she twisted her body in agony at our touch. If we set her aside in her seat, she would scream to be held again, only to kick and tear herself away when we brought her near. I had dealt with tantrums on airplanes before. Meghan had initiated me early when an unknown ear infection had made her miserable on a trip to visit my parents. I cuddled and cooed my way 3,000 miles and apologized to all around me. I had thought then that I had accomplished something heroic but it was nothing compared to this. Casey's experience with Ana after I left Colombia must have been similar, and I began to understand his ordeal more with empathy than with the previous sympathy I had shown before. Sympathy is much easier.

At one point, Alesia managed to climb out of my arms and run down the plane aisle. I followed and she led me up one side, through the flight attendant station, and down the opposite side. She created her own little racetrack. As she walked her "hobblety" walk and I followed, she calmed down. Up and down, up and down we walked for an hour. Casey and I took turns trudging behind. People began to ask her name and say hello when she passed. One woman handed me a cup of water as if I were a marathon runner in the middle leg of a race. I was. I prayed Alesia would tire of the walking, then was sorry when she did. She resumed her fearful screaming, hold-me-don't-hold-me routine—with an added twist. She began biting and scratching me. I had teeth marks up and down my arms. The flight attendants tried their best to placate her with crackers and other treats. They kept asking, "What can we do to help?"

"I wish I knew."

Alesia spit in our faces. In that moment spitting was a much greater insult to me than biting or scratching. My immediate reaction was to spit right back. Thankfully, I stopped myself. Instead, I cried.

During one of Casey's turns, a Russian man offered some advice on child care. "I am a father," he said, "I am familiar with children. I think I can help." Casey let him try. He talked to Alesia in Russian. She screamed louder, then kicked him in the chest.

While I was holding Alesia in the flight attendant's station (to give the other passengers around us a break) a woman came up to me and said, "I am a psychic. I can feel much strength from this child."

"Oh yes, you are right," I said. "And you should feel her bite!"

"I will send her calming energy," she told me with a kind smile. "It will help."

"Thank you." We would accept any help. I'm confident that the passengers of all faiths and spiritual beliefs were saying a prayer for this child—and for a strong tailwind!

I was never so happy to see New York. As they passed us outside the terminal, passengers said goodbye to Alesia. Several flight attendants said, "God bless you," as we left. One man just looked at us and said, "Wow!"

And we still had to fly to San Francisco.

Something about solid ground seemed to console Alesia. We let her wander around the airport lounge as we waited for our next flight. Casey's sister came to the airport to meet her new niece. "She's so sweet," she exclaimed.

"Oh yes," we replied, completely spent, "she can be very sweet."

Chapter 18

❧

LIFE WITH FOUR CHILDREN

Meghan's depiction of our family's Christmas.

November 20, 1994

> *Last night I dreamt I was at some kind of medical clinic with the girls. I couldn't remember which one needed the medical help, so I brought them all. After passing through long corridors, we finally arrived in two huge rooms with closets and toys. The girls scattered and began to run around and play. A doctor, a therapist, and a nurse came in and asked me whom we were there to see. I said, ``Well, I think Ana needs some help with her speech and some testing.'' Then I remembered Nadia and realized she needed something—but I wasn't sure what. Then I thought about Alesia. Wasn't she due to have her foot checked? Meghan must surely need something. But as hard as I tried, I couldn't match the right child with the right doctor. I couldn't keep track of who needed what and where everybody was. It was a huge mess. I struggled to call Casey on a pay phone but I kept dialing the wrong number. Finally, I woke up—drained.*

Alesia didn't like the flight from New York to San Francisco any more than she had any of her other flights, but twelve hours of travel were beginning to slow her down. Her bites no longer drew blood, and by the time we'd crossed the Rocky Mountains, she was asleep. So it was a dazed and sedate Alesia that our family met at the airport upon our arrival. Alesia was unimpressed with her siblings. I don't think she understood they would all be living in the same house. As we headed to the baggage claim area, I looked like a mother duck with four ducklings gathered around trying to attach themselves to me so I wouldn't swim away. Meghan, Nadia, and Ana were much more preoccupied with keeping Casey and me in their sights than they were with getting to know their new sister. I think I was still shell-shocked from the plane ride from hell. What I really wanted to do was climb aboard the luggage cart and be carried off to my big, comfortable, American bed and sleep for about a week. But we had a celebration to attend and four girls who probably wouldn't calm down for another fifteen years or so.

Those first days back were a time of huge adjustment for everyone. Alesia's "honeymoon period" must have come and gone the day we met in Russia. Her strong personality showed itself in everything she did. I loved the way she stood up for herself in every situation, but her sisters didn't find it endearing at all. Rather than sit back and watch what our family life was like for a while, she immediately joined in, adding her own dimension to how things operated. But her energy was contagious and soon she was an important element in the girls' games. Like everything else she did, when she played, Alesia played full tilt. She would try to speed down the hallway with her Alesia run—two hops on her right foot, and one long stride with her left.

After a while, Alesia seemed to love having sisters, but she was so used to ruling the roost that soon she was giving more orders than she was taking. While Meghan balked at this idea (and retreated into a book or another room), Nadia and Ana seemed to accept, for a few months at least, Alesia's two-year-old "bossiness" with good humor.

Alesia still loathed going to sleep and fought it for as long as possible. We developed an elaborate ritual to get her to wind down and rest but it often took over an hour to complete. We had a crib set up for her in our bedroom for the first few weeks, but knew that wasn't going to be the long-term solution. Soon, she'd have to get used to sleeping in the same room with her sisters so Casey and I could have our privacy back. I didn't know how the other girls would be able to fall asleep with the commotion she created in trying to calm herself. Eventually, like Nadia, she would rock herself to sleep, but instead of humming softly, she sang out in a loud voice.

We began to see other effects from Alesia's arrival on the scene. Both Ana and Nadia were wetting their beds at night and Ana would often wet her pants during the day. Meghan was starting to have nightmares of car wrecks, plane crashes, earthquakes, and other disasters out of her control. So, between changing sheets, quieting the opera diva, and soothing bad dreams, I was beginning to experience symptoms of sleep deprivation. It got to the point that if one of the girls didn't need me, I would wake up, just before reaching REM sleep, wondering what was wrong.

Ana now wanted to be held continuously. But Alesia didn't want to share her new mom. They fought often and hard over who would get to sit in my lap. When I convinced them there was room for both of them, they fought over who got the biggest piece of "lap real estate." Nadia, and finally Meghan, would join in the struggle, and while there was possibly room for two, three or four were out of the question. What had been a hard situation with three children became even harder with four. My solution was simple; I rarely sat down.

Thanksgiving approached, and while things were hard, we were truly thankful for our intense and often crazy home life. I would really be thankful to have one full night of uninterrupted sleep. I put the request on my early-bird Christmas list.

We didn't waste any time setting up medical appointments for Alesia. We went in to see Dr. Morgan first thing for a complete physical and took the usual parasite tests. She gave us a referral to Dr. Rinsky of the Lucille Packard Children's Hospital to look at her foot. Considering that Alesia had only been in the United States for two weeks when she first met Dr. Rinsky, she did pretty well cooperating with his examination. His verdict on her foot, however, was not what we'd expected.

"Alesia's foot hasn't grown correctly," Dr. Rinsky told us. "I can try to reshape it surgically over the next ten years. Although it would look much more like a normal foot, it wouldn't be very functional. She would have to have numerous surgeries and would never have full use of her leg. The other option is to amputate her foot just above the ankle and fit her with a prosthetic device that would allow her the full use of her leg."

After asking a few more questions, we quickly made our decision: amputation. We could see how important being active was to Alesia. We asked Dr. Rinsky to perform the amputation and prayed that Alesia would agree with our decision when she was older. Even though she had never let her dysfunctional foot stop her before, she had never run, or danced without an awkward limp. Eventually, with a prosthesis, she'd be able to move freely.

On the other hand, what a horrendous surgery to perform on a child who was just learning to trust her parents. How could we possibly help her understand what was happening without the benefit of a common language? How many two-year-olds would understand the concept anyway? We thanked God for our strong-willed and active child. We knew she had the personality to overcome what was in store.

Alesia would need an initial surgery to remove the callus build-up on the bottom of her foot. If that went smoothly, we were advised to schedule the amputation as soon as possible.

Ana's adoption was finalized in court that December. We had the same judge as we had had with Nadia, but this time we had Alesia with us too. We were just as scattered as we had been during Nadia's finalization, even with our good intentions of being more organized. ("See you soon," we said again as we left, which didn't seem to surprise the judge at all.) Ana was proud of her certificate and all the attention she received, but even though we tried to explain what was happening several times, she seemed unsure as to what the day in court had meant. She went on a crying jag that evening and would not let us comfort her. We could only sit by her and wait for the storm to pass. She had so many conflicting emotions. We were important to her now and she was afraid to have anyone be too important in her life. Everyone who had been important to her in the past had left her. She was protecting herself by blocking us out—yet wanting our love desperately. I ached to make her understand that our love wasn't going away, but she wasn't yet able to grasp the concept.

Alesia watched Ana's crying fit from the safety of the hallway. She knew the language of tears. I don't think she'd ever seen another child throw a fit as big as her best and Ana's intensity scared her. After that incident, I noticed that Ana and Alesia seemed closer. Maybe it was because Alesia could see that Ana had many of the same powerful emotions waiting to burst forth. Nadia took her turn by "bursting" a few days later. Not to be outdone, Meghan took her turn frequently and helped Nadia refine her door-slamming technique. In a call to Marge during that emotion-filled time, I moaned about the fact that the girls blew up one after another. "I never get a break between blow-ups," I said.

"Isn't it nice that they take turns with their tantrums," she replied brightly. "Just think how impossible it would be to care for them if they were all out of control at the same time."

I had to agree with her logic and appreciate her optimism, even though I had been hoping for a little more pity. My kids were supportive of each other when they weren't the one screaming. While they often bickered over Casey's and my attention, when one of them was in the middle of a meltdown, the others would stand clear and give us time to soothe her as best we could.

Casey and I worked very hard to make sure each child got some individual time away from the rest of the family. We called it "special time." This helped a lot to overcome some of the competition each was feeling when we were all together. If I went to the grocery store, I'd invite one of the kids along. Meghan and I often went out for dinner on Wednesday nights after her dance class. Whenever one of the girls had a doctor or dentist appointment—and one of them always did—I would schedule time around it to spend doing something on our own. The expectation of time alone with Mom helped make the dreaded medical visits something to look forward to.

The night before Alesia's first surgery, I paced through the house with the cellular phone, getting reassurance from my mom long-distance. Casey wasn't able to be with us at the hospital, which made it the first time one of the kids would have a major medical treatment without both of us there. But the surgery was supposedly a simple procedure. She wouldn't have to stay overnight in the hospital, but she would have to be put under a general anesthetic. The Lucille Packard Children's Hospital is a state-of-the-art hospital in Palo Alto on the Stanford University campus. With Dr. Rinsky, Alesia was in the best of hands.

I was still nervous.

At the hospital, I held Alesia while the anesthesiologist explained that he would give her a mild sedative and showed me the mask they would use to administer the general anesthetic. I showed the mask to Alesia and she practiced on a doll. Even sedated, when the time came to place the mask over Alesia's mouth and nose, she was not a willing patient. She fought it at first, but eventually she gave up her struggle to stay awake. I knew how she hated to go to sleep. I could hear the blood pounding in my ears when I was directed to wait in the adjoining room. My head ached. I thought about her past Russian surgery. Had they been able to prepare her then? I had heard stories of limited supplies of anesthetics and of children strapped into adult-sized beds to prevent them from falling. What kind of hospitals would be available to orphanage children? Was she remembering that other surgery today? What kind of pain would she be in when she woke up?

I was jarred out of my reveries by Alesia's screams. I recognized them immediately and was almost out the door when a nurse ran in and rushed me into the post-op recovery room. "She woke up screaming," she said. "Try to calm her down." Alesia was lying on her back in a hospital bed with metal guard rails surrounding her. She reached up to me but fought as soon as I had her in my arms. She grabbed my eyeglasses off my face and threw them across the room. She began spitting at me but her mouth was dry. This infuriated her and she began scratching me and trying to bite me and pulling at her IV. "What's the matter with her?" yelled one of the nurses. "I've never seen a child act this way. Why is she being so bad?!"

I didn't respond. I had my hands full. Luckily, another nurse came to our rescue. "She isn't being bad," she said, giving the first nurse a stern look. "She's afraid." She pulled a chair over for me to sit with Alesia. "My, isn't she a strong child." She smiled at me.

While my body and ego were bruised, that nurse's smile reassured me that Alesia was going to be okay. "Yes," I replied proudly, holding Alesia's arms and legs so she wouldn't hurt me and saying once again, *she is a very strong child.*

It took forty minutes, but finally, Alesia calmed down. Casey had missed a big one.

Meanwhile, I was having many vivid dreams. Often, I would dream of being trapped inside an elevator. No matter how hard I tried in my dream, I couldn't get it to work properly. The doors would open between floors with not enough room to crawl through. This dream always ended with the elevator breaking free and plummeting full-speed to the bottom of the shaft. I would wake up just before it crashed, with my heart pounding in my chest.

I also dreamt of being back home in Iowa and living at my mother's house. In my dream I would be looking for apartments I liked and thinking about getting a job. But I didn't feel any pressure to do anything. I was thinking about maybe going out on a date, maybe seeing a movie and starting up an old romance. Then suddenly I'd remember: I have a husband and four children waiting for me in California! "I really should call them," I'd think, "but then I'd have to tell Casey when I'm coming home. Would it be wrong if I went out a few more nights and maybe lived here awhile longer before I went back?

"How can I call them? What if they've moved? Well, maybe I'll take that job after all." Then I'd wake up and check to see if Casey had caught me dreaming of a life without responsibilities. "Maybe if I close my eyes real fast," I would think, "I can go back for a while."

I didn't need a Freudian or a Jungian to tell me my dreams were stress-related. Since bringing Alesia home, my overactive conscience was reminding me that since I had wanted this child so badly, and since it was our choice to go through with each adoption, I shouldn't ask for help. We already depended so much on family and friends just for day-to-day support, I didn't feel comfortable asking them to give more of their time just so that I could sit and relax. As they say in Iowa: "I'd made my bed, now I had to lie in it." Oh, if only I could—lie in a bed, that is. Of course with all those dreams, I must have been sleeping some. It just didn't feel like it.

People began telling us how special—how amazing—we were. "Those children are so lucky to have you take them into your family!" we would often hear.

"We're the lucky ones," was our standard reply, which I meant with all my heart. Their comments made me uncomfortable. After all, people never told us how lucky Meghan was that I gave birth to her.

I didn't *feel* special. And I knew that I wasn't necessarily the great person their comments suggested. I was yelling at my kids just like other parents do, probably four times as much. I began to worry a little. Do I have to be a great and special person for these adoptions to work out? If so, I wasn't sure I was up to it. Luckily, that hasn't proven to be the case. "Consistent ordinariness" has seemed to suffice so far.

Sometimes people don't think about what they're asking.

"Which one is your real child?" people who have heard about our family but don't know us well will ask (usually in front of the girls).

"They are all our children," we answer.

Usually people realize their mistake, but if they continue to question us as to our *real* daughter, we look them squarely in the eyes and repeat with emphasis, "They are *all* our *real* children." I've told the girls that it's our job to educate people—children and grown-ups alike—about adoptive families.

One day a little girl looked at Ana, looked at me, and then asked, "Why is her skin dark and yours isn't?"

"Because she's lucky," I replied.

"It just is," said Ana and held on to my hand tightly.

Another day while on a bus during a field trip, a child in Nadia's class who knew she was adopted asked, "How much did you pay for Nadia?"

"She's priceless," I answered happily. Nadia beamed.

"That's right," she said.

Later that night, Nadia asked me what "priceless" meant.

Another Christmas arrived. We didn't have the gathering of out-of-town visitors that had celebrated with us the year before. After all the excitement of the past eighteen months, it was nice to focus totally on our new family—a world of love by itself. Casey took the girls to the Santa Cruz mountains to cut down our Christmas tree that year. As we decorated it, I told the girls a story about each ornament. We lit a candle on Winter Solstice and took turns telling what had made us happy about the past year.

Meghan and Nadia gave holiday advice to Ana and Alesia. "You must go to sleep or Santa won't come," Nadia said wisely. Meghan enjoyed being the one who knew the "truth" about Santa (wink wink) and helped us create the holiday world of miracles, family, and gifts for her sisters.

On Christmas Eve, we read the story of Jesus' birth and tried to explain the concept to our girls, who had not had any previous religious exposure. I wasn't sure whether they grasped the concept of God's Son.

"Maybe baby Jesus was adopted," Ana suggested.

Chapter 19

HOSPITALS

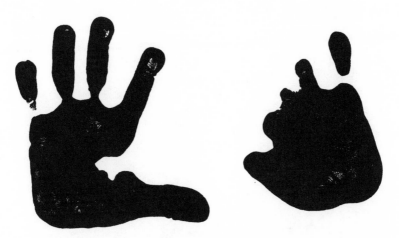

Alesia wanted to make hand prints in paint just
like her sister Ana had done in preschool.

December 25, 1994

> *Christmas day. Alesia's surgery is tomorrow. I wish I could protect her from all the pain that lies ahead, but that's a gift I can't give. I keep trying to picture Alesia's amputation. I sometimes imagine how it must feel from her perspective:*
>
> *My new parents take me to the hospital. When I leave the house I have a foot. My parents give me to some doctors and I fall asleep. When I wake up, my foot is gone and I hurt. Is this what all parents do?*

Alesia seemed happy as we drove up to the hospital, even though I had to wake her up at 5:00 A.M. I hadn't slept much and it showed. Casey and I had gotten into an argument the night before. Merry Christmas. He wanted to know what the schedule for the surgery was so he could plan some work. I was upset that he didn't know what was happening, and that he was asking at 11:30 the night before! Tit led to tat and soon we were taking out our fears on each other—which was becoming a recurring theme. In the morning, though, our minds were focused on Alesia and that meant supporting each other. Usually for Casey and me it's the anticipation that is hardest to deal with together. In an actual crisis, we work as a team.

Once on the surgery unit Alesia trotted off to the playroom as if she owned the place. After the first surgery, I guess she figured she had claim to it. She played awhile, was examined by the anesthesiologist, then we went back to the playroom to wait. Minutes later, Alesia took a running leap and smacked into the bookshelves—with her face. She screamed and we applied ice. Not a great way to start her morning. A large bruise sprang up on her cheek—she looked as if she had already begun the war.

She was given a liquid sedative but spit a lot of it back at the nurse. Lucky nurse. Later it would be me.

We asked the doctor to give her more medicine with the hope that she wouldn't have the severe reaction she'd had the last time she was put under. "Did I mention that she had a severe reaction to the anesthesia last time?" I asked him again. I remembered only too well the scene after the last surgery and I didn't want a repeat performance.

"Yes, Mrs. Conroy, and I read about it in her chart. Don't worry, we'll give her a medication that will help ease the pain and will also take away any memory she might have of the procedure."

"Great," we said, "can we have some too?"

At first we didn't think the sedative was working. Alesia was playing normally and seemed unaffected, but I followed close behind her in case she lost her balance. The doctor came in and said they would be ready to start the surgery in five minutes. I was doubtful that *she* would be ready by then, but when I next looked down at Alesia, she looked like a flower child at Woodstock. She was mesmerized by the colors on a plastic castle. "Wow, cool, man," her eyes said. Casey and I couldn't help but chuckle. She looked intensely at the trademark and bent closer, closer, until her head touched the castle balcony. Then she looked up at me, smiled a brilliant but goofy smile, and fell back into my arms. With half-closed eyelids she whispered, "Tickle tickle tickle . . ." with the last tickle trailing off. Even though *I* wasn't ready to let her go, *she* was definitely ready for dreamland. As I watched them wheel her down the corridor, I felt my heart contract. Had we made the right decision?

Casey and I waited. Casey rested while I read a *People* magazine. We waited some more. After almost three hours the nurse came in to tell us that Dr. Rinsky was finishing up and Alesia was fine. "Thank God," I whispered and then prepared for postsurgery battle. This time I wanted to be there the instant she woke up. When we entered the recovery room, Alesia was woozy but awake enough to cry softly. She reached out to me and I imagined that she was wondering why we had let them do this to her. A myriad of tubes led from her foot, hand, and arm. A bag was filling with her blood and an IV hung by the bed. Her left leg was completely wrapped in bandages, and her left hand, which they had also made some surgical corrections to, was wrapped in gauze from fingers to elbow.

Alesia began to cry harder, pumping her legs up and down, while I held on and spoke softly to her. Casey was trying to comfort her with soothing words. Dr. Rinsky was instructing me not to hold Alesia's leg down because it would cause more pain. Two nurses were trying to get morphine into the IV. A third nurse was getting a chair for me to sit in that would allow me to lie down with Alesia, who was getting frantic. She got hold of my eyeglasses and threw them off. (When would I learn to take them off myself?) She squirmed and tried to get comfortable but couldn't. I couldn't get in a good position without squeezing off several tubes in the process. It was a comedy of errors but eventually with the help of Casey, the nurses, and a cherry popsicle, she calmed down.

I don't remember much about the rest of Alesia's hospital stay. My most vivid memory is of a children's wooden wagon with a red railing on each side. It was outfitted with a special holder for an IV pole. We tucked pillows and Alesia's many tubes and bags into the wagon and then placed her gently in the middle. The hospital is built around an inner courtyard with the different units extending from a central, circular hallway. We began our trek, pulling Alesia in the wagon around the hall, passing other children in other wagons. The wagons were popular with the patients— the movement eased their pain and boredom. I wonder if the architect knew that this central hallway would become a constant walkway for parents and their recovering children. Casey would pull and then I would pull, around and around. Whenever she was hurting, around and around we would go. We must have put ten miles on that little red wagon that night.

Children recover at an astonishing speed. We were able to go home the next day.

"Don't be alarmed when you see her stump," Dr. Rinsky instructed. "It'll look a little like raw ground hamburger meat."

"Okay," I answered. ("You mean I have to look at it?!" I wanted to say.)

I have always been the pillar of strength when it comes to other children's blood and guts. As a preschool teacher I accompanied a three-year-old girl to the hospital to get stitches in her hand. I sang songs to distract her from the painful shots of Novocain. "This doctor sews so well," I said, "I bet he makes all his own clothes." The girl smiled. "Maybe he would sew a dress for your cat when he's finished with your hand."

"Not for a *cat*," she giggled.

The doctor said. "You must not be her mother, you're much too calm."

Now I was the mother. My stomach turned over just thinking about changing Alesia's bandages myself. I worried Alesia might notice my aversion. I was afraid I might hurt her or forget some important procedure. But I had to buck up. I had no choice.

"Don't let her do too much," the doctor cautioned as he left. Right.

Two days later, she was sliding around the hardwood floors on her butt with her leg held high in the air, chasing her sisters around the room. Don't let her do too much.

The girls were curious about Alesia's surgery, and at first they were very helpful in trying to feed her (since her right hand had only one finger and her left hand was in bandages, holding a fork or spoon was a major challenge). But after a while they got bored with their invalid sister and Alesia began finding ways to help herself. She was ingenious in finding ways to pick up objects and get from one place to another. To pick up a toy from the floor, she would use her forearms to stand it up, balance it, then push it up the table leg and finally over the top with her knee. She never complained or asked me to get anything for her. She was determined to do things herself and we let her.

After the surgery, Alesia blossomed. She was outgoing and friendly to everyone. She still had her almost nightly tantrum, but during the day she was a joy. She began picking up English words even though no one except family members knew what she was saying. Of all the children, she had the hardest time pronouncing English words. We soon learned to interpret her unique language and got into the habit of listening and then translating back to her what she had said in "our English."

We went for weekly visits to Dr. Rinsky, who pronounced that her stump appeared to be healing nicely. At first Alesia wanted as little as possible to do with Dr. Rinsky. *"Nye, bulna!"* she would cry, meaning "Don't hurt me."

"No *bulna,* I'm just going to look today," he would answer.

She didn't like to look at her stump and would look away whenever I changed the dressings. At first, I felt awkward and clumsy trying to wrap the bandages around the wound. But with time it became second nature to both me and Casey, who took turns playing nurse. Alesia even began to enjoy the quiet time we would spend cleaning her stump, applying special ointment, and reapplying the gauze and bandage. We looked forward to the day she would be fitted with her first prosthesis.

It was late January when, as I was cleaning Alesia's stump, the stitches opened. I tried to hide my panic as I took a closer look. I could see her leg bone. Was that really bone? Mothers shouldn't see their baby's bones unless they are looking at an X-ray. There should be skin and muscles and all sorts of stuff between me and her bones. What was happening? I called Casey. I called the hospital. "I'm sorry to bother you"—I took a deep breath— "but I can see my child's bone through her open incision! I don't think this is supposed to be happening." I'm sure the nurse I spoke to appreciated my medical savvy. She called the doctor right away. The wound had only healed on the surface—not inside. So the next day, Dr. Rinsky performed another procedure to close the stump again before the bone or the area around it became infected. This was Alesia's third surgery. We'd been her parents for only seventy-three days.

I like to think that, deep down, Alesia knew these operations were for her benefit. Her hospital stay was longer this time. When Meghan, Nadia, and Ana visited, they were very impressed by the seemingly unlimited supply of popsicles and the large playroom open to them as well as the patients.

"Could I please schedule an appointment to have my appendix removed?" Meghan asked one of the nurses.

"This is the life," Nadia told Ana.

After several weeks, Alesia was able to have her bandages off during the night while she slept. One night she was lying beside me while I was reading in my bed. For the first time she looked intently at her stump. She stared at it and began to touch it gently with her hands. I put down my book, looked at her, and said,

"You know, it's really getting better. It is actually quite beautiful." I put my hand on it momentarily, then took it away. She reached over for my hand and placed it back on her stump. I held my hand there and then began touching the stitches and the scabs. "This is a part of you, so I love it too," I said gently.

I know Alesia didn't know all the words I was saying but she understood. The deformity that had seemed so frightening in the past simply became another part of Alesia.

"I don't care if my baby is a boy or a girl as long as it has ten fingers and ten toes," I remember saying when I was pregnant with Meghan. Now I knew that ten fingers and ten toes aren't that important.

I gave Alesia's stump a kiss. "Your leg is beautiful," I said, and as strange as it seems, it really was. From then on, she always wanted to help administer to her leg. It was hers again.

As soon as Dr. Rinsky was sure the incision was healing properly, Alesia was fitted with a cast. Since it was obvious we weren't going to be able to slow her down, he decided to apply the strongest barrier possible—which meant a cast instead of a bandage. She had to have it cut off and replastered each week for four weeks and then every three weeks after that for another two months. After a few weeks Alesia loved her cast because it was the closest thing she had ever had to a normal leg. Interns would apply the casts and soon began building up the bottom with extra plaster to even up her stance. There is nothing more dangerous than a two-year-old with an attitude and a cast. If Alesia was in a bad mood we did our best to steer clear of her new weapon. "No! You may not kick! Don't swing that leg at me, young lady!"

Although Alesia seemed unbothered by her missing fingers and foot, other people weren't always as comfortable. For example, one day when we visited a clothing store, the girls were running around and Alesia was crawling, trying to join in as best she could. Her dangling pant leg completely covered up her amputated foot. She had one foot and shoe sticking out and one pant leg just dragging along. A man came into the store with his little girl and he began playing with Alesia. He tickled her, saying, "Oops, somebody lost their foot. Somebody stole your foot. Where did your foot go? You lost your foot."

Alesia just smiled, enjoying the fun. Then Ana, who had been standing by, told the man, "You're right, the doctor cut off her foot."

Suddenly he realized that Alesia's pants weren't just coming down, as he had first thought—she really didn't have a foot. His face turned a deep shade of red. Alesia didn't care. She liked the attention. She knew she didn't have a foot. It was no big deal.

Chapter 20

❧

LEARNING TO WALK

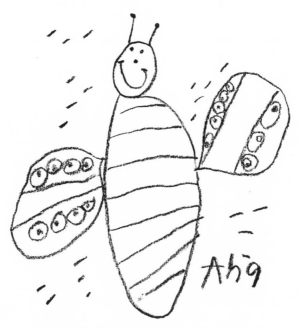

Ana's drawing of a bee or a butterfly
(depending on the day you ask).

February 2, 1995

   Nadia stomps around. She slams the door. When I ask her to do something, she just stands there. If I get upset, she is belligerent. ``I'm doing it,'' she screams, but she hasn't moved—pushing me until I feel over the edge. I try to speak nicely to all the girls. For good behavior I give them small rewards like a quarter or a trip to Burger King (although Meghan now tells me that we must boycott Burger King and McDonald's because they are destroying the rain forest). I finally decided that I couldn't rely on positive reinforcement to keep the girls from killing each other. The only thing that works is to split them up, but there aren't enough places in the house to put them all.
   On top of that, yesterday I cleaned all day and the house still looks like a disaster area. This weekend I did laundry—for two days solid I did laundry—in and out, in and out. I had to put a whole hamper full of clothes back because they didn't get washed.

Late that winter, we experienced a total breakdown of behavior at our house. "It looks like the inmates are running the asylum," one of my friends said.

"Thanks for pointing that out."

I cried often now. I couldn't help it. I had no control over my tear ducts. The more settled and physically strong Alesia became, the more Meghan, Nadia, and Ana fought and bickered. Meghan argued with everything we said.

"Why can't I have a friend spend the night?" she'd ask.

"Because it's a school night."

"No it isn't, it's because I have too many sisters!"

or:

"Will you please take me shopping tonight to buy some new jeans?"

"Not tonight, Meghan."

"Why, because of my sisters?"

"No, because it's nine o'clock and the stores are closed."

"You never take me shopping anymore, you're too busy with all my sisters."

Every problem was blamed on her sisters. Meghan seemed to have too much homework because of her sisters. She didn't have any friends anymore because of her sisters. She didn't have anything to wear because of her sisters. She couldn't get her hair to stay back because of her sisters. *Nothing was right anymore because of her sisters!*

Ana was also having difficulty, especially adjusting to a new sister who kept going to the hospital and getting all kinds of attention. She had regressed in the past, displaying behavior more appropriate for a much younger child, but now she regressed even more. Her preschool teacher was concerned. Ana wasn't able to sit still even for a minute. We noticed it mainly at the dinner table. She was unable to sit long enough to eat her food. Sometimes she would even fall off her chair in the middle of a bite. She would slide off to one side, then the other. She would get up to go to the bathroom a couple times, then stand for a while when she returned. No amount of table manner coaching, pleading, or even threats worked. She was physically unable to keep her body still for any length of time.

She couldn't sit in my lap either. She only seemed interested in my affection if one of the other children wanted it. If I tried to hug her or reach out to hold her hand, she'd withdraw. But if any of her sisters wanted to be cuddled, she begged to take their place.

Ana became fascinated with babies. "Does the baby's mommy love her?" she would ask if she saw an infant. She was so curious I worried that she would hop into the stroller along with the baby. "Does the mommy change his diaper? Does the mommy give her a bottle? Could I have a bottle?" She would stare at the child's mother as if trying to discern whether this mother would treat her baby lovingly.

She would fall into dark moods which neither Casey nor I

could predict or prevent. She would make faces and tease one of her sisters until they would get angry enough to yell or hit. Then she would sit back and wait for her sibling to get in trouble. Meghan was an easy target. Ana knew she would fly off the handle at the slightest provocation.

"Ana, you're an idiot!" Meghan would scream. "Leave me alone, you dork!"

"What's going on?" I would say, coming into the room.

"Ana wrecked my markers and I told her not to play with them before."

Meghan considered this another invasion of her property. I would look over at Ana. I could almost see a halo glimmering above her head. "I didn't do anything," she'd say sweetly.

"Why you dirty—" Meghan would say, lunging at Ana.

"Be quiet, Meghan."

"Why should I, Mom? I saw her do it. I saw her wreck my marker. She did it on purpose!" Then Meghan—overwhelmed at the injustice—would begin screaming at me. "You always side with her! You never listen to me! Nobody ever listens to me! Nobody loves me! I wish I were never born!"

"Meghan, calm down and stop screaming at me. We'll work this out," I would say, trying to keep my voice low. All this over a set of markers?

"No, you won't. Nobody cares. My life is ruined and you don't even care."

"Go to your room until you can settle down."

"Fine, punish me! I can't believe this! I hate you!"

"Go to your room."

Off Meghan would stomp, slamming as many doors along the way as possible.

"Ana," I would say, "did you play with Meghan's markers?"

"No."

"Then how did they get out here on the table?"

Each girl was trying to carve out and understand her place in this new family structure. I started to see them fall into roles that I didn't feel good about: Meghan the wronged, belligerent sister; Nadia the too-good-to-be-true sister; Ana the hyperactive, sneaky sister; and Alesia the injured, demanding sister. I wanted them to develop the other aspects I knew were an important part of their personalities, though not as active lately: Meghan, artistic and precocious; Nadia, sensitive and creative; Ana, effervescent and adventurous; and Alesia, tenacious and fun-loving.

Casey and I tried our best to praise positive behavior, even if in retrospect it seemed like a stretch—"Alesia, you started to bite me and you didn't, that's great!"—and downplay less desirable behavior—"Meghan, I can't listen when you scream at me." "Nadia, it's our job to make sure everyone is wearing a coat to school, not yours." We began teaching our children what it means to be a family unit—the benefits *and* the responsibilities. This forced Casey and me to crystallize our own family values more than we had ever had to do in the past. When Meghan was an only child, we could teach morals, ethics, and right behavior as her life experiences presented themselves. Now we had to play catch-up with our other daughters, who had limited, and wildly divergent, life experience. When we finally came to terms with what we were dealing with, we were able to begin establishing in everyone's mind three things:

- Casey and I would now be their parents forever—like it or not, they were stuck with us for the long haul.
- We loved them always, no matter how ridiculous their behavior.
- There would be natural consequences for anyone who didn't follow the family rules and expectations.

We had no choice—we had to get serious. Now we were outnumbered.

It was time for Alesia, as well as our entire family, to begin to walk on our own. Although Alesia had been running around on her cast for a couple of months, she wouldn't have complete control of her leg until she was fitted with a prosthetic device.

How do you interview the person who is to create your child's leg? What questions do you ask? Neither Casey nor I had any idea how to select the best "prosthetic maker." Would the choice determine how much Alesia could achieve physically? Dr. Rinsky referred us to a clinic that worked with the children's hospital in Palo Alto, but if possible, we wanted to try to find someone closer to home. Casey's personal doctor told us about a man named

Mike Norrell who ran a prosthetic business that his father had started.

While we were waiting to meet Mike, I peeked into his workroom. I couldn't believe what I saw. Shelves and workbenches lined three of the four walls and they were filled top-to-bottom with artificial body parts—arms, legs, feet—of various sizes and shapes. In one corner of the room, a leg was wedged tightly into a vise on a workbench. (My leg felt pinched.) On the floor lay pieces of flesh-colored plastic. Nuts and bolts were packed in rows of small boxes awaiting their role in the production of someone's new knee. It certainly looked like a good place to start our search for Alesia's "prosthetic engineer." I have no idea if we asked any of the right questions, but we liked Mike's answers. Quiet but confident, he took great pride in his work.

"Nothing is impossible. I look at each missing limb as a challenge. How can we provide the most function with the best form? If I can't find what I need, I'll design it myself," Mike said.

I knew if it were me, I wouldn't want a generic leg that came off an assembly line. I liked Mike's creative style. Alesia was sure to test the limits of durability with any device attached to her.

When I brought Alesia to meet Mike, the first thing he did was measure her legs. Each measurement had to be taken from the same part of the hip. It had to be exact. Unfortunately, Alesia couldn't stay still long enough to assure any kind of accuracy. Finally, with the help of several Tootsie Pops (not to mention a few threats from me), we were able to begin making a mold of her stump. Mike put a panty hose on her stump (she then had to have one on the other leg, just like Mom) and wrapped a plaster gauze over the lower portion of her leg up to her knee. After it had dried a bit, Mike slipped it off. He would use this mold to create an inner liner made of pelite (a flexible but firm, foam-rubber-like product) that would slip on between her leg and the plastic prosthesis. The liner would have a slit running up the side to allow it to open just enough to be put on over the rounded ball of her stump. Once the prosthesis was in place, the liner slit would close, creating a tight fit (but not so tight that it hurt). Alesia wouldn't have to hold her leg on with any belts or straps.

Alesia would also have a special foot, created out of a material similar to what diving boards are made of, for "give." It took about six weeks for the leg and foot to be completed, but soon Alesia and I were coming in for the big day!

We weren't the only people excited that day. The entire Norrell office staff was on hand to watch Alesia receive her leg. There were some minor adjustments—cutting down the top to make a more comfortable fit, building up the bottom of her other shoe to make up for the growing room that had been added to the prosthesis—but soon she was allowed to walk down the hall. After her first few tentative steps, and a few more adjustments, she ran, she danced, she hopped, and she—beamed with pleasure.

I didn't miss my baby's first steps, I saw them that day in Mike's office. Alesia finally had two operative legs and feet.

"Go outside!" she shouted, heading for the door.

"Wait for me!"

The chase had begun. She hasn't really slowed down since.

We went to pick up the other girls at school, excited to show them Alesia's new prize. I was carrying her because I wanted her to go in the direction I was headed, which didn't appeal to her newly won freedom of movement. When we got to Nadia's classroom I began to put her down.

"Oops, Mommy," she said.

"What?" I looked down. Her leg was gone. "Oh Alesia, where's your leg?"

Alesia pointed toward the playground.

"It fell off?" I asked stupidly.

Her $6,000 leg was missing? We'd had it less than an hour! I grabbed her and took off to retrace our steps. Sure enough, there in the middle of the playground was a bright, shiny new . . . leg. Wouldn't that have been a surprise for a child strolling back to the classroom? We would obviously need some practice and maybe another pair of socks inside the prosthesis for a tighter fit.

Alesia's leg was a constant source of curiosity among other children. Kids would come up to her and touch it. They would ask her what it was and why she had it. She was, and continues to be, very matter of fact about the whole thing. She will answer the big question once—"It's my leg"—and then she doesn't want to be bothered about it.

One day, after she had gotten used to her new appendage, we were at the park. I was pushing her on a swing when a group of children surrounded us.

"What's that?" one girl asked me, pointing to Alesia's prosthesis.

"It's her leg," I answered.

"Why is that her leg?" a boy asked.

"What happened to her real leg?" another child chimed in.

"Does it hurt?"

"What's it made of?"

Alesia looked back at me and smiled. "Okay!" she shouted and somehow on the next up-swing she released her prosthesis and sent it flying through the air. The children's eyes went wide and their hands shot up to their mouths. The first little girl let out a scream. Alesia just laughed . . .

. . . then the children began to laugh too. One of the kids retrieved her leg and I put it back on while everyone watched. After that the kids didn't ask any more questions. They just thought Alesia was extra cool.

Chapter 21

❧

A FOREVER FAMILY

Our family at the park.

June 18, 1995

Today I looked out the back window and saw Meghan teaching the girls how to do cartwheels. They didn't fight, yell at each other, or break anything. Could this be the faint light I've been waiting for at the end of a very long tunnel?

I can't say when it happened. One day we were a family of strangers with one biological child and three adopted children. The next we were a family like any other. I was beginning to have faith that our lives might one day be manageable again. We were now a family—a unit. Six individual souls living together as a whole. A bond has formed that, through arguments, tension, and uncertainty, through laughter, comfort, and joyous celebrations, will always remain.

Casey and I have lost our potential sainthood status. We are boring, regular parents just like everyone else we know. Our family and friends know we couldn't have survived the last few years without them. Saints are much more independent.

My relationship with Casey has been tested as never before. Sometimes Casey gets depressed over the amount of money we owe from adoptions, surgeries, and loss of work. Each adoption ranged from $15,000 to $20,000—a far cry from the $10,000 we feared during our initial meeting with Bee. We borrowed from every source we could tap. "We'll be in debt forever," he sighs.

"Not forever," I tell him with a smile. "Just for the next ten or twenty years."

He doesn't usually smile back.

I worry too, more about stamina than money, but I know we'll work things out. We've reversed roles, Casey and I. Now I'm practicing our "faith in the universe" and he is mourning his loss of control over our large family. As one of my friends would say, "This, too, shall pass."

Both of us have had to reevaluate and examine our idea of what marriage and family are supposed to be. (How could we not, when our whole family structure has been blown out of the water?) But with examination comes strength. As we have survived this awesome amount of change, I feel confident that we can survive anything. Casey and I have worked together to bring our children home, and though the adjustments have been rough and sometimes painful, the rewards have been well worth every minute of upheaval.

I'm certainly not the same person who started out wanting a second child seemingly a lifetime ago. I've learned that I'm capable of much more than I had previously imagined, and that love isn't something to be taken for granted. Each of us has prospered tremendously during this family growth spurt.

Meghan often is asked how she likes having her new sisters. "I don't," is sometimes her reply. But no one outside the family better mess with her sisters or they will have her to deal with. When she was in fourth grade, she wrote a composition about herself and her family.

> Hi. I'm Meghan Conroy. I belong to a very adoptive family. I am the only biological child in my family because all of my sisters are adopted. Two of my sisters are from Russia and one is from Colombia.
>
> . . . My mom and dad have to travel a lot when they adopt children. When they went to Russia they got to sample Russian food and drinks. They didn't go for pleasure but they still had a good time.
>
> . . . When I graduate from high school I'm going to go to a college to learn how to be a journalist, or a reporter. After that I'm going to work at a newspaper for at least a year before I find a better job. I'm not going to get married until I'm really old like twenty-seven and I'm not going to have any kids.

One day while we were in the process of adopting Alesia, Meghan turned to me and asked, "Mom, could you get me a list of all the children living in Russian orphanages?"

"Why would you want that?" I questioned, surprised by her interest.

"So I can check off their names as we adopt them."

She's still adjusting. Now, as Meghan approaches adolescence at the speed of light, she continues to vacillate between enjoying her new sisters and wanting her own apartment in New York where no one knows she has a family.

As things quieted down after Alesia's last surgery, Ana's "wounds" began appearing. One day my mom found a stash of schoolbooks in the back of Ana's dresser drawer. It turned out that more than twenty-five books from her classroom were hidden in different drawers. Nadia noticed some of her allowance missing. I suspected Ana but Nadia was certain that Ana would *never* take something of hers. I found the money later in Ana's piggy bank. Two days later I got a call from the school principal: Ana had been caught stealing from a boy's lunch money envelope. When confronted, she lied, claiming she had no idea how the money ended up in her jeans pocket, even when another child saw her take it. I picked her up from the principal's office, where she sat terrified, told her that stealing was wrong and unacceptable, and let her think things over in her room for the rest of the afternoon. She cried buckets of tears in remorse. I felt that surely we would have no more stealing after such an ordeal.

The next day, I found a child's billfold and a toy I hadn't seen before in her backpack. "Where did you get this?" I asked.

"My friend gave them to me," she answered.

"Your friend gave you a billfold with five dollars in it?"

"Yes! Why don't you believe me?"

"Well, I need to call your friend's mother and tell her that we can't accept this gift."

"No! You can't. Maybe it accidentally got in there somehow." Ana was beginning to panic.

"Ana, please tell me the truth," I said in a quiet voice.

"I am!" she shouted and began to cry.

The teacher confirmed that the billfold and toy had been stolen. I found a children's therapist who had experience working with adopted children. After I briefly told her of Ana's history and the stealing, she said, "It sounds like Ana has been with you almost as long as she's ever been with one family. She might be getting ready to leave. She's collecting what she might need if you send her away."

It made sense. It also broke my heart.

"Let Ana know that she is an important part of your family now and that people in her family don't steal," the therapist continued. "Don't give her the chance to lie by asking her about things you find. Make a rule that, while she is learning not to steal, you will look into her backpack each day, and if you find anything, it will be returned by her along with an apology. Let her know that you know how hard it is for her not to steal right now. Assure her that you will help her learn how to be a member of the family. Speak often of future family events and of her place as a family member."

"Ana," I said later that night when we were alone. "I love you and will help you learn how to be a member of this family. I'm going to help you stop stealing."

Ana looked at me as her eyes filled with tears. Finally she whispered, "But what about my next mommy?"

"Oh, Ana," I cried, hugging her, even though she stiffened in my arms. "I will always be your mommy! I'm your mommy forever and ever. I love you with all my heart. You are an important part of our family and you always will be." Casey heard the commotion and came into the room. Ana started sobbing. Casey held us both. We all stayed locked together as we rocked gently back and forth. "I love you, too," Casey said. "We will always love you no matter what."

It was a cathartic experience. "As hard as that was to hear," I told Casey later that night after Ana was asleep, "now maybe she understands that we aren't going to leave her."

The next day Ana took money and candy from her cousin, Ashton. "Thief," he yelled when she was discovered sitting on the stolen goods.

This wasn't going to be easy.

With continuous backpack searches, therapy, love, and reassurance of her place in our lives, Ana has curbed her urge to stockpile for future needs. In fact, she caught me the other day telling Casey I wasn't going to eat any more chocolate. "In this family we don't lie," she told me seriously, showing how well she understands our family rules as well as my eating habits.

One day Ana told Casey she loved him. We both stopped and

stared. "Did you say what I thought you said?" I asked, incredulous and thrilled.

Ana blushed, lowered her eyes, and nodded her head.

"I love you too!" Casey exclaimed and we all exchanged high fives, hugs, and kisses. Ana was so proud of herself, she glowed.

Alesia continues her "leg pranks." Last Christmas I took her along with the other girls to visit Santa at a local craft shop. Since it was early in the day, we were the only visitors to see Mr. Claus. He lifted Alesia, Ana, and Nadia all onto his lap and listened as they recited their wish lists. Since I could see that this might take a while, I asked one of the store clerks if I could browse around while the girls were occupied with Santa. Two minutes later, I heard a loud, "Ohhh, Ho, Ho, Ho!" and the clerk rushed over to find me. "I'm afraid your daughter's leg is off," she told me breathlessly. "Is that all right?"

I hurried back to find Alesia's leg, which she had grabbed from inside her overalls, shoved in Santa's face so he could take a closer look. "See, I do it," she said gleefully.

"You're supposed to keep your leg on," admonished Nadia.

I guess since it was her first visit, she wanted Santa to know everything about her.

In January I enrolled Alesia in a dance class. I couldn't hide my pleasure as I shopped for her tiny size 3T leotard. I adored picking out ballet shoes that would fit both her right foot and her prosthesis. I was as excited as she was when I dropped her off with Miss Lisa and Miss Marie, her teachers. Alesia had watched Meghan, Ana, and Nadia during their classes and now it was finally her turn. She didn't waste a second being shy. She joined in immediately as I knew she would. I'll always love watching her dance.

I couldn't help comparing Ana and Alesia's adjustment and realizing that emotional scars are far more difficult to overcome than physical scars.

Recently, I saw a mother I didn't know watching Nadia play basketball with her son. I had a sudden urge to say to her, "A few years ago my daughter didn't even know what a basketball was, she had never heard of a place called the YMCA, and she had never worn a pair of tennis shoes." The woman would surely wonder what I was talking about, but I would continue. I would want her to know what this game meant to my child. I would want to remind her to be sure to appreciate her child. I would want to remind myself to appreciate the gift that my children are to Casey and me.

"If you knew my daughter's history, you would know what it means for her to be playing basketball with your child. She's running, smiling, and playing just like your child runs, smiles, and plays."

Nadia has something she never thought she would have. She has a mom, a dad, three sisters, and a grandpa and grandmas—an entire family—forever and ever.

HV
875.5   Conroy, Maggie
.C65   Francis
1997
        A world of love

DUE DATE   D704   23.00

092083
5049 6042

001 942   000 019